ADVANCE PRAISE

"*Just Mercy*, the story of a grieving mother whose teenage daughter is brutally murdered, exquisitely portrays the complexity and difficulty of forgiveness and its power to take us to the inescapable truth that we are all connected. Bernadette Baker and her family will touch your heart and shake your soul so that, regardless of your position, you will never feel the same about the issue of the death penalty. *Just Mercy* is grounded in Dorothy Van Soest's insight about the role of grief in the lives of both victims and offenders and the healing potential of restorative dialogue. This family drama is a must-read that teaches us about the true nature of justice and our very humanity."

— Sr. Helen Prejean, C.S.J., Author of *Dead Man Walking*

"*Just Mercy* is a moving, fast-paced read that artfully sweeps us up in the journey of forgiveness."

— Leslie Neale, Director/Producer of acclaimed documentary
films, *Road to Return, Juvies, & Unlikely Friends.*

"A stunning achievement. From the first page to the last we are taken on a journey through surprising twists and turns, as a family shattered by the heinous murder of their youngest daughter, Veronica, struggles to come to terms with their shock and grief. When Bernadette, Veronica's mother, goes to the prison to witness the execution of the woman who murdered her daughter, something quite unexpected occurs, launching her on a quest that will unearth life-altering truths about herself, her dead daughter, the remaining members of her family…and her own relationship to the killer. I won't reveal the details that trigger this quest, nor the stunning truths she uncovers, for fear of spoiling the story for other readers. Suffice it to say that Bernadette's unrelenting courage allows us, in the (relative) safety of our armchairs, to delve into human issues as far-reaching as love, grief, justice, forgiveness, vengefulness, and the intricacies of our own private worlds. Dorothy Van Soest is indeed a masterful storyteller. I eagerly await her next book."

—Hal Zina Bennett, bestselling author of *Write From the Heart: Unleashing the Power of Our Creativity*

"*Just Mercy* reads like a motion picture ... bringing home the horror of the death penalty and the complexities of how compassion arrives in unexpected ways. Raelynn Blackwell's story is the voice of so many on America's death row. Raelynn has come to accept responsibility for her actions, as does Bernadette Baker, leaving the reader on both sides of compassion. *Just Mercy* is ultimately a passionate, well-written book about our sense of humanity, and where crime and justice stand in the way."

—Jarvis Jay Masters, Author of Finding Freedom: *Writings from Death Row and That Bird Has My Wings: The Autobiography of an Innocent Man on Death Row*

"*Just Mercy* shares the compelling and intense journey of a family struggling with the horrors, trauma, and grief associated with the murder of a family member and the death penalty. It offers important insight into some of the additional harms a death sentence can inflict on a victim's family and the varied ways different family members process, grieve, and heal following the murder of a loved one."

—Marcelle Clowes, Member Engagement Coordinator, Murder Victims' Families for Reconciliation (MVFR)

"Dorothy Van Soest has eloquently envisioned and deftly delivered a compelling tale that will tug you through grief, horror and hope as you witness instinct and ethics locking horns through a senseless tragedy and its legal outcome. The author touches on a range of timely topics with grace and clarity while centering on the question of 'bad behavior' and its appropriate punishment. In the end, it is love, compassion, and acceptance that prevail. In a word, just mercy."

—Sarah W. Bartlett, co-editor, *HEAR ME, SEE ME: Incarcerated Women Write* and founding co-director of writing inside *VT*.

"*Just Mercy* takes us inside a family's struggle for justice, revealing the complexities and quandaries inherent in capital punishment. After reading the book, it is impossible not to feel compassion for everyone who is impacted by the death penalty system--condemned prisoners and murder victims' family members alike."

—Jen Marlowe, author, *I Am Troy Davis*

"In *Just Mercy,* victim Veronica Baker's family is divided between those who support, oppose or are painfully ambivalent about capital punishment. Dorothy Van Soest's gentle portrayal of their struggle in the face of cruel circumstances makes for a compelling read and the plot twist is up there with the best of them."

—Dave Avolio, Board Member, Washington Coalition to Abolish the Death Penalty

"*Just Mercy* asks a heart-wrenching question: how can a mother whose daughter has been murdered respond to and even feel some connection with the murderer, and what will it mean for her family if she does? This book captures in vivid and believable detail the aftermath of a murder and the ways that a family could be bitterly divided about the right thing to do, and in doing so, asks important questions about the meaning of the word justice. This book is a page-turner that makes you think, and that will stay with you long you after finish."

—Irene Sheppard, author, *Restorativity* blog

Early in the narrative the story's main character, Bernadette Baker, chastises a reporter in response to questions about her position on the death penalty, "Don't go there; it's complicated." But Dorothy Van Soest does "go there" while still honoring the enormous complexity and soul-crushing grief compulsory in homicide and its aftermath. As individual family members struggle to find meaning in their beloved Veronica's murder, the state's response to that crime and ultimately what they understand about the killer, they are at times aligned and at times in utter opposition to one another and their communities further illustrating the complexities faced by survivors. What makes a family and how families undertake and define healing is explored in this candid, utterly suspenseful and captivating novel."

> —Marilyn Armour, Ph.D. LICSW, Professor and Director,
> Institute for Restorative Justice and Restorative Dialogue, The
> University of Texas at Austin

"*Just Mercy* faithfully captures the emotional complexities surrounding the death penalty – particularly the toll it takes on and among victims' families – and confronts our notions of justice, punishment, and forgiveness. It presents a challenging, multi-faceted response to a question that can't be answered in the abstract: What would you do if your family member were murdered?"

> —Kristin Houlé, Executive Director, Texas Coalition to Abolish
> the Death Penalty

"Dorothy Van Soest magnificently holds and embodies the value, in each of her characters, of how healing happens when opposing contradictory experiences are held together in a sacred space. *Just Mercy* is a fitting title for a relationship between unlikely advocates that manifests the principles of the victim offender dialogue process in a riveting family drama."

> —David Doerfler, founder and facilitator, Concentric Journeys

In this compelling story of forgiveness and redemption, Dorothy Van Soest brings the insight and experience of her distinguished career as a social worker and scholar to a story that reveals the complex nature of people's relationships and the multiple dimensions of contemporary social issues. Her writing reflects both an understanding of the human heart and how place and circumstances shape a person's life chances. *Just Mercy* is a powerful call for breaking down the barriers that separate us and for recognizing the value of every human being."

> —Michael Reisch, Ph.D., Daniel Thursz Distinguished Professor
> of Social Justice, University of Maryland

"An exciting and compelling look at how a family faces the ultimate punishment. *Just Mercy* will take you on a journey through the Texas criminal justice system that you will never forget."

> —Larry Fitzgerald, former Public Information Officer,
> Huntsville, Texas Department of Criminal Justice.

"A mother has no idea what will unfold as she seeks to understand how another human being could take the life of her daughter. Part mystery, part spiritual journey, *Just Mercy* shows the surprising ways that human lives intersect and the roles that compassion plays in coming to terms with tragedy and loss."

> —Jane Gilgun, Author, Professor, University of Minnesota

JUST MERCY

a novel

JUST MERCY

a novel

Dorothy Van Soest

Apprentice House
Baltimore, Maryland

First Edition

Printed in the United States of America

Paperback ISBN: 978-1-62720-022-6
Ebook ISBN: 978-1-62720-023-3

Design by Cody Barber
Cover Photo Illustration by Cody Barber

Published by Apprentice House

Apprentice House
Loyola University Maryland
4501 N. Charles Street
Baltimore, MD 21210
410.617.5265 • 410.617.2198 (fax)
www.ApprenticeHouse.com
info@ApprenticeHouse.com

"We are one, after all, you and I, together we suffer, together exist and forever will recreate one another."
— *Pierre Teilhard de Chardin*

ONE

May 3, 2001

Veronica stared at the back of the downtown #20 bus, knowing full well that if she'd left Natalie's house even just a few seconds earlier she wouldn't have missed it. No matter. It had been totally worth it. Standing at the bus stop, she dropped her backpack to the ground and unzipped the outside compartment, holding her long blonde hair out of her eyes with one hand while pulling out her cell phone with the other. Her mom answered on the third ring.

"Hey, Mom, I just missed the eight o'clock. Next one's in half an hour."

"Okay. I'll reset my worry alarm to nine o'clock, then."

"So funny. See you soon."

Even though she laughed as if it was a joke, Veronica knew full well that at nine o'clock sharp, her mom would start worrying for real. She'd learned that the hard way two years ago, when she was fourteen, the first time she missed her curfew. It wasn't like she was trying to sneak in late when she crept up the stairs on her tiptoes that night; she was just trying not to wake her folks. And she wouldn't have if it weren't for that squeaky step. When she'd reached the dark hallway at the top of the stairs, her mom had appeared out of nowhere, her fists gripping the hem of her cotton nightgown, her eyes flashing fear and anger.

"Thank God you're okay! Don't you *ever* scare me like that again!"

"Sorry, Mom. I thought you were sleeping."

"Next time, call. Don't *ever* forget that, young lady." Then she turned on her heels, went into her bedroom, and closed the door.

"Hey, sis," her brother Fin had said the next day, "don't you know Mom doesn't go off duty until she hears the last foot hit the squeak?"

"We all know that," she said, "but this is the first time that old step turned against me."

They'd both laughed then, unbothered by their mom's controlling nature, understanding it for what it was: a sign of her love for them.

Their older sister, as usual, had a totally different reaction. "You weren't grounded?" Annamaria had asked when she heard about what happened. "How come you get away with being late? I never did, that's for sure."

Later, when Veronica asked why she didn't punish her that night, her mom said, "Disappointing me was punishment enough for you."

So true. After that night, she'd never forgotten her mom's number one rule: if you were going to be late, the first thing you did was call. Even times like now when there was nothing to worry about.

The night air was warm and sticky, and Veronica reached for the water bottle in the side pocket of her backpack. Taking a long drink, she leaned against the signpost, liking the way the metal pole felt cool on the bare spot of her back between her crop top and her hip huggers.

She glanced at her watch. Ten minutes after eight. Since it took the bus twenty minutes to get from the east side of Austin to the west side, she'd be home in plenty of time to finish her essay on homelessness for her political science class. Tomorrow, when she read it to the class, someone—most likely a guy—would probably snicker or call her a bleeding-heart liberal. She didn't mind. It wouldn't be the first time. And, besides, she loved watching her favorite teacher, Miss Malone, whenever that happened. Even in that mousy gray suit she always wore, she would somehow manage to make herself look real tall and imposing; then she would roll her eyes up over those black horn-rimmed glasses of hers and say, "Write a rebuttal, sir. I'm sure Miss Baker would welcome an *intelligent* debate."

Debating was one of Veronica's favorite things, and she always wished someone would accept the challenge. But no one ever did. She didn't fault them, though. Writing didn't come easy for everyone like it did for her. Nothing about school came easy for her friend Natalie, that's for sure. It wasn't fair that she had to work so hard just to get Cs. But it could be so frustrating sometimes. Like tonight, when Nat had struggled with one lousy algebra question for such a long time that Veronica offered to just give her the answer.

"No," Nat had said, stomping her foot on the floor. "I have to do it myself."

Veronica felt bad about getting impatient and suggesting a shortcut, but it had turned out all right in the end when Nat solved the problem on her own. "I did it! I did it! I did it!" she yelled, laughing and jumping up and down with her chest all puffed up like she'd reached the top of Mount Everest or something. It was totally worth missing the bus for that.

She looked at her watch again. Eight twenty. Might as well organize her backpack now so she wouldn't have to do it in the morning. She sat down on the sidewalk and took everything out: from the main compartment came her math, science, and English books plus her all-purpose notebook divided into sections by subject; from the outside part came her inhaler, cell phone, pencil case, and post-it notepad, all of which she put back in; and from the side pocket came stuff to throw out. She rearranged the books to match her class schedule and slipped her notebook in behind them, then zipped up the backpack and left it lying on the ground. It didn't take more than two strides of her long, slender legs to get to the trash can into which she dropped an empty apple juice bottle; a Snickers wrapper; a banana peel in a plastic baggie; and some crumpled papers, notes from friends passed to her in class.

By then it was eight thirty. She stepped off the curb and looked down the street. Where was that bus, anyway? It couldn't be stuck in traffic; only two cars had passed while she waited. She reminded herself to call home again if it didn't come in a few minutes and stepped backward and up onto the curb without looking behind her. She bumped into something and turned around to see a woman on the verge of falling into the gutter. She grabbed the woman's arm and pulled her up just in time.

"I'm so sorry. I didn't see you. Are you okay?"

The woman swayed back and forth, staring into space through hollow eyes ringed with black. Stringy matted hair—it was too dirty to tell whether it was brown or blonde—clung to her cheeks. She probably looked older than she was, her body sunken inside ripped and filthy jeans that were falling off her hips and a faded blue tee shirt with holes in the front that looked like they came from cigarette burns. If Mom were here, she'd try to figure out how to clean the woman up and get her a change of clothes. That was Mom, Veronica thought with a smile, always trying to fix everyone—not the worst thing in the world.

The woman tilted forward, then tipped backward. Veronica reached out to steady her. She looked sick. She must be homeless.

"Do you want to sit down, ma'am?"

The woman turned and started to stagger off but tripped on the curb and almost fell again.

"Here, let me help you."

"Don't need no help." The woman's voice was hoarse, growl-like.

"You look like you're about to pass out."

The woman glared for an instant before her eyes went blank again. Veronica watched her reach into the pocket of her jeans and pull something out. Something shiny. She heard a click. Then she saw it. Why did the woman have a knife? And where would a homeless woman get a switchblade, of all things? She had read about the rapes and assaults against the few women who lived alone on the streets of Austin. Of course. That explained it. The woman needed the knife for protection.

She kept her eyes on the switchblade dangling at the woman's side, quivering in her hand as if it were a living thing. Click. Veronica jumped. The blade disappeared. Click. It shot out again and pointed at the ground. Click. Gone. Click. Click. Click. The knife opened, closed, opened.

"I think you should put that away," she said in a careful, calm voice.

But instead the woman brought the knife up to within inches of her own face. She squinted at it as if trying to figure out what it was. Then she pressed the tip of the blade into her hand and studied the thin line of red oozing from her palm. With surprising precision, she pressed the sharp point of the blade into the tip of each of her fingers. One by one she brought her fingers to her lips, her tongue darting in and out, licking the blood.

Another staccato click and the blade disappeared. Click—open. Click—close.

Veronica's breath was coming in ragged spurts now. Why hadn't she put her inhaler in her pocket?

"You're hurting yourself," she gasped, holding out her open hand. "Here, give the knife to me."

The woman raised her hand high in the air. The knife hovered over her head. Click. The blade shot up toward the night sky. Click. It was gone. She tucked in her chin and narrowed her eyes. Click. Her left eye twitched. Her lips sneered.

"Please, let me help you." Veronica's voice shook. Where was that bus, anyway? What could she do to calm the woman down until it got here?

"What makes you think I need help? Huh? Huh?"

At the feral look in the woman's eyes, Veronica's heart started hammering against her chest. "It's okay. It's okay. I just don't want anyone to get hurt." She raised her palms in front of her.

"Like you? Huh? Huh? Like you?"

When the woman took a step forward and pointed the knife at her, Veronica raised her hands again. She lifted her left foot up and in slow motion set it down behind her. Then she lifted her right foot and set it down, repeating each tiny step and going as slowly as possible in order to reach her backpack without setting the woman off. If only she could get to her cell phone. She needed her inhaler, bad.

Too late. With a terrifying howl, the woman charged at her. Veronica tried to push her away and felt the blade slash her fingers. She raised her hands to cover her face as the woman screamed and lunged at her again. Then the blade was everywhere, tearing into her arm, her shoulder, her face. It flashed over her as she fell to the ground. With each stab, she screamed and begged the woman to stop. The pain was excruciating until suddenly, gratefully, she felt nothing.

TWO

July 15, 2011

Nothing turned out the way Bernadette thought it would on the day she went to Huntsville to witness the execution of the woman who murdered her daughter. She'd expected a large crowd, but not this large. Yellow tape divided more than a thousand screaming people into separate camps: protesters against the death penalty on the left, supporters on the right, media in the middle. Uniformed police were scattered about to maintain order and discourage violence.

The walk to the building known as The Walls wasn't what she expected, either. The space between the two opposing crowds was nothing but a narrow path, the building seemed miles away, and the steps up to its entrance looked too steep for her stocky legs, strong as they were, to manage. Just as she wiped away the beads of perspiration that were bubbling up and causing strands of her gray-nutmeg hair to stick to her forehead, someone to her right waved a homemade sign in her face that said "It's about time."

"Give the bitch hell, Mrs. Baker," a young crew-cut-headed man screamed as others around him joined in.

Bernadette cupped her arthritic fingers over her ears, cursing the Texas heat—well over a hundred degrees in the mid-afternoon sun—and striding forward as fast as her thick ankles would permit.

"We're praying for you, Bernie!"

"God be with you, Bernie!"

She turned toward the familiar voices on her left and saw Father Gilpatrick's ruddy Irish cheeks and Sister McDonald's sweet oval face smiling up at her from where they knelt on the pavement.

"Bless your heart, hon."

Bernadette's soft, blue eyes filled with tears. It was Eddie Silas, president of the Texas Coalition Against the Death Penalty. Even though "bless your heart" could mean any number of things, no one had to explain to her what he meant by it. She didn't blame him for being disappointed in her. After she canceled her membership in the coalition ten years ago, she had refused his calls and ignored his plea-filled letters until he gave up on her. He was a dear soul. They all were. But there was no way they could understand what had happened to her. Even her own children couldn't.

"Kill the bitch!"

She turned to her right. The crowd cheered. She recognized some of their faces. How strange to see them smiling at her now. What would they think if she told them she wasn't there to support their cause any more than she was there to support the cause of the coalition?

She kept walking, her head down, her eyes turned away from both the devout and the hate-filled, her ears closed to both the earnest cries for mercy and the vindictive screams for justice. With her fingernails digging into the fleshy palms of her clenched fists, she stumbled down the ever-narrowing path, wishing she were as certain about why she was here as everyone else seemed to be.

Regis Dorfman steered her through the jostling crowds with his hand on the small of her back. He was wearing brown slacks and a short-sleeved beige shirt—thrift store purchases, no doubt, and years out of style, yet a perfect fit for this man who had come to know her so well over the past year. She turned to him and he gave her his deep-dimpled smile, which she interpreted to mean just what she wanted it to mean: that all the tears she'd shed, all the pain and rage he'd guided her through, would soon bring the healing for which she longed. That after tonight she would be able to move on, to live again.

Swarms of microphones and television cameras were thrust in her face and Regis darted in front of her, transforming his body into a protective shield.

"Mrs. Baker! How do you feel?"

"Are you glad your daughter's murderer is finally going to be executed?"

"What do you think her last words will be, Mrs. Baker?"

Bernadette tripped and started to panic, but when she grabbed the back of Regis's shirt to keep from falling, the familiar spiciness of his Aqua Velva cologne calmed her. She stopped to look at the reporters' hungry faces and couldn't help but want to feed them something. She stood up straight and gave them her sturdy, tough, midwestern housewife look.

"Don't even go there," she said. "It's not that simple." Her voice rang with a strong maternal authority that rendered the reporters mute; even she turned to see if the words had come from someone

other than herself. But when she looked down at her hands, she saw
that they had begun trembling. The reporters must have noticed,
too, because they went back to bombarding her with questions.

"Will you be happy to see Raelynn Blackwell die, Mrs. Baker?"

"No."

"Do you support her execution?"

"Yes."

"Have you changed your position on the death penalty?"

"No."

"Then what do you hope to get from witnessing the
execution?"

"Yeah, Mrs. Baker, why are you here, then?"

"Enough." She glowered at them. If they were going to insist
on taunting her, she would refuse to answer any more questions.
Not that she could have answered them anyway. She raised the
palms of her hands in a peremptory gesture, and much to her
surprise the reporters fell away, like the Red Sea parting. She flicked
the short, coarse strands of hair off her cheeks, placed her hands on
her thick hips, and forged her way along the path before her.

With the reporters and cameras now focused on the crowds,
the mob's screaming reached a fever pitch.

"The whole world is watching! The whole world is watching!"

"Justice now! Justice now!"

"Shame on Texas! Shame on Texas!"

"An eye for an eye! A tooth for a tooth!"

Bernadette craned her neck and looked back at the crowd, her
heart leaping when she spotted a handsome young man with wavy
multicolored hair. He looked like Fin. She squinted and saw that

it wasn't her son, after all, but she knew he was there and worried about him being alone.

"Texans don't cotton much to executing women," Regis said.

Bernadette nodded. She knew only two women had been executed in Texas before tonight. The first, Chipita Rodriguez, had been hung from a mesquite tree in San Patricio on November 13, 1863—falsely accused, it was later established, of robbing a man and murdering him with an ax. It would be 135 years before Texas had the stomach to execute another woman, and when Karla Faye Tucker was put to death on February 3, 1998, for murdering two people with a pickaxe, almost two thousand people from all over the country and even other countries had protested the execution. Bernadette had been there, too, shivering in the rain outside, standing next to Chipita Rodriguez's ghost—who, with the noose still hanging around her neck, wailed at the crowd's back-slapping, cheering, and spontaneous rendition of "The Star-Spangled Banner" once the official death announcement was made.

Now, as Bernadette lifted one foot after the other up the steep steps to the main entrance of the Walls Unit, she wondered if Chipita's ghost would be here tonight. And Karla Faye's, too. The media had been obsessed of late with the fact that another woman was going to be executed. They were fascinated by the similarities between Raelynn Blackwell and Karla Faye Tucker: how both had stabbed their victims multiple times—had admitted their guilt— were close to the same age—had been drug abusers and prostitutes until religion found them on death row and turned them into model prisoners. How both had suffered sad and sordid childhoods.

Thank God none of the reporters had asked Bernadette about

any of that. If they had, she would have told them in no uncertain terms that none of those comparisons mattered, that Raelynn Blackwell had killed her Veronica, her precious baby girl, and that made all the difference.

"You got your ID?" A hefty bald man behind a glass window inside the front entrance held his hand up for them to stop—or was he waving at her?

"So many people out there," she said as she slid her driver's license through the slot at the bottom of the glass.

"Yes, ma'am. Crowds big as all hell and half of Texas," he said with a grin. "Some damn Yankees, too, seems like. Looks like it's fixin' to happen this time."

She wondered if the man was smiling because he was glad another murderer was going to get her due. Or maybe he was one of the guards she'd heard about who liked, even respected, Raelynn Blackwell, in which case his smile could be a cover for sadness. Then again, maybe he was just being Texas friendly.

"So dang hot out there, the fire aints don't even sting," the man said as he swept the back of his hand across his dripping brow. "Now y'all know you cain't have no cameras or tape recorders or nothing of that sort in here, right?"

She clutched her purse under her arm. Did he really think she wanted to take pictures? Just then, Amy Whitehall—a counselor and the only woman on the trauma team—appeared. Both her clothes—a sleeveless silk paisley blouse and tan linen slacks—and the pained expression on her face distinguished her as a transplanted easterner on a mission to humanize Texas.

"I'll take it from here, Henry." Amy Whitehall was out of

breath when she reached out to shake hands. "I am so terribly sorry, Mrs. Baker, that I wasn't here… in time to… escort you in. We'll go to the Turnout Room now. Witnesses for the condemned are kept in another building, so we don't have to worry about bumping into any of them."

Bernadette was about to explain that that wouldn't be a problem, but the sight of the massive enclosure adjacent to the stairway with its floor-to-ceiling walls of brass bars stopped her short. She stared open-mouthed at the prisoners—there must have been at least a dozen of them—who stood on ladders of varying heights as they polished the brass.

"That's the bullring," Amy said. "It used to be the point of entry for new arrivals. Staff use it now to come into the prison through that walkway in the middle."

"Good lord, I'm not ready for this." Bernadette clutched her stomach.

"No one ever is," Regis said.

"I never saw anyone die before," Bernadette said. "I was eleven when my mother passed." Why did she say that? Raelynn Blackwell's death tonight would be nothing like her mother's had been—though all she remembered about that was her father describing her mother's death rattle at the end, and how Bernadette was glad she hadn't been there to hear it and then had felt guilty about being glad.

When they reached the Turnout Room, she saw that, as with everything else that day, it was nothing like she expected. The room's walls were bare, and plastic chairs—must have been fifty of them—were scattered around. A sixty-cup coffee urn sat on a Formica table in the corner, surrounded by way too many Styrofoam cups. She sat in one of the uncomfortable chairs and set about fixing things in her head: there should be a cozy conversation area with a soft leather couch and matching chairs, photographs of Texas bluebonnets and Indian paintbrush flowers on the walls, a multicolored cloth on the Formica table, and a twelve-cup coffeemaker and some clear glass mugs instead of the urn and Styrofoam cups. She would top it all off by adding a plate of homemade chocolate chip cookies with macadamia nuts. She glanced up at the way-too-big numbers on an institutional clock hanging on the wall and wished it wouldn't tick so loudly. It was four o'clock. Two more hours to go.

"Are you okay, Mrs. Baker?"

She jumped at the sound of Amy Whitehall's voice.

"Raelynn Blackwell is in a holding cell now," Amy said, trying to read Bernadette's mind and not even coming close. "The chaplain is with her. At two o'clock she would have been allowed a phone call, at three a visit with her attorney. Between three thirty and now, she would have been served her final meal."

"So, each step of her death is being engineered to ensure as little pain and emotion as possible, isn't it?" Bernadette said. "Well, my Veronica had no time to prepare, no witnesses to choose, no favorite last meal to eat, no final statement to make the night she was killed, did she?"

"I'm sorry," the trauma counselor said. "We're here to help in any way we can."

Then tell me why I'm doing this, Bernadette wanted to say. But that was a question even she couldn't answer. Maybe there was no answer—at least not one that made sense.

"I brought you this," Amy said, handing her a folder that said Public Information in bold letters on the front. "I'll be right back …in case you need me for anything before …or after."

Bernadette waited until the counselor was gone and then whispered to Regis, "She seems awfully cautious, don't you think? I thought this trauma team was supposed to be the best in the country."

"Well, this is a bit unusual for them," he said.

She glanced down at the familiar blue Texas Department of Criminal Justice logo on the folder's white cover and opened it to the first page. She ran her forefinger down the names of the official witnesses and newspaper reporters until she got to the list of Raelynn Blackwell's personal witnesses. There her finger lingered on her own name and Regis Dorfman's before moving further down the page to the Victim Witnesses list, where it stopped once again at her own name. So that was why Amy Whitehall seemed nervous. She must have been surprised to see Bernadette's name on both lists.

Well, no one could have been as surprised as she was the day she got the letter from Raelynn Blackwell. "Dear Mrs. Baker," she had written on elementary-school lined paper, "I am writing to ask wud you be a personal witness for me? I am asking Regis too. I no I deserve to die and I dont deserve for you to say yes but I hope you will think about it. Sincerely, Miss Raelynn Blackwell."

She had sat down to respond right away. "Dear Raelynn," she wrote, "I hope having me as one of your personal witnesses will help you. But you must know that even if I agree to be a witness for you, I still think execution is the right punishment for the murder of my daughter." But then she crossed out the second sentence, crumpled up the paper and started again. "Dear Raelynn," she settled on after several tries, "I will be there to witness your execution. Bernadette Baker."

She turned to Regis now and, as usual, his eyes compelled her to say more about what she was thinking. "I must be crazy to do this," she said. "I keep wondering why I said yes to Raelynn right away when I got her letter. She prints like a child, you know, maybe that's all it was. Maybe Annamaria's right that I'm just a soft touch."

Regis's eyebrow went up, which she knew was his way of letting her know that whatever she had to say was okay, that it didn't matter if he'd heard it before.

"I still don't understand why she only asked the two of us when she's allowed five personal witnesses."

"You have doubts about saying yes to her?"

"Yes. No. Oh, I don't know. Annamaria asked me how I could be a witness for someone whose death I was hoping for and I didn't have an answer for her. I'm surprised she's talking to me at all anymore."

Bernadette took a deep breath and folded her hands on her lap. "I wish I could get her to talk to you. She clings to her desire for vengeance as if she's clinging to Veronica herself. When Marty and I adopted Veronica, Annamaria was thirteen years old. She said if we wanted another kid so bad I should just have one myself. There was no reasoning with her. She's stubborn, that one. Always was. She even swore she'd run away. But when we got Veronica, that girl fell more deeply in love with her baby sister than anyone could have even imagined. She's really soft inside, people don't realize that."

The door opened then, and Amy Whitehall walked back into the room, glancing in their direction with a worried expression.

"I don't need her here," Bernadette said under her breath.

"She won't impose," Regis said. "They're here just in case they're needed."

"But I have you."

"It takes a village," he said.

She smiled at the predictable Regis expression. "And to think I was terrified of you at first," she said.

It seemed like such a long time ago when she had first learned about Regis from an interview with him in the *Austin Chronicle*. After that he'd seemed to pop up everywhere: in an article about his restorative dialogue program from the University of Texas's online magazine, in victims' reports on Internet blogs, in a television documentary that featured victims and offenders talking to each other. Yet the more she learned about his program, the more adamant she had been that it wasn't for her.

"To even think about doing something like that turns my stomach," she'd said to Marty.

She knew she felt that way because she was tired, so bone tired that for nine years she hadn't been able to pick up the phone to call a friend to go to lunch or stop in at the women's bookstore she used to support for a cup of tea or to pick up a book—but then, she'd stopped reading anyway. She'd still managed to shop for food and cook dinner for the family on Friday nights, but the joy had gone out of it.

Then one day while mopping the kitchen floor, she'd happened to hear Sister Helen Prejean on National Public Radio say, "The only way I know what I really believe is by keeping watch over what I do." Bernadette would never understand why on that particular day those words quickened in her a desperate desire to live again and an urgent need to rid herself of the grief, pain, and anger that kept her from doing so. All she knew was that she had picked up the phone and called Regis. That was well over a year ago. An eternity.

She looked at Regis now, at his compassionate hazel eyes with that mysterious tinge of sadness around the edges, his thinning brown hair with specks of gray covering his ears, the upturned corners of his mouth, and, of course, those dimples that made him look as if he was smiling even when he wasn't.

"What would I do without you?" she said, squeezing his arm.

He smiled at her but he looked worried. Amy Whitehall kept glancing at the clock with an anxious look on her face, too. Best not to look at either of them, Bernadette thought. She fidgeted with the public information folder on her lap, turned the page to the Offender's Rap Sheet:

> *Raelynn Blackwell. Age and race (39 White), DOB (03/03/72), Date of Offense (05/03/01), Date of Arrest (05/03/01), Age when arrested (29), Height (5'3"), Weight (100), Eyes (blue), Hair (blonde), execution date (July 15, 2011), amount of time on death row (3,732 days – 10 yrs., 2 months, 20 days).*

Bernadette's eyes stung. This wasn't anything like the other rap sheets she'd seen over the years. This one was personal. She flipped the page. There was no need to read the facts of the crime when the excruciating details of that day were forever engraved in her very being: the police officer at the door telling them Veronica had been found lying in a pool of blood by the bus stop at 8:45 p.m.—she and Marty clinging to each other after identifying Veronica's body—carrying her backpack to the car, her inhaler falling out of the side pocket and onto the ground—the police calling later that night to say a squad car had picked up a crazed and bloodied woman staggering around the east side of Austin, gripping in her hand a gold necklace with the initials VB on it—forensics later determining that the blood on Raelynn Blackwell was a combination of her own and Veronica's.

The door opened, and Bernadette brushed away the tear making its way down her cheek. She recognized Warden Fredrick's round face from a picture that was hanging on the wall downstairs. But why was he here? And why was Amy Whitehall still looking askance at her from the opposite side of the room? She looked at her watch. Six fifteen. They should all be in the death chamber by now. Her stomach knotted up. The muscles in her neck went on alert, her imagination running wild with a herd of all things that possibly could have gone wrong.

"Welcome, Mrs. Baker," the warden said with a warm Texas smile. "I came to see if there's anything you might be needing." His thick fingers were soft against hers when he shook her hand.

"Something's wrong, isn't it?" she said.

"Just waiting for the governor's call," he said. "Shouldn't be long now."

He patted her shoulder in a gesture of sympathy and she shrugged it off with a frown, but when he brought her a cup of acidic-smelling coffee, she saw that under his bushy salt-and-pepper eyebrows his blue eyes were kind like Marty's and she didn't have the heart to refuse it. After he left, she set the cup on the floor under her chair.

The folder sat open on her lap. Years ago, when she was active in the anti-death-penalty movement, she'd gotten her hands on a similar packet, so she already knew what was in it—a list of scheduled executions, execution methods and procedures, the Texas capital punishment code, criminal and witness procedures, Texas death row history and facts. She had no need to read any of that, not now.

Right after she closed the packet, a man she'd never seen before walked into the room. She cringed at the sight of the gaudy tie hanging loose around the folds of his crimson neck and coming to rest on his protruding belly, his bulbous nose marinated in sweat.

"There's been a slight delay," the man said in a raspy voice, "nothing unusual. Just make yourselves comfortable." Then he turned and left as quickly as he'd come, slamming the door behind him.

So much waiting time gave space to Bernadette's natural impulse to worry, and it didn't take long for her to succumb to it. She started with Fin.

"Be careful what you wear," she'd told him that morning on the phone. "Don't make yourself a target."

He'd said what he always said: "Don't worry, Mom, I can take care of myself just fine."

Of course he could. Her drop-dead handsome son was no longer the sweet little curly-headed, red-cheeked boy who had been every bully's target. He was thirty years old now, six feet tall, like his dad, and as capable as they come. Still, she worried about him. She couldn't help herself.

"I bet Marty's got his nose in a book right now," she said to Regis. "It's his way of losing track of time until I call to tell him it's over."

Good old solid Marty. She knew her attention to detail and her tendency to micromanage things drove her philosophy professor husband crazy sometimes, but she had never had cause to question his love for her.

"I thought he would come with you today," Regis said.

"I told him not to," she said.

Regis looked at her with that raised eyebrow of his again.

"He said he would come, but I know he would only be doing it for me," she said. "It's a good thing Annamaria decided not to come. She'll be frustrated enough having to wait for it to be over. Just so she doesn't take it out on Patty. The two of them fight about everything as it is, just like me and Annamaria did when she was sixteen, and my granddaughter has enough teenage angst already without having to fight with her mother over this tonight."

They fell silent then as her thoughts turned to Raelynn Blackwell. The tie-down team should have secured her to the gurney in the death chamber by now. Or was she still in the holding cell? Bernadette looked at her watch. Six thirty. She pressed her fingers into the sides of her head and massaged her temples.

"What are you thinking about?" Regis asked after a few minutes.

"If Veronica were here, she'd tell me to stop worrying. She was the opposite of me, always so easygoing. When she was three days old, already she was smiling, and I knew it wasn't gas, no matter what people said. The terrible twos never happened for her, either. And she was sailing through her teenage years without the torment that Annamaria and Fin suffered at that awkward stage until… until…"

Regis rested his hand on hers. She wiped a tear from her eye, took in a breath and released it. Raelynn Blackwell would soon pay for what she did, and then it would be over.

THREE

Fin's muscular arms throbbed from holding his homemade sign high in the air for four straight hours, and when his fingers tingled and then finally went numb, he had no choice but to let the poster drop to the ground. He propped it up against his sinewy legs and rubbed his hands together to bring his fingers back to life.

"Want me to hold it, bro?" Chuck asked.

Fin smiled at his best friend. Even though Chuck shied away from any kind of protesting or political activity, he had taken off work to be with Fin today, something neither of them did often. They had so much in common and were together so much that some people started to think they even looked alike—both tall, handsome, fit—seemingly ignoring the fact that Fin was white with purplish morning-glory blue eyes and Chuck was black with deep brown eyes. It was their unwavering dedication to helping preteen boys stay out of trouble—Chuck at the Big Brothers Big Sisters program, where he matched at-risk boys with men who served as mentors and role models, and Fin at the Communities in Schools program, where he counseled middle-school boys—that brought them together, and Fin considered the day the two of them met to be the best day of his life. Tears of gratitude filled his eyes now as he handed his poster over to Chuck.

"Wish I could cry at the drop of a hat like that," Chuck said with a grin.

Fin shrugged, embarrassed. He looked down at his watch. It was after six o'clock. He ran his fingers through his thick, wavy hair and hopped from one foot to the other. The sweltering heat was getting to him.

"Come on, any time now," he said. "Mom said she'd let us know as soon as it was over."

"You and your mom," Chuck said with a shake of his head, "two peas in a pod."

"Not about this, we're not," Fin said. "She shouldn't be in there. I don't get it. I don't get her."

The crowds were getting more and more restless, which made Chuck fidgety. Fin studied the people standing and kneeling nearby, a varied bunch of young, old, and middle-aged, with men and women in about equal numbers, most white, a few Latinos, no blacks except for Chuck. Fin felt bound to those who came to protest the execution, yet set apart from them at the same time. No one else was like him. No one else was Veronica's brother.

"Do it! Do it now! Do it! Do it now!"

"Hateful Sam Houston U students," Fin mumbled, "hateful and ignorant."

"Finbar Baker, my dear man." The sound of Father Gilpatrick's soft Irish brogue made his ears burn. Ten years ago Fin had cursed the priest and stormed out of the confessional, and he hadn't set foot inside St. Austin's or any other church since then. He noticed that the priest's back was now curved, his face covered with deep wrinkles, his thick hair a shocking white.

"How are you, my boy?" the priest asked.

Fin bit his tongue. *Just say you're fine,* he told himself. But it was ludicrous to think anyone could be fine tonight, so he shrugged and left it at that.

"It's hard," Father Gilpatrick said.

"You were wrong." Fin's body tightened as the words snuck out through his pursed lips.

"What?"

"It wasn't a sin to blame myself for what happened."

Father Gilpatrick's eyebrows went up, and he tilted his head to the side.

"It wasn't," Fin said. "It isn't. Veronica would still be alive if I hadn't moved into my own apartment while she was still in high school. I should have been there to drive over and pick her up that night when her bus was late."

"I see. I see." The priest looked as if he was about to say something else but changed his mind. "Well," he said, "please do give my regards to your mother for me, Finbar."

"Did you see her go in?"

"Yes. I would have liked to talk to her."

Father Gilpatrick patted Fin's shoulder then and disappeared into the crowd. Fin wanted to call him back, say more, tell him he knew what Veronica thought—that he knew what she thought because they both thought the same things and always had—that he was working hard to make right all the things that needed to be made right in this world because he had promised his sister he would not only do his part but her part, too.

"Getting pretty late, isn't it?" Chuck said.

Fin looked at his watch and his breath stuck in his throat. He grabbed Chuck's arm and squeezed it.

"Ouch! Why'd you do that?"

"It's six thirty."

Fin crossed his fingers. He pressed his hands over his stomach. Glanced down at his watch again, just to be sure. He blew his breath out through his lips, not daring to say out loud what he was thinking, what he knew Veronica would be thinking, too, if she were here.

FOUR

The butterflies in Annamaria's stomach had been there since she woke up. She'd thrown herself into her work both to keep them at bay and so that she would appear to her colleagues to be the same competent attorney today that she was every other day. She tugged at her amber corkscrew curls—a habit she'd started as a child in a futile attempt to straighten them—and pushed her chair back, her eyes glued to the legal folder that lay open on her desk. No one wanted the Hinson case. Now she knew why. Jacob Hinson had been set up big time, and it was up to her to prove he wasn't guilty. Volunteering to take the case would help smooth some of the feathers she'd ruffled at the last office meeting.

"Check his estranged wife's holdings," she'd insisted when they were discussing the troublesome embezzlement case. "That's where the money is. You'll see."

No one had listened to her, but, of course, it turned out that she had been right—again. Because her always being right grated on her colleagues' nerves, she tried to mollify them by working longer hours than anyone else and taking on cases they didn't want—like the Hinson case. If she played her cards right, she could make partner by the time she was forty, one year from now. Not an easy feat at a law firm as prestigious and competitive as Benton and Smith.

But that's not what she'd been thinking about all day. Her frenzied focus on work was more about containing her anxiety than about promoting her career. Or was it excitement she felt? It had been ten long years, after all, and she'd often doubted that this day would ever come. Well, now it was here. At last.

At five o'clock, early for her, she closed the Hinson file and gulped down what was left of the white zinfandel in her glass. Most days she had only one glass of wine at the end of the day to relax, but today she had two. She didn't keep any alcohol at home, not because she worried about her own consumption or because of her mom's warning that alcoholism ran in their family or even because of her ex-husband Roberto's drinking problem, but because it just seemed wise not to have the stuff around with a teenager in the house.

There was no line at the KFC drive-through when she picked up dinner for herself and Patty, so by five thirty she was already turning off Balcones Drive and pulling her BMW up the long sloping driveway and into the garage of their modern Hill Country house. Another half hour and it would be over.

Her keys clinked as they collided with Patty's oversized key ring in the glass bowl on the marble-topped table in the front hall. There was a strong smell of disinfectant in the house, a sure sign—along with the extra gleam to the wood floors and special shine to the glass walls—that Guadalupe had been there. How fitting that today was cleaning day. She kicked off her three-inch heels in the hallway,

noting even today, as she always did, the contrast between her
thick ankles (which she'd unfortunately inherited from her mom)
and her reasonably long, slender legs (which she'd fortunately
inherited from her dad). On her way to the kitchen, Annamaria
set her designer briefcase down on the dining room table next
to the freshly cut flowers from the backyard, careful not to leave
her fingerprints on the shiny teak surface. Everything had to be
perfect—just as a new beginning should be.

Patty bounced into the all-white kitchen just as Annamaria
dropped the KFC bag onto the glistening island counter.

"Tell me you did *not* go outside looking like that," she said
when she saw her braless sixteen-year-old daughter wearing a
too-tight tank top and cutoff jean shorts.

"Like I would, Mom."

Annamaria reached over and stroked the silky black hair and
smooth, golden-brown cheeks that Patty had inherited from her
handsome father. Sometimes she wished Patty's father were still here
to protect her, especially during these difficult teenage years, but
Roberto Gonzales was long gone, having disappeared to El Paso or
Mexico or wherever the hell he went fourteen years ago. It was one
thing to run away from her and their drunken fights, she got that,
but she could never forgive him for abandoning his two-year-old
daughter. Though she had changed her name from Gonzales back
to Baker when they divorced, Patty's official name remained the
same: Patricia Roberta Gonzales. Her middle and last names—in
addition to those brown-sugar eyes and long, curly eyelashes—were
all she had left of her father although none of that seemed to matter
much to Patty.

Annamaria looked at her watch. Twenty minutes to go. She reached inside the glass cabinet for two plain white plates, the good ones, and the fancy glass goblets.

"The good linen napkins, too?" Patty closed the door of the doublewide stainless steel refrigerator with a kick and plopped two cans of Diet Coke on the counter.

"It's a special occasion."

"Fine, but, like, I'll just help myself from the boxes, if you don't mind." Patty pulled the KFC containers from the bag and loaded her plate with a chicken breast—extra crispy, just the way Annamaria knew she liked it—coleslaw, mashed potatoes, gravy, green beans, and an individual-sized apple pie. She gulped her Coke from the can.

Annamaria looked at her watch. Five forty-five. *Try not to think about it*, she told herself. *It'll be over sooner that way*. But she couldn't help herself. She looked at her watch again. Still five forty-five. And again. Five forty-six.

Patty mumbled something through the two huge spoonfuls of mashed potatoes she'd stuffed into her mouth, in response to which Annamaria rolled her eyes and pursed her lips, then proceeded to pick at the food on her plate. She glanced down at her watch. Five fifty. Patty muttered something else that could have been anything from "Don't worry" to "Fuck you," for all Annamaria could tell.

"Don't talk with your mouth full, young lady," she said.

Patty grinned and bit into a piece of chicken. It was five fifty-seven.

"Shore is finger-lickin' good, Ma." Her daughter chewed with her mouth open, then swallowed with an exaggerated gulp.

"What... are... you... *doing?*" It took all the effort Annamaria could muster to not stab her chicken breast but instead slowly lower her fork onto her plate. Why the hell was Patty acting like a four-year-old? She didn't need this. Not tonight of all nights.

"So it's working, ain't it?" Patty shrugged and set about building a mound of mashed potatoes in the middle of her plate, scooping out a hole in the top and pouring masses of gooey brown gravy into it. With a sideways glance at her mother, she carved rivulets into the sides of her potato mountain, then watched the gravy flow down like lava from a volcano.

"Stop it, young lady." Annamaria grabbed Patty's hand. The potato mountain collapsed.

"*You* stop it already." Patty motioned at her mom's watch with a flick of her head.

All right. She would try. She would show her daughter that she was the adult in the room. But after a few minutes that seemed like hours, she couldn't stand it anymore. She glanced down at her watch and gasped. It was past six thirty.

"Your grandmother should have called by now."

"She'll call when she's ready to call." Patty reached across the counter and grabbed Annamaria's wrist.

Annamaria peeled her daughter's fingers off her delicate gold watch and peeked at it again. Six thirty-seven. She reached for the remote control and clicked on the kitchen TV. Shit. The local news was already over.

"That monster better be dead by now," she muttered.

"Mom . . . Gran says . . ."

Annamaria leaped to her feet, yanked open the kitchen drawer behind her, and pulled a yellowed newspaper from under the phone books.

"See this?" She stabbed her finger on the picture of a skeletal woman with black-ringed eyes and dirty, matted hair. "*This* is a monster. She killed your Aunt Veronica. I don't care what your grandmother says."

"Don't start, Mom." Patty's eyes glistened with tears.

Annamaria took a deep breath. "I didn't mean to bad-mouth Gran."

When Patty's lips started quivering Annamaria no longer saw a pouty teenager but a little preschooler with eyes full of complete and total devotion hugging her grandmother's legs. After Roberto left, Patty's loyalty to her Gran was forged when Annamaria's mom cared for Patty full time so Annamaria could work at Macy's in the mall at night and go to law school during the day. While their bond was beautiful to Annamaria, it saddened her at the same time because it was such a contrast to her own stormy relationship with her mom.

"Like, Gran's more courageous than anyone, *ever*," Patty said. "And that man that's been helping her?"

"Please, Patty. I don't want to talk about that right now." Annamaria closed her eyes and pushed against her temples with the heels of her hands.

"What's his name again?"

"Regis Dorfman. And for the record, your Gran hasn't been in her right mind since she got involved with that man."

She shoved the newspaper with the photo of Raelynn Blackwell to the side. Who in their right mind would want to do what her mom had done, what her mom was doing? How could she be so naïve? And confused; one minute she thought one way, the next minute she thought another way. Once it was all over—*Dear God, let it be over*—maybe she'd come to her senses.

"Gran says he's amazing."

"What's amazing, young lady," she said, "is that it's almost seven o'clock and we have no idea what the hell is going on."

FIVE

"I need to do this alone, Marty. You shouldn't feel guilty about not coming with me."

That was the last thing Bernie had said to him that morning before she left for Huntsville. And his response—"Of course I won't"—had been truthful. He respected Bernie's preference for doing things on her own and in her own way. It was the way she was, always had been. If she needed him to do something, he knew she would tell him. He liked that they were so different: her hair straight, his curly; her body short and soft, his tall and sinewy. He had always believed each of them had important, yet different, roles to play in their partnership as well. His was to keep the home ship steady, and though he knew that males in general were no better at it than females, the stalwart role came naturally for him. It was just who he was. He and Bernie balanced each other out, just as his parents had. She, like his mother, was the intuitive doer and he, like his father, was the thinker and meaning maker. Not that Bernie wasn't his equal in the thinking department; in fact, he enjoyed thinking of himself as Jean Paul Sartre to her Simone de Beauvoir.

While they formed an equilibrium that, Martin reasoned, was

essential to the healthy functioning of any system, sometimes he envied Bernie's spontaneous earth mother passion. But on the few occasions when he wondered out loud if he might be deficient in the emotions department, she would say, "Come on, Marty, you're the most well-adjusted one in this family." He knew, of course, that that was only partially true. The whole truth was that Bernie was the most self-actualized and authentic person he knew. Or at least she had been until everything changed.

Right after Bernie left that morning, he removed the list of household chores from under the rainbow-colored Keep Austin Weird magnet on the refrigerator door. The list was in his handwriting and thus indecipherable to anyone but him. It wasn't that he knew what things needed to be done around the house and added them to the list on his own. Bernie would always have to point them out first, and then he'd write them down.

He studied the list now. They were little chores, things no one but she would notice. Nothing too demanding. He was glad for something physical to do while he waited today. This wouldn't be the best time to try to concentrate on something like preparing for the new philosophy course he was scheduled to teach in the fall semester. No, today, it was best to keep active.

He decided to tackle the outside chores first: hose out the garbage cans, wash the sliding glass doors to the deck with vinegar water and newspaper as per Bernie's instructions, clean the barbecue grill, wipe down the deck furniture, drown the colony of fire ants in the backyard with Bernie's mysterious mixture of dishwashing liquid and citrus oil, weed the flower bed in the back corner of the yard. He listened to pianist Van Cliburn play Rachmaninoff on his iPod as he worked and so the morning passed quickly. But by noon all his bones hurt. He wiped the sweat from his brow and blamed his discomfort on the sun sizzling over his head in the endless Texas sky. His khaki shorts hung low on his hips. He yanked them up, remembering what the doctor had said about his lack of appetite. But this wasn't the time to think about that.

He bit into the turkey sandwich Bernie had left for him in the refrigerator.

"What will you eat for lunch?" he'd asked her before she left.

"I'll pick up something," she'd said.

Thank goodness he'd had the sense not to make a joke about the killer burgers that were served at the restaurant across the street from The Walls. He was still appalled at himself for even thinking about it.

He put his sandwich, the bulk of it untouched, back into the refrigerator and set about crossing off all the outside chores completed so far. He found he'd finished them all and was ready to tackle the inside ones, glad to be in the air-conditioning at this time of day. While he was cleaning the AC filters, he thought about how glad he was that Bernie wasn't alone, that Regis was at Huntsville with her. Still, while he was dusting the ceiling fans, he found himself second-guessing his agreement not to go with her. But of course she would be fine.

While he was arranging the paint cans in the garage by color, setting aside for disposal the ones Bernie had labeled as being more than five years old, he wondered how Fin was doing. It was quite unlikely, he decided, that Bernie would see him there. While he was vacuuming the coils in back of the refrigerator, his thoughts turned to Annamaria. At that, all he could do was shake his head, turn up the volume on his iPod, and make a concerted effort not to worry about the children today. What was the point when Bernie did enough worrying for both of them?

It's not that she worried in a futile way. He never thought of Bernie as an anxious person. In fact, his wife was the strongest, most courageous woman he'd ever known. And he'd known some powerful women in his lifetime, starting with his own mother and continuing to the present day with the few women professors in his philosophy department at The University of Texas at Austin who were tough as they come. They had to be to survive in his field, of course, but even they couldn't hold a candle to his Bernie.

At five o'clock, after he'd finished cleaning the dead bugs from the light globes on the ceilings in the entryway and kitchen, he sat at the round oak table with his list. One chore remained undone. He'd saved the best for last.

He headed for the living room and the 1902 mahogany bookshelves that had sealed the deal for him when they decided to buy the house decades ago. He looked around the room for a few seconds, admiring the old oriental rug Bernie had found at a garage sale, the original dark woodwork, the way the eclectic mix of modern and traditional paintings blended so nicely with all their family pictures. Everything was impeccable, as usual, thanks to Bernie; even the multi-colored pillows on the dark maroon leather couch were lined up in sharp precision.

With the sound of Beethoven in the background, he set about his remaining task with relish, rearranging the existing volumes on the bookshelves in alphabetical order and making room for the books he'd finished reading. As he worked, he introduced the authors to each other, assuring them that they would make good neighbors and colleagues, and thought about the times when he and Bernie would sit out on the deck, reading. He favored philosophy books by Kant, Hegel, Marx, Foucault, and Kierkegaard, while she preferred the latest literary novel, *New Yorker* short story, or political commentary by the likes of Molly Ivins and Jim Hightower. Every so often, she would interrupt him to share some poignant or laugh-out-loud turn of phrase, like when Ivins wrote that if a certain Texas congressman's IQ slipped any lower, you'd have to water him twice a day.

"What is intelligence?" he remembered asking her.

"When you can walk and chew gum at the same time. I doubt this guy can," she'd retorted.

How he missed times like that, when he would ask her about some lofty concept just to hear her pithy Midwestern take on it, always practical. But that was all before. Before she stopped reading altogether. Before she quit engaging in causes about which she used to feel so passionate. Before she reverted to her old habit of trying to manage everyone and everything. Before Veronica was murdered.

It was a few minutes after six o'clock when Marty slipped the last book into its proper place on the bookshelf, right next to *The Other America*. He pulled Michael Harrington's book out and caressed its cover, reliving the dinner debate it had spawned when Veronica had been assigned the book for school.

"I can't imagine what it must be like," she'd said, "to be trapped in a vicious cycle of poverty and not be able to get out of it."

"Right," Fin had chimed in.

"Can't you guys see," Annamaria had said, taking the opposite point of view as usual, "all that's happened since that book was written? The Great Society, the War on Poverty, civil rights legislation. Social Security and Medicare have all but eliminated poverty among the elderly."

"Come on, you can't be serious," Fin had said.

"What about all those high-rise public housing projects?" Veronica added.

"There but for the grace of God," Bernie had said.

"You would see it that way," Annamaria had retorted.

At that point Marty had chimed in, rubbing his chin in thoughtful reflection. "So what do you think about the argument that poverty is caused by cultural pathology?"

"Pretty funny," Annamaria had said. "That was considered a liberal idea in the 1960s, and now it's the conservatives who see it and the liberals are suddenly blind."

"It's not right to blame poor people for being poor." Veronica's voice had gone up several octaves higher by then.

"Critical thinking leads to right actions," Marty had said.

"Follow your heart, is what I say," Bernie had said.

As he put Harrington's book back on the shelf, Marty thought about how many dinnertime discussions just like that one they'd had over the years. No matter the topic, the debates always played themselves out in a similar fashion, with members of the family assuming predictable roles. His favorite times were when he and Veronica continued the conversations while doing the dishes together. He remembered the last one as if it were yesterday. How tenacious Veronica had been that night.

"Health is a basic human right," she'd declared with a certainty so characteristic of the young.

"Maybe access to health care could be considered a right, but not health itself," he had countered.

"I *know* the difference, Dad," she'd said.

Overcome with delight at his baby girl's passion and knowledge about things most teenagers wouldn't even bother to think about, he had folded her in his arms. "That's my girl," he'd said as she rested her head on his shoulder. No one could have known then that they had just finished the last debate they would ever have.

He swallowed hard to push down the lump in his throat. How could everything have changed in an instant? The worse part was when Bernie fell apart during the months right after Veronica was killed; she did nothing but clean, scrubbing down all the walls and ceilings—cleaning out every single closet, cabinet and drawer—mopping the floors every day—scrubbing the toilets and sinks several times a day. What a terrible time that had been. How hopeless he'd felt, how lost he was without Bernie to lean on. How relieved he'd been when her obsessive cleaning finally stopped, when she started cooking again. How hopeful he'd been when they started to have the kids over for dinner again on Friday nights. But even as, to this day, they gathered weekly around the same table where their debating skills were first honed, nothing had ever been the same again without Veronica.

He sighed and looked at his watch. Well, things were about to change again, and for the better. Soon he would have his Bernie back. They would go on vacations again, join or start a book club, reconnect with old friends, take walks around Town Lake. Maybe she'd renew her license and teach again, maybe even take a few classes at the university. He didn't care if she still put herself in charge of everything. He could live with that.

At six thirty he went into the kitchen to microwave the plate of spaghetti with meatballs that Bernie had left for him in the refrigerator. But, finding he still wasn't hungry, he sat down at the table with a cup of coffee instead. The coffee tasted bitter on his tongue, and he pushed it to the side. He read over the list of chores, looking for just one more to keep him busy. He told himself to relax. Bernie would call as soon as she could. Everything would be all right. He just needed to be patient. He picked up the latest philosophy journal and leafed through its pages but found it impossible to concentrate. Soon he found himself doing nothing but staring at the phone, willing it to ring. And when it did, he almost jumped out of his skin. He pulled himself together. This was it. A new chapter was about to begin.

"Dad, what the hell is going on? Has Mom called you yet?"

"I thought you were her," he said with a heavy sigh. The last thing he needed right now were Annamaria's hysterics.

"It's after seven, for Christ's sake."

"I'll call you as soon I hear anything," he said.

"There better not be a problem," she said, "not again."

"I'm sure nothing's wrong." He hoped nothing was.

"Right, nothing's wrong, nothing's ever wrong, is it, Dad? Well, not this time."

"Try to calm down, okay?"

"At least Fin could call."

"I'm hanging up now so Mom can get through."

He cut off the phone before she could say anything else. It was always the same with Annamaria when it came to Raelynn Blackwell. Something would set her off: news coverage about another appeal filed or lost, another prominent figure speaking on Raelynn's behalf, the setting of an execution date, another delay. It didn't matter what it was. Just the mention of Raelynn Blackwell's name would get her going. It often happened over dinner. And as soon as Annamaria started to rant, Fin would take her on, always with the same arguments: the death penalty wasn't working; it would be a whole lot cheaper just to lock people up and pitch the key; it was only a matter of *when* it would be abolished, not *if;* it was immoral to murder anyone, whether by the state, a person, or an army. He always ended the same way: "Come on, it's just plain inhumane."

"Inhumane?" Annamaria would scream. "Don't you see there's nothing inhumane about going to sleep and not waking up? What about us?"

At that point, Bernie would typically intervene. "You know how I feel," she would say. "Raelynn Blackwell needs to be punished. Doing the right thing is the only way this can end."

Bernie's words rang in Marty's ears now. What if it didn't end after tonight? What if he still didn't get his wife back? Why hadn't she called yet? Was she too upset to talk about what happened? He should have gone with her, made sure she was okay. At seven fifteen, he dropped his head onto the table, too tired to think anymore.

SIX

Bernadette folded her arms across her chest, unfolded them. Her skirt stuck to the plastic chair. She tugged it loose. Pulled the hem down over her knees and crossed her legs. Looked at her watch. Seven o'clock. She uncrossed her legs. The trauma team hovered around the coffee urn, wariness and stress now added to the pain on Amy Whitehall's face. What was Fin doing outside? He must be getting worried. Annamaria would be beside herself by now. Even Marty would be starting to wonder what was going on.

Maybe she should call them. But what would she tell them? Not to worry? That there was no problem, they were just waiting for the governor's call, that's all? But how could she do that when her gut was churning with an unmistakable certainty that something had gone wrong? No, calling would create more worry. Maybe they'd figured out by now that these things sometimes take time. Maybe they didn't even expect her call yet. She glanced at Regis, who looked his usual calm self.

"Good lord, what is going on anyway?" She tried, without success, to keep her voice from rising.

Regis patted her arm. "I'll go see."

He approached the trauma team. They shook their heads in unison, then turned toward Bernadette as if one body. She looked at her watch, double-checked it with the clock on the wall. Seven fifteen. Something had to have gone wrong. Maybe the tie-down team had trouble securing Raelynn Blackwell properly because she was so small. Maybe there was a technical problem of some kind. She thought about the simulated execution she'd seen earlier on the video the trauma team had showed her during the witness orientation session: the injection team inserting an intravenous tube in each arm of the mannequin lying on a gurney, the right one a contingency in case the left one malfunctioned; the narrator describing how "the first lethal dose of sodium thiopental renders the offender unconscious, then a dose of pancuronium bromide collapses the diaphragm and lungs, and finally a dose of potassium chloride stops the heart. It takes only about seventeen minutes from the time the offender is restrained until he is pronounced dead." Any number of things could have gone wrong, she thought now, at any point.

Just then the door opened and in came the man she'd found so repulsive earlier. "It's time," he said. "Will the witnesses please follow me?"

She released the breath she hadn't realized she'd been holding in, pushing it out of her puffed-up cheeks as she followed in the wake of the man's sweat-odor trail. Someone squeezed her shoulder. She shrugged the hand off and, out of the corner of her eye, caught a glimpse of a retreating Amy Whitehall.

At the door to the death chamber, two somber guards nodded and stepped aside. A muscle twitched in her jaw. This was it. A crushing wave filled with doubt, fear, and panic almost knocked her to the floor. She couldn't move. She tasted vomit in the back of her throat.

"It's fast." Amy Whitehall was back, whispering in her ear. "Don't worry, it won't last long."

"Such a comfort," Bernadette retorted.

At least the sound of Amy's voice had the effect of jump-starting her legs so she was able to walk on her own. Once they were inside the small viewing room, the hair on top of her down-turned head brushed against the glass window. She closed her eyes and leaned against Regis as images of impending death flashed, unbidden, through her head: a Vietnamese prisoner executed at point blank range during the 1968 Tet Offensive, a Liberian soldier looming over an unarmed man lying face up in a ditch, bodies falling from the burning Twin Towers on 9/11, a young boy herded from the Warsaw ghetto by a Nazi wielding a machine gun.

"Take your time," Regis said, squeezing her shoulder.

The images went away. But she couldn't look at what was on the other side of the window. Not yet. She ran her tongue over her dry lips. This was the right punishment, she knew that, but watching someone die might be quite another thing altogether. Her body trembled even more than it had two weeks ago at Gatesville when she confronted Raelynn Blackwell. She didn't know which was harder, facing the murderer of her daughter then or witnessing that murderer's execution now.

"She looks peaceful," Regis whispered.

Bernadette balled her hands into fists, and the muscles in her neck tightened as she willed her eyes to open. The first thing she noticed was how Raelynn Blackwell's ankles disappeared under the thick restraints that secured her to the massive silver gurney and how her shins, thighs, waist, and chest were dwarfed under the brown leather straps and huge metal buckles. For some reason, Bernadette hadn't expected everything to be so white: Raelynn Blackwell's laundered and pressed prison garb, her socks under what looked like brand-new white tennis shoes, the makeshift pillow under her head, a towel folded in thirds. Her arms were extended on boards, her hands and fingers covered with white bandages. Intravenous tubes protruded from the bandages around her wrists, snaking under the gurney and disappearing through a hole in the wall just below a one-way window.

Raelynn Blackwell turned her head toward the viewing window. A radiant smile brightened her face, and her blue eyes twinkled under trimmed bangs; even the blonde curls tickling her flushed cheekbones glowed. Bernadette's eyes fixed on the silver cross resting on the woman's throat, and she gritted her teeth just as she had the first time she'd seen it.

"Not *your* God!" she had screamed that day at Gatesville while Raelynn Blackwell sobbed on the other side of the Plexiglas window. "You don't get to have the same God Veronica had. I won't allow it!"

A cold fist closed over Bernadette's chest now and her legs buckled, but still she held Raelynn Blackwell's gaze, pressing against the window to hold herself up. Just as she had been determined not to turn away from Raelynn the first time she'd laid eyes on her, she refused to turn away from her now.

Warden Fredrick stood at the head of the gurney with the chaplain at the foot, his hand cupping Raelynn Blackwell's right ankle. Both men stared at the floor as a large microphone descended from the ceiling and stopped within inches of Raelynn Blackwell's lips. Bernadette braced herself. Soon the microphone would receive her final words, the warden would give the signal, and the chemicals would be released. Soon, Raelynn Blackwell would be dead and it would all be over.

She looked into Raelynn's tearless eyes and remembered how strange it had seemed to her that, in spite of the ninety-five degree temperature in the visiting room at Gatesville that day, the woman hadn't even broken out in a sweat.

"I'm ready to die," Bernadette remembered her saying. "It's what I deserve."

Just as the heat hadn't bothered Raelynn Blackwell that day, so too death was going to come easy for her now—unlike the cruel, painful death she had inflicted on Veronica. Bernadette clenched her jaw. Maybe this wasn't the appropriate punishment after all. *Shouldn't she have to suffer more than this?* She bit her lower lip and felt the heat of shame on her neck. After all her work with Regis, all those hours confronting Raelynn Blackwell, had it all boiled down to this—to her wanting Raelynn Blackwell to suffer as much as Veronica had? Bernadette started to cry. It wasn't right, it just wasn't right for Raelynn Blackwell to be at peace with herself and her god when Bernadette wasn't. Not only was it not right; it wasn't fair. But, then, what did it matter? Nothing could make things right again. Nothing could bring Veronica back. There could be no redemption.

Just then, the curtain snapped shut across the viewing window. The repulsive man stormed into the tiny room, out of breath.

"Sorry, folks," he said, "if you'll just follow me, I'll take you to the warden."

SEVEN

The pro-execution crowd, fearing the worst, grew angrier by the minute, while the anti-death penalty crowd, hoping for the best, became more subdued. Just as Fin's eyes were darting between two opposing signs—"Die, Bitch, Die!" and "The Only Solution Is Love"—a burly bald man with bulging eyes jumped in front of Chuck and waved a noose right in his face. The noose was fastened to a sign that said "Raelynn Blackwell, It's Your Time." Fin threw himself in front of Chuck, and a police officer pulled the man away shortly after, leaving the two of them shaken.

"Time to step back a bit, maybe?" Chuck said, his eyes wide with fear.

They tried to move, but with so many people crammed together, getting away from the growing chaos proved to be impossible. At the sound of scuffling and shouting several feet to their right, Fin and Chuck stood on their toes and craned their necks to see what was going on, increasingly afraid that things might soon spiral out of control.

"She's a child of God." A white-haired man waved a tattered Bible in the face of a young man with a crew cut.

"She's a cold-blooded murderer." The young man waved a sign back in the old man's face. The sign said "No Special Favors For So-Called Believers."

The crowd behind the young man started to chant: "Justice, not religion. Justice, not religion."

The police moved in and dragged the young man away, and the man with the Bible fell to his knees.

"Pray for those who despise you," Chuck muttered.

Fin didn't say anything. Religion was one of the things about which he and Chuck didn't see eye to eye, to say the least. Fin berated organized religion for inflicting pain on people in the name of God, while Chuck still attended services at the Baptist church in which he'd grown up, where he felt loved and accepted. Fin loved Chuck, yet there was something other than religion that kept them from being more than friends; while Fin dreamed of adopting a couple of kids someday, Chuck showed no interest in being a father. Not that they'd ever discussed the matter openly. Fin was too afraid.

"Kill the bitch! Do it now! Kill the bitch! Do it now!" The crowd's chants reached a hysterical level.

Chuck cringed and took a few steps back. "They want blood," he said.

Fin put his arm around Chuck's shoulder. "But there's at least four times as many on our side," he said, pointing to the growing numbers of people who were now getting down on their knees on the pavement to pray that Raelynn Blackwell's life be spared. Fin crossed his fingers, closed his eyes, and prayed in his own way along with them.

EIGHT

Bernadette was stunned as she stumbled out of the death chamber, sure that her heart was going to hammer holes right through her ribs. She looked at Regis, behind her, and his face told her that he had no idea what was happening, any more than she did. With robot-like steps that matched the guard's hollow footsteps in front of her and Amy Whitehall's sighs behind her, she filed into a large open room along with everyone else.

Tap, tap, tap. Warden Fredrick stood in the middle of the room, his thick fingers thumping against his chunky thighs. Beads of perspiration dotted his forehead and a circle of sweat radiated out from the underarms of his light blue shirt. Bernadette searched his face for a clue about what was going on, but her intuition seemed to have gone as quiet as the room. All at once, several men exploded through the door, press tags flying from their necks, their edgy voices and shuffling feet shattering the silence as they vied for the best position near the warden. She glared at them. Who invited them, anyway? Shouldn't the media be kept away?

A fidgety circle formed around the warden. His face looked depleted and his eyes haunted as he expanded his chest as if he was trying to fill himself with courage. He raised his hands, and the room fell silent.

"The governor stopped the procedure," he announced.

A burst of adrenaline shot through Bernadette's veins and tightened around her throat. A chorus of gasps echoed through the room—and then havoc broke out.

"What did the governor say?"

"Why did she stop the execution?"

"What's going on?"

The warden raised his palms and the reporters fell silent, notepads and pens at the ready.

"The governor didn't call at six o'clock like she usually does." He cleared his throat. "At seven o'clock, we called her office. Her staff said we could expect to hear from her any minute." He cleared his throat again.

"When did she call?" A reporter interrupted, his voice loud, demanding.

"Tell us what happened," another one said.

"Offender Blackwell was out of appeals." Warden Fredrick tried to shout over the reporters' voices but quickly gave up and pressed the palms of his hands into the air to restore order.

"We fully expected the governor to give the go-ahead. That's why we broke with policy just this once and prepared the offender. That's why I made the decision to bring the witnesses into the viewing room."

He took a deep breath and looked at Bernadette, speaking to her as if she were the only person in the room. "I didn't want you to have to wait any longer than you already had. That was poor judgment on my part. I should have waited. I'm sorry. I never should have put you through all that."

Then he cleared his throat again and sighed, looking around the circle as if resigned to the attacks that were certain to follow.

"Why did the governor stop it?" a reporter blurted out.

"Yeah, what happened, anyway?"

"Does this mean her death sentence is commuted?"

"I reckon Mr. Pearl over there is the one to do the rest of the explaining here," Warden Fredrick said.

A man who had been leaning against the wall stepped forward and joined the warden in the middle of the room. With suspicion, Bernadette eyed his buzz cut, his round head, and his ruddy face that seemed oddly placed on top of his lean body, a flaming red bowtie incongruous next to his impeccable gray linen three-piece suit.

"I'm Attorney Jimmy Pearl, y'all," he said, "and I've been on Miss Blackwell's defense team from the start. The warden here is right that we had run out of appeals. But I decided to give it one last shot and sent a letter to the governor. I reckon she didn't see it before tonight. And now it seems like it gave her enough grief to grant us a thirty-day reprieve."

"So you expected the execution to be called off the whole time." It was a challenge, not a question, from a baby-faced reporter with a badge around his neck that indicated he was from the *Austin American-Statesman*.

"Actually, young fellow, I did not. I expected my letter to be ignored."

"You... don't... really... expect... us... to believe that."

Bernadette's words came out in ragged bursts. Her face felt hot and pinched. She pressed her fingers against the vein pulsing in her neck and tightened her lips into a thin, angry line.

"What was the basis for the appeal?" the reporter asked.

Bernadette didn't wait to hear the response. She stormed across the floor and hurled herself out the door. With her square shoulders pulled back and her sturdy shoes striking the floor like two jackhammers, she charged down the hall.

"*Por dios,* señora." A brown-skinned guard jumped as she hurried past. "Where is it that you are going?" he asked.

"Home," she snapped.

"*Lo siento,* señora, but you cannot go alone. *Un momento.* I will take you."

He reached for his cell phone but kept his eyes fixed on her so that, as much as she wanted to bolt, she didn't dare. She gritted her teeth, pursed her lips, and beat the floor with her foot.

A hand touched her shoulder. She twisted away from it.

"Are you okay?" It was Regis, sounding winded and looking alarmed.

"Why didn't you warn me? You *should* have known. *Somebody* should have known."

Regis reached for her hand, but she waved him away. He drew back with a nod.

"Señora," the guard said, "we will go now."

She stomped after him, rivulets of sweat flowing between her breasts and soaking her armpits. Regis stayed a safe distance behind until they approached the main entrance, at which point he jumped in front of her.

"Hold on," he said, blocking her path.

She stopped and stretched to look over his shoulder. Outside, camera lights blazed against the dusky sky, the irate crowd roared. She crouched behind Regis, a chill running up her spine.

"Good lord," she said. "They don't know."

***

Fin spotted his mom's white 1996 Volvo station wagon right where Regis had said it would be. He bent over to catch his breath and his eyes landed on the bumper.

"Mom, did you scratch that off yourself?" he'd asked her when he first noticed her End the Death Penalty bumper sticker was missing. She hadn't answered, and he'd never asked again.

He could still hear the frenzied cries of the crowds in the distance. Thank goodness Chuck left at the same time he did. Poor guy was scared to death that all hell was going to break loose any minute. It still might. It all depended on what had happened inside, and Fin still didn't know what that was. All he knew was what Regis had told him on the phone a few minutes ago: that they were getting his mom out through a back door and he should meet her at her car. He punched the redial button on his cell phone.

"Where are you?" Regis asked through the crackling static.

"At Mom's car."

"Don't let her drive, okay?"

A few minutes later, a white van with the blue Texas Department of Criminal Justice logo on its side rolled to a stop next to him. His mom jumped out.

"Let's get out of here," she said. Her hands shook as she fumbled in her purse for the car keys.

"Let me," Fin said.

"I am *perfectly* capable," she said.

The keys fell to the ground and Fin snatched them up, held them out of her reach. Then he led her over to the passenger side of the car and opened the door.

"Damn them!" A vein jumped up and down her neck as she slammed herself back against the seat.

"Who?"

"All of them. The protesters. The governor. The warden. Regis. The attorney. Raelynn Blackwell. *Especially* her."

"What happened?"

"I can't get it out of my head." She squeezed her temples and closed her eyes, opened them, blinked, closed them again.

"It must have been horrible," Fin said. Of course she couldn't get it out of her head. How could anyone? But why was she so angry? Was it because Raelynn Blackwell was dead? Now that it was over, did she have regrets about it? He reached over and touched her cheek. She turned away from him and straightened up.

"Are you okay, Mom?"

"Does it look like I'm okay?" Her body was rigid, her voice cold as ice. "Does it?"

He tried to imagine what it must have been like for her to watch Raelynn Blackwell die. It made him sick to think of her standing there, just letting it happen.

"She knew. Don't tell me she didn't."

"Who? Knew what?"

"Annamaria's right. A leopard never changes its spots."

Fin was stunned to see his mom's face twisted with such intense rage. What could Raelynn Blackwell have done before she died? Was it her last words?

"That's why she was so calm."

"Come on, Mom. I don't know what you're talking about. Can you just tell me what happened?" He gripped the steering wheel tighter, expecting to hear something bad. Something very bad.

"You mean what *didn't* happen."

"*What* didn't happen?"

"The execution, Fin. The execution."

His heart lurched, then sped off without him.

"What?"

"The governor called it off."

"Thank you," he whispered.

"How *dare* you!"

He felt for her. A lot. But he still couldn't help but give silent thanks to whatever force in the universe had answered his prayers.

"It's not *fair*," she said.

"Why did the governor stop it?" He tried to keep his voice calm, to sound neutral, but he was so beside himself he could barely sit still.

"She was in on it."

"Who? In on what?"

"Raelynn Blackwell, that's who. She worked the system, that's what. She had it all planned. She knew she wasn't going to die." With each angry spurt, his mom smacked the top of her leg like a drum, her voice growing louder with each beat.

"Come on. That just doesn't sound right." He reached for her hand, hoping to calm her down so he could reason with her. But she snatched her hand away and stared stone-faced at him.

He looked out the window at the passing rural landscape, at what he could see in the dark of the tin-roofed houses with ramshackle porches sagging under the weight of old refrigerators and trailer parts, red barns with hand-painted roofs advertising Brahman bulls and Suzie's Bar-B-Q, ubiquitous Don't Mess with Texas signs. This part of Texas had always been scary to him, but right now it wasn't anywhere near as scary as what he was about to say. Still, he had to say to it.

"I'm sorry, Mom, but I'm glad."

There, he'd been honest. At least there was that. They'd always been honest with each other. Mom would have it no other way. She could at least appreciate that, couldn't she? But she shook her head and waved him away. Her face, twisted into an angry coil, looked disfigured in the dark. This was not his mother. What was happening to her?

"If I could get my hands on her right now, I would …"

"What? Kill her?"

She slapped the seat between them. His hand flew up to his cheek as he realized, for the first time in his life, that not every slap is physical. His face went numb, and he felt sick to his stomach. Tears stung his eyes. Whatever had happened tonight had been too much for her. He saw that now. He reached over and touched her shoulder.

"I'm sorry," he said, "I shouldn't have said that."

She didn't speak for the rest of the way, just sat rigid and stared out the window. When they got home, Fin walked her to the front door and told her he loved her. She stormed into the house and slammed the door behind her without even saying good night.

NINE

Marty poured himself a fresh cup of coffee and sat down at the kitchen table, propped his head up with his hands, and sighed. Most of the night, Bernie had kept him awake, saying over and over that Raelynn Blackwell had known what was going to happen all along, that everyone else knew, too, that she'd been a fool. And yet, after all that, he still didn't know what had happened, only that Raelynn Blackwell was still alive this morning. But how could a murderer orchestrate the timing of her own execution? Down to the last minute, no less. Nothing Bernie said made any sense, and he didn't know what to make of it. His wife was a lot of things— headstrong, passionate, bold, practical, courageous—but never crazy, never delusional. This wasn't like her. Not like her at all.

"Hi, Dad. I brought Mom's car back." Fin dropped the Volvo keys on the table, then ran his fingers through his disheveled hair and stretched his neck up and down, side to side.

"You look like hell," Marty said.

"Have you looked at yourself in the mirror this morning? How's Mom?"

"She's asleep. Finally."

Fin reached for the *Austin American-Statesman* lying untouched in the middle of the table. "It's the lead story," he said as he unfolded the newspaper.

A picture of Raelynn Blackwell taken the night she was arrested was on the front page next to a photograph of now-retired judge Vera Jean Groundtree and former district attorney Frank O'Grady at some glitzy fundraising event.

"Here, I'll read it to you," Fin said.

That crooked grin of his, plus an almost-twinkle in his eyes, made Marty sit up and take notice.

GOVERNOR HALTS EXECUTION

Huntsville—Convicted murderer Raelynn Blackwell, who brutally stabbed 16-year-old Veronica Baker to death at an Austin bus stop 10 years ago, got lucky last night. Blackwell was already strapped to a gurney with intravenous needles in her arms when a call from Gov. Libby Kopecky halted the execution.

The governor's action was apparently a surprise to Blackwell's attorney, Jimmy Pearl, who had written a letter to the governor claiming that retired Judge Vera Jean Groundtree, who sentenced Blackwell to death, and former district attorney Frank O'Grady, who prosecuted Blackwell, had an intimate relationship for several years.

In the letter, Pearl claimed that "the intimate sexual relationship between the judge and the district attorney began several years prior to Miss Blackwell's trial. While

*Mr. O'Grady and Judge Groundtree have different
recollections as to when the affair ceased containing a
sexual component, there is no doubt that the relationship
was sexual in the years immediately leading up to the time
that the Judge had jurisdiction over Miss Blackwell's case."*

*Pearl said the pair kept the relationship secret. "The
judge never disclosed it to a single litigant or lawyer
who appeared before her, and she never recused herself
from hearing a single case because of her affair," he
wrote. "Similarly, the district attorney never disclosed the
romantic relationship to any of his adversaries, nor did
he recuse himself or his office from prosecuting the case
because of his affair with Judge Groundtree."*

*"We filed a motion about the situation before, but the
charges were never taken seriously, nor were the allegations
ever properly investigated," Pearl said in the letter.*

*Governor Kopecky called for just such an investigation
and granted Blackwell a thirty-day reprieve.*

*When the announcement was made that there would
be no execution, pandemonium broke out among the
estimated 2,000 death-penalty protesters and supporters
who were gathered outside the Walls Unit.*

*Bernadette Baker, mother of the murdered girl, was
in the viewing room to witness the execution when it
was unexpectedly halted. She could not be reached for
comment.*

"So that's it," Marty said as Fin lowered the paper. "But it doesn't say what Raelynn Blackwell's last words were."

"Maybe that's what Mom is so mad about. I've never seen her like this."

"She's not making any sense."

"Tell me about it. She wouldn't even talk to me most of the way home." Fin took a sip of coffee. "Ewww, did you make this stuff?"

"She's not herself." Marty shook his head. He'd never known Bernie to get mad at Fin for anything, much less stop talking to him.

"I think I know how she feels, though," Fin said. "I'd feel deceived, too, if I believed Raelynn Blackwell knew this was going to happen."

"Delusional thinking," Marty said.

Fin didn't say anything. He seemed deep in thought. "Remember Timmy Lee Brown?" he finally asked.

Marty nodded. He remembered Bernie telling the story about the two things Timmy Lee, a mentally retarded man on death row, loved most: bird coloring books and a parakeet named Tipper that some sympathetic guards had given him. The poor guy was so deficient in mental capacity that when they escorted him to the death chamber, he asked if he could color in his book after the execution was over.

"Remember," Fin went on, "how no one seemed to care about Timmy Lee dying, but people were so worried about Tipper that offers to take the parakeet poured in from all over Texas?"

"What are you getting at, Fin?"

"Well, I keep thinking maybe we're worrying about Mom like people worried about the parakeet instead of worrying about Timmy Lee. It's not that I don't feel for her. I do. But it's just that, well, she's not the one they're trying to kill, is she?"

Just then, the phone rang. "Good thing I thought to turn it off in the bedroom," Marty said as he picked up the receiver.

"Can you believe she pulled it off *again*, Dad? Give me Mom."

He held the receiver a few inches away to protect his eardrum from Annamaria's piercing voice. "She's asleep," he said. "She had a rough night."

"Well, of course she did. She's *upset*. How did that bitch manage this, anyway?

He sighed, promised Annamaria he'd have Bernie call her back, and hung up.

"So we now have consensus that Raelynn Blackwell is in control of the world," Fin said with a sarcastic snort.

"Since with your mom someone has to be responsible for everything that happens, she apparently thinks that this time it's Raelynn Blackwell."

"At least for once maybe she doesn't feel that *she's* responsible."

"It's the way she was raised," Marty said with a sigh. He knew only too well how Bernie had struggled with her overdeveloped sense of responsibility, rooted deep as it was in her mother's addiction and early death and her father's unrealistic expectations of her as the oldest of six kids. Dealing with it hadn't been easy on her or on their relationship over the years.

"Maybe that's what makes Mom so good at everything," Fin said, just as the doorbell rang. "That's Chuck to give me a ride home. Show Mom the article. Maybe it'll help."

Good idea. Fin left, and Marty looked at his watch. Maybe Bernie would be awake by now. He poured her a cup of coffee, tucked the newspaper under his arm, and went upstairs. He opened the bedroom door and saw a pile of rumpled covers on the bed but no Bernie, so he knocked on the bathroom door.

"Bernie? Hon?"

No answer. "Bernie?"

He pushed the door open and found her lying in the tub with her eyes closed, her arms at her sides, an inflatable pillow under her head. He fell to his knees and put his fingers on her neck to feel for a pulse. It was steady. Thank God. She started shivering then. No wonder. The water was cold, meaning she'd been in here a long time. He should have checked on her earlier. He touched her cheek, and her eyes opened.

"It's never going to end," she whispered, staring up at the ceiling.

He pulled her from the tub. She didn't resist, but she didn't help, either, so it was a challenge for him to hold her up and dry her off while trying to warm her with the soft, thick bath towel at the same time. He half carried her to the bed with her feet dragging along behind, her head pressed against his chest. He laid her down and pulled the sheet over her. She sighed and he felt the warmth of her breath in his ear.

"It's not over," she said.

He kissed her cheeks and her eyelids, then caressed her head until a change in her breathing assured him that she had fallen asleep. He ached to have her back as his lifelong companion, the one person in the world he had always been able to count on. He felt as desperate as if he'd lost her for good—until he reminded himself that she had reached her limits like this once before, but that the day *had* come when he arrived home from the university to a house that no longer reeked of disinfectant. Just as she had come to her senses then, she would come to her senses now, too, once she got some rest. He tucked the covers up around her neck and tiptoed from the room.

TEN

Annamaria was beside herself. Dad kept telling her to call back later, but now their phone didn't even ring when she tried. Probably disconnected. She could just see the newspaper reporters all over this, pestering her folks to death. But what the hell was she supposed to do? She had to talk to someone, now, someone in the family. Fin would have to do. He wouldn't see things her way—he never did—but at least she could count on him to listen.

"You are not to talk to strangers under any circumstances," she said to Patty after a heated argument over whether Patty should come with her to Fin's house or go to the mall with her friend Kitty instead. "Call me every hour, do you understand? *Every* hour."

With a final warning, she dropped Patty off at the mall and then headed for the freeway.

"God, I hate this road," she grumbled as she steered her car around the broken pieces of asphalt in the merge lane.

I-35 was notorious for its confusing exits and entrances and its poor condition, but mostly Annamaria hated it for what it symbolized: the duplicity of the politicos who built it right down the middle of Austin to avoid the 1960s' school-desegregation mandates. Now, four decades later, the neighborhoods east of the freeway—where most of the black, Hispanic, and poor people still lived—served as receptacles for the city's growing pollution and waste. Because she and Fin agreed about this, it was unfathomable to her why he—or anyone else, for that matter, with the means and any common sense—would choose the east side's untended potholes and dusty streets over the west side's prolific live oak and pecan trees.

But that was just what Fin insisted on doing. Two years ago, when he first came up with the harebrained idea of buying a small fixer-upper on the east side, she'd done her best to talk him out of it. But, of course, he wouldn't listen.

"People should live near their jobs," he had said. "I can walk to school this way, see the kids I work with around the neighborhood, play soccer with them, watch out for them, talk to their parents at the corner grocery store."

Well, that's my brother, she said to herself as she navigated the confusing exit off the freeway. She did give him credit for choosing to live near the Eastside Café, the upscale restaurant popular with westsiders like her who enjoyed strolling through the prolific organic gardens out back after a gourmet lunch before heading back to their cushy jobs on the other side of the freeway.

Also to his credit, Fin had transformed the ramshackle house into an elegant home, all done on the cheap with the help of flea markets and friends' cast-offs. The outside, royal blue with rust-red trim, was too garish for Annamaria's taste. But she had to admit that his little house, right down to the name Casa Azul—painted above the front door, in honor of his favorite artist, Frida Kahlo—suited Fin to a T.

She pulled into his unpaved driveway and parked alongside his front yard, which was filled with blooming red and pink bougainvillea and Hill Country penstemon. The two pink flamingos watching over his xeriscaped garden oasis looked as out of place next to the neighbor's rusty cars and parched crabgrass as did her BMW and pale yellow linen shorts suit. Every time she came here, she marveled at how it could be just a ten-minute drive from this little bungalow to the Victorian house in the historic Enfield neighborhood where they grew up, when the two places were worlds apart.

Fin waved to her from his front porch swing, shirtless and handsome in faded cutoff jean shorts and looking very much like he belonged right where he was. Ordinarily, his warm smile and those blue eyes of his melted her heart, at least initially. But today they served only to make Annamaria pause and wonder, and then only for a minute, if last night's development had helped him to understand what she'd been trying to tell him all along. He was, after all, more complex than most people realized. Yes, he was the kind, down-to-earth social worker who didn't own a car, loved working with kids in the Communities in Schools program even though God knew it paid next to nothing, and walked the two blocks to his job at East Austin Middle School at the same time every morning in his worn and patched (though impeccably pressed) jeans and political tee shirts.

But there was another Fin, a man of refined tastes with a diverse collection of white, black, and Hispanic male friends who were connoisseurs of fine art and wine, who listened to classical music and had season tickets to the opera. All his friends were gay and—to Annamaria's great amusement—seemed to fit every stereotype. When it came down to it, she loved her brother to death. His political proclivities were the opposite of hers, that was true, but he wasn't one of those strident, self-righteous leftists. At his core, Fin was more compassionate than ideological, for which she thanked her lucky stars.

"I just *knew* something was going to screw it up again," she said as she breezed past him into the living room, waving the morning newspaper in the air. "What the hell was O'Grady thinking, to mess around with a judge? I thought he knew better. Geez!"

"I knew you'd be pissed," Fin said.

"And that damn Groundtree!" Annamaria poked her finger at the face of the judge in the photograph. "I've been in her court a few times, and anyone can see she's not the brightest light on the porch. I never would have guessed that old hag had a sexy bone left in her body. She's a grandmother, for Christ sake! Shit, she's old enough to be a *great*-grandmother. Old enough to have a *little* bit of sense, anyway."

"Want some coffee, Sis? Better yet, how about some Calming Yogi tea?" Fin's grin expanded into a smile.

"Don't be funny. You got something stronger?" She followed him into the kitchen and headed for the sink to wash the newsprint from her hands.

"Never in a million years would I have expected Governor Kopecky to do the right thing," Fin said as he opened the refrigerator. "People can sure fool you sometimes."

Annamaria stared at her brother. He was so naïve, as bad as their mom. "Can't you see Kopecky's just covering her ass?" she said. "You know she's as solid a Republican as they come. Hell, that's why I voted for her."

"So you don't think there'll be an investigation?"

"Oh, there will be an investigation, all right. *Many* investigations. Every case that O'Grady brought to Groundtree's court will be called into question now. Wait until you see how many appeals there will be. Believe me, attorneys all over Austin are going nuts right now, poring through the Texas Rules of Appellate Procedures like vultures in search of anything they can find in the carcasses of the all the cases they lost. It's more than just a scandal. It's a legal nightmare, you'll see."

"But what happens to Raelynn Blackwell now?"

"I'll tell you exactly what will happen. A panel will be assigned to review her trial, and the results will show that the evidence in the case didn't change because of Groundtree and O'Grady's stupid little liaison, that she had admitted guilt and the mitigating circumstances were fully vetted at the punishment phase of trial. That will put a lid on it. Not to worry."

"Not to worry?" A splotch of pink moved up Fin's neck and started to take over his face.

"Nothing is going to change," she said.

Fin's hands trembled as he picked up the teak tray on which were arranged two glasses of wine, a plate of sliced apples and cheese, and two bright red- and yellow-flowered cloth napkins. Annamaria followed him into the living room, grabbed a glass of wine, and sank back into the soft purple couch cushions.

"You're wrong," Fin said, tears now welling up in his eyes. "I know you're wrong." He shook his head and lowered himself into the chair adjacent to the couch.

"Sometimes, Fin, I think you care more about that monster than you care about what it's been like for us. How many claims has she made so far, do you think? I stopped counting. Guess we were duped into thinking she'd run out of them this time. Trust me, she knew she wasn't going to die last night."

"So you and Mom finally agree about something."

She shot up from the cushions. "Really? Mom gets it now? She knows she was lied to all this time?"

"She feels betrayed."

"I bet she's pissed. Tell me she's pissed, Fin."

"No need to gloat about it."

She sat back on the couch. *Could Mom and I find common ground at last?* It was almost too much to hope for. She couldn't remember the last time they had agreed about anything.

"Well, I've got her back on this one," she said with a smile.

"You're both wrong."

"I have to see her."

"Don't go rushing over there."

"Why not?"

"Just *don't.*"

She scowled and sat back on the couch. What was with Fin sounding authoritative all of a sudden instead of trying to smooth things over like he usually did? And who did he think he was, anyway, telling her what to do? Besides, he was the one who was wrong. Dead wrong.

"Mom is too well-meaning." She articulated her words as if explaining a complicated concept to a child. "She doesn't see it.

Neither do you. But criminals are master con artists. I'm not saying Mom shouldn't keep looking for the good in people if she wants to. You, too, Fin. Just don't be so naïve about it. At least next time maybe Mom won't be so easily fooled."

"Don't expect her to agree with you," he said.

"Why not? She always said the punishment should fit the crime."

"That never included murder, and you know it."

"The punishment does fit the crime for that monster."

"You know what Mom says about you always calling her that."

"No, I don't."

"Well, if you ever listened to her, you would know she thinks that when you demonize Raelynn Blackwell, you're letting her off too easy, not holding her accountable to the same moral standards as other human beings."

Annamaria's face flushed. "Oh, I hold her accountable, all right, and justice *will* prevail."

"Retribution, you mean."

"That's justice."

"No, it's not."

"You're just like Mom, thinking forgiveness is the same as justice."

"Mom says confronting Raelynn Blackwell with her inhumanity forced her to face what she did. Isn't that a form of justice?"

"Not in my book, it isn't," she said. "And just for the record, I was against Mom getting involved with that dialogue shit from the start. I sure would never do it myself."

"I guess it's not for everyone," he said with a sigh.

"Don't worry, I'll get my justice in thirty days, thank you very much."

"Not if I can help it." Fin's eyes drilled into her.

Annamaria held his gaze with an intensity intended to match his. Let there be an explosion, if there had to be. She wouldn't back down. But after several minutes, Fin's face softened a little and soon his lopsided grin was back. She welcomed her conciliatory brother back with a smile of her own.

"So how's my favorite niece?" he asked.

Her stomach clutched up. She looked at her watch. Why hadn't Patty called yet?

"Something wrong with her?" Fin tipped his head to the side, a look of concern on his face.

"No, no, she's fine. Still a handful, of course."

"Like most sixteen-year-old girls," he said. "Veronica was an outlier that way. She was always so good."

At that, Annamaria's stomach tightened even more and then went into full-throttle churn. Why was Fin comparing Patty to Veronica when they were both good kids; neither was a hell-raiser like she had been at that age, that's for sure. And what did being good have to do with anything, anyway? It hadn't kept Veronica safe, hadn't made life just and fair the way Fin thought it should be, didn't make life predictable, either, no matter how much she wished it could. Life was a crapshoot, and it always would be.

"What's wrong?" Fin asked.

"Do you think Mom's still asleep?"

"Don't bother her," he said. "Wait for her to call you."

Annamaria stared at her brother's tightened jaw, his lips pursed into a threat. It wasn't like him to give orders like this, but then, neither was it like her to take them from him or anyone else. Yet that's just what she did. She took her hand out of her purse and reached for her wine glass instead of her cell phone.

ELEVEN

The curtains were drawn tight, and in the dark bedroom Bernadette couldn't tell what time it was. Not that she cared. Her head throbbed from last night's nightmare that wouldn't end, its images, like a hangover, refusing to go away: the gurney, the smile, the slammed curtain—gurney, smile, curtain—metal buckles and brown leather straps—IV tubes—but mostly Raelynn Blackwell's victory smile. How could she have been so foolish as to assume she knew what that smile meant? Everything had been nothing but a sickening lie. She should have known. It's not that she hadn't been warned.

"You'll see, Mom," Annamaria told her a year ago. "She'll meet with you just to avoid the needle."

"I'm not doing it for her," she had replied, "I'm doing it for me."

"Fine, but just don't go drowning in sympathy like you always do, Mom."

Bernadette rolled onto her back and stared up at the ceiling. Annamaria had been wrong about one thing. She had accused her of considering a bad childhood an excuse for murder, and that just wasn't true. Bernadette had even told Regis, at least at first, that she didn't want to hear anything about Raelynn Blackwell's childhood. And she *had* been cautious every step of the way. Hadn't she? Still, she should reconsider whether some of what Annamaria said was true, whether she'd missed something critical that might have made a difference. She thought about how she almost didn't call Regis at all. That was being careful, wasn't it? And then, when she did call, she had questioned him about everything. She'd even insisted that her confrontation with Raelynn Blackwell not take place until there were no more appeals left and the execution was scheduled, so there would be no room for manipulation.

No, what Annamaria had said wasn't true. She had been *plenty* skeptical. Take Raelynn Blackwell's discovery of religion on death row as an example.

"Everyone who's looking for Jesus should go to prison," she remembered telling Regis. "Seems to be where he hangs out. Those crazy fundamentalists are crawling all over the place looking for jailhouse conversions. Like somehow that makes every crime okay."

She had, right away, apologized to Regis for saying that, because he was a Protestant minister—at least he had been one before he left the church for some unknown reason she would never ask him about, not wanting to pry into his personal life—and since she didn't know what religion meant to him, she was careful not to offend by sharing her opinion that Raelynn Blackwell's conversion was a cheap form of grace. She didn't understand people's passion about religion. To her it was about ritual and tradition more than anything else—although she credited the Catholic Church with instilling in her the moral objection she'd had to state-sanctioned executions before Veronica's murder, and to abortion, too, although that was another matter and something she kept to herself.

She rolled onto her side and closed her eyes, still wondering if, in the end, there was some truth to Annamaria's accusations. Maybe she *was* naïve. Yes, she'd questioned what religion might mean to Raelynn Blackwell, but had she really given enough serious consideration to the possibility that the woman had used both religion and the dialogue program just to avoid being executed?

She set about reviewing the details of their face-to-face meeting two weeks ago. Were there warning signs then? If there were, she wouldn't be at all surprised if she had missed them. During a tour of the Gatesville prison compound the day before their meeting, she had found the incongruous beauty of the place disconcerting: the attractive foliage in front of the Mountain View Unit, the resilient vine that crept up the red bricks of the low building and embedded itself in the crumbling mortar. A testimony to life, it had seemed to her at the time.

Then there was the inside of the building. It was clean and well kept, with colorful painted murals of children and inmate art in a display case that made the place look like a cheerful retreat center. Officer Handley, a ruddy-faced man dressed like a camp director in gray slacks and a pale green polo shirt, had welcomed her and Regis and talked on and on about this and that (she wondered now if it had been nervous chatter) while escorting them around the place. Everything, from the unexpected setting to the cordiality of the staff, camouflaged the true purpose of the Mountain View Unit as the place where death-row women waited to die.

The massive visiting room, a sterile and empty space where her meeting with Raelynn Blackwell was to take place the next day, had been altogether different. While there, she'd imagined what it would be like during visiting hours, with a line of women convicts sitting on one side of the long row of tables, and their mothers, fathers, spouses, children, and friends sitting on the other side, the bulletproof window with several inches of wire mesh at the bottom prohibiting any kind of touch. She could almost hear the buzzing echoes in the room, people shouting to hear each other over the din. No privacy. No holding of hands or hugging. Good lord. Annamaria *was* right. Bernadette had already been drowning in sympathy before she even laid eyes on Raelynn Blackwell.

"I don't want to meet here," she had told Regis.

"It's what we agreed to, remember?"

Of course she remembered. Every aspect of her meeting with Raelynn Blackwell had been worked out in advance: the rules to be followed, goals of the session, how long it would last, what each of them wanted and needed from the meeting. They'd even signed a contract that included Raelynn Blackwell's wishes: no special arrangements would be made for her, she would not be treated differently from other prisoners by having the meeting in the chapel or another place besides the visiting room, which was the only place other prisoners were allowed to interact with people from the outside. What a fool she'd been, Bernadette realized now, to think of all that as evidence of Raelynn's remorse, as her way of accepting responsibility for what she'd done.

Then there was the meeting with Raelynn Blackwell the day after the tour. Had she missed something critical then, too? A plump, pleasant woman with short frizzy hair the color of carrots had shuffled her and Regis to the visiting room while balancing a pitcher of ice water and two glasses on a tray. When they sat down, the screeching sounds of their metal chairs scraping on the concrete floor echoed through the massive room, shattering its glassy silence. Bernadette thought about how fidgety she had been, how she'd stared at the Plexiglas divider, waited for Raelynn Blackwell to appear. Still, she had been convinced at the time that she was ready; at least she thought she should have been, after all the work she'd done to prepare.

When a handcuffed Raelynn Blackwell was led to her place on the other side of the Plexiglas, Bernadette's first impressions of her had been so startling that she could see her now just as vividly as then, looking childlike with her blonde hair pulled back in a neat ponytail, her cheeks flushed a natural pink. Except for the white prison jumpsuit, she looked like someone you might meet on the street or in the grocery store, maybe even smile at, say hello to, strike up a conversation with about the weather or the price of food these days. Those first impressions surely must have clouded her judgment.

It's not that she hadn't known at the time how unsteady she was. She'd hardly listened to Regis as he clarified the role he would play in the session and reviewed the rules. All she'd been able to do was stare at Raelynn Blackwell while gripping the plastic pouch that hung from a ribbon around her neck. Inside it was a picture of Veronica in her cheerleader outfit with arms outstretched, a maroon and white pom-pom in each hand, a radiant smile on her innocent face, her pink cheeks glowing with excitement.

***

"Do you have any questions?" Regis asked. Neither of them did. "Okay, Bernadette, whatever you want to say." The oversized round clock on the wall ticked away the minutes. "Whenever you're ready," he said. "Take your time."

She brought the picture of Veronica up to her lips and kissed her daughter's face. It was time. She saw fear in Raelynn Blackwell's eyes and remembered what Regis had told her the day before.

"She's scared," he'd said, "of being torn apart by your rage. Or by her own shame."

It was a good thing Bernadette had been forewarned. Otherwise it would have been too hard to look such fear in the face and still do what she had to do. She took a deep breath and, with trembling fingers, pressed Veronica's plastic-encased picture against the window.

"This is my daughter," she said. "This is the beautiful girl you killed."

Raelynn Blackwell lifted her hands to wipe away the torrent of tears that broke loose then, flooding her cheeks and her neck, seeping into her mouth. Her hands shook, her silent lips trembled. Minutes passed. The clock ticked. Yet not once did Raelynn Blackwell turn away from Veronica's picture or do anything to interrupt her accuser.

Bernadette gulped in a mouthful of air and let it out through her nose, then opened her mouth, but the words she'd rehearsed— *Look at her, dammit, look at her*—no longer seemed right and wouldn't come. She coughed. Cleared her throat. Searched for new words. Raelynn Blackwell's pain burned through the Plexiglas window and, with it, Regis's words.

"I won't let Raelynn meet with you," he had said many times, "until she has worked through the many layers of shame and guilt from her past. Don't worry, it won't be enough for her to admit guilt and take responsibility. She will have to be willing to be accountable to you if there is to be any healing."

That's why she doesn't turn away, Bernadette told herself. *She's being accountable.* She lowered Veronica's picture a few inches and took another deep breath, in and out. Then she placed the plastic holder on the table with the picture facing her. When she looked down at it, she could swear she heard Veronica say, *Look at how courageous she's trying to be, Mom.*

The women's eyes locked, and a magnet of pain pulled Bernadette into the center of Raelynn Blackwell and melted her heart so that all she saw was the lifetime of shame and guilt that was the woman who murdered her daughter.

"I know this is hard," she whispered.

***

Bernadette shivered. She pulled the sheet up to her neck in the dark bedroom, and its coolness enveloped her bare skin. Never in a million years would she have expected to hear herself utter the words *I know this is hard.* Had she made herself, at that moment, a victim of her own compassion? Had she made it easy for Raelynn Blackwell to carry out the plot to use her and the dialogue program to get her death sentence commuted? The sinister duplicity of it all left her reeling. But it was her own fault. Hadn't she put herself on the line? Hadn't she set herself up to be betrayed? Why, she'd even dared to ask the question she'd been most afraid to ask. Even thought she'd been prepared for the answer. What a fool she'd been.

***

"I need to know what it was like for Veronica at the end," Bernadette asked Raelynn. "Did she suffer? What were her last words?"

Raelynn Blackwell stared down at her hands.

"Answer me! I need to know!" Bernadette hit the table with her fist, and a sharp pain shot up her arm.

"I'm sorry," Raelynn Blackwell said. Her face was hidden in her chest, her voice muffled. "I didn't see her."

"How *dare* you—?"

"I wish I could tell you, Mrs. Baker, but I don't remember none of it. I was on so much junk that night…crack, pills, heroin, booze…whatever I could get my hands on."

"But you *saw* her."

"It was like I weren't even there. The police told me what I done. I didn't want to believe it. But I saw the blood on me. It tasted like metal on my tongue. I smelled it. I took a shower but the smell wouldn't go away." Raelynn Blackwell picked away at the skin on her fingers with short jerky snatches, as if she were still trying to get rid of the blood.

"Did she have trouble breathing? Did her asthma flare up?"

"I'm sorry, Mrs. Baker. I'm so sorry."

Bernadette fell back in her chair and closed her eyes. So there it was. She would never know if Veronica's death had been swift and painless, as she hoped, or if her daughter had felt every piercing, brutal slash of the knife as she gasped for breath, which is what Bernadette had feared all these years. No one, not even her murderer, had borne witness to Veronica's last minutes on earth. It was too much for Bernadette to bear. She was afraid she couldn't go on. Regis, who had stayed in the background all morning, put his hand under her elbow then and helped her up. A walk over to the door and back helped her regain her composure. She sat back down and took a deep breath.

"I'm not excusing you," she said, "but I understand."

Raelynn Blackwell's face was red and swollen. "I am responsible for your daughter's death," she said with a fierce shake of her head. "My not remembering don't make it no different."

"No, it doesn't," Bernadette said. "I'm not saying it does."

***

Bernadette rolled onto her stomach in the dark bedroom now and buried her face in the pillow. After Regis had helped her to see that knowing the truth about Veronica's death would be better than not knowing and she'd found the courage to ask, in the end there had been no answer. Or was that all just a lie, too? Had it been another way for Raelynn Blackwell to get sympathy or to avoid taking responsibility?

Bernadette decided then that the evidence was clear. As careful as she might have been to not allow sympathy to compel her to step into Raelynn Blackwell's shoes, that's exactly what she had done. She'd done herself in.

She squeezed her eyes shut and moaned into the pillow, "no, no, no, no, no," realizing as she did so that she sounded very much the way Raelynn Blackwell had when she moaned, "I'm sorry…I'm sorry…I didn't mean to make things worse. I'm sorry…so sorry… so sorry."

She turned onto her back again and wiped the wetness from

her cheeks with the backs of her hands. She sat up and dragged her legs over the side of the bed. She was cold; goose bumps covered her nakedness, and she folded her arms over her breasts. She must have been too tired to put on a nightgown after taking a bath last night. Or was it this morning? Everything had been such a blur. She reached for her robe and wrapped its softness around her. Then she walked over to the dresser and retrieved the plastic-encased picture of Veronica from her purse.

"I tried, sweetheart," she whispered as she brushed her lips over the picture. "I tried."

Sometimes, when she talked to Veronica like this, she believed she actually heard her daughter talking back to her. But now she wondered if it was only her imagination. Had Veronica really told her Raelynn Blackwell was being truthful that day or had Bernadette simply wanted to believe it so bad that she had imagined hearing Veronica's voice? And if the latter was true, did that mean she had betrayed her daughter by going on to tell Raelynn Blackwell so much about her?

***

It was near the end of their time together that afternoon, and Bernadette held Veronica's picture up to the window for Raelynn Blackwell to see one more time.

"I want you to know who you murdered," she said. "I mean, really *know* her. Look at how pretty she was. Look at that brilliant smile. You snuffed that out and don't even remember doing it."

Bernadette's pulse was racing as she continued.

"Do you know what she was doing the night you killed her? She was on her way home from helping a friend with her homework. She started out tutoring Natalie as part of a service project, and the two of them became good friends. She took the bus to the east side of Austin all the time to see Natalie. She was getting ready to go to her first prom. She would have been the prettiest girl there. That's the hardest thing to think about: everything she missed, everything she never got to experience."

She stopped to catch her breath and saw that Raelynn Blackwell was trembling so hard the table shook and that her eyes were so puffy they were almost closed. But the memories rushing through Bernadette made it impossible for her to stop even if she'd wanted to.

"She always gave people the benefit of the doubt. Like in middle school when this one girl called her a nasty name. Veronica said the girl must be unhappy or she wouldn't try to make others unhappy. She wondered if the girl's father beat her or if her mother yelled at her too much, or if maybe she felt ugly. Annamaria told her she should be nasty right back, but Veronica said that would make the girl even more miserable. My baby girl didn't have it in her to be mean to anyone. She had the biggest heart of anyone I know. Just think about all the good she could have done if she had lived."

Bernadette blew her breath out through her mouth. Raelynn Blackwell was squeezing the chain that held the silver cross around her neck so tightly that it made her veins pop out. Her suffering evoked pity in Bernadette, the way a friend's pain does. She removed the picture of Veronica from the Plexiglas and laid it on the table.

"It wasn't personal," she whispered. "You didn't mean to kill her."

"No. But I did." Raelynn Blackwell's voice shook, but her resolve was unmistakable. She wiped her face with the upper part of each arm in turn.

"Veronica never did any drugs or alcohol," Bernadette said with a sigh.

"I wish I never done any."

"When did you start?"

"I'm guessing I were about five."

"Good lord." Bernadette shook her head.

"It were my job to clean up after Ma's parties. There was always butts in the ashtrays and booze left in the glasses. Pills, too, sometimes."

"Your mother didn't know?"

Raelynn shrugged. "She gave me junk herself." Then she frowned and looked into Bernadette's eyes. "Don't get me wrong, Mrs. Baker. None of that don't excuse me for what I did."

"I'm not saying Veronica was perfect. But she knew there were consequences for her behavior. So did Annamaria and Fin. I can't count the number of times I had to ground one of them or take away their privileges."

"That's what good mothers are s'posed to do," Raelynn said, "I wish..." She brought her hands up and covered her mouth as if holding back forbidden words.

Bernadette bit her bottom lip. Regis smiled at her. He looked satisfied. She heard the ticking of the clock on the wall and looked up at it, wondering where the time had gone.

"I know I should forgive you," she said.

"I don't deserve your forgiveness."

"It's not about what you deserve or don't deserve. It's about what I need."

***

Still sitting on the edge of the bed, Bernadette rolled her shoulders and then stretched her arms above her head. When she had left Gatesville that day, she was convinced that things would never be the same again, that she had forgiven Raelynn Blackwell. But had she really? Right now, she wasn't sure. She wasn't sure about anything.

"Is it even possible," she said aloud, "when someone does something so brutal, so cruel? Is it even possible?"

"Who are you talking to?" It was Marty, coming into the room with a tray of food.

"Just thinking out loud."

He put the tray down on the bed and rested his hand on her forehead as if checking for a fever.

"What time is it?" she asked.

"Breakfast time for you. Dinnertime for the rest of the world."

The smell of scrambled eggs and two pieces of buttered whole-wheat toast made her realize how famished she was. She couldn't remember the last time she'd eaten anything.

"Freshly brewed," Marty said as he handed her a pottery mug shaped like a troll, her favorite, the one he bought her when they were first married. She cupped it in both hands, ran her fingers over the rough texture of the troll's silly face on one side and its behind on the other. She ran her tongue over its rim before taking a sip of coffee.

"You had me worried, Bernie."

"I was terrible to Fin," she said.

"He understands. Eat. Before it gets cold."

The eggs, tasting of goat cheese and fresh ground pepper, melted in her mouth. Smile lines crept across Marty's face, and his shoulders relaxed a bit as he watched her take a bite of toast and a gulp of coffee.

"I keep going over it all in my head. Was it a sham, Marty? The way Raelynn Blackwell cried? Was all that an act? Wouldn't Regis have known if it was?"

"Do you still think she knew what the governor was going to do?"

"What else would make her smile in the face of death like that? You think I'm crazy, don't you?"

"Let's just say it isn't like you." Marty smiled as he picked up the newspaper from the tray. "Here," he said, handing it to her. "It's on the front page."

She read the article in silence, stopping every once in a while to shake her head. When she was finished, she laid the newspaper down on her lap.

"I don't understand," she said. "Why didn't Raelynn Blackwell tell me her lawyer sent a letter to the governor? Why would she keep that from me?"

TWELVE

It had only been a few days since the governor postponed the execution. Marty had warned Bernadette that it might be too soon, that she might not be ready just yet, but she couldn't wait. She had to find out. From the passenger seat, she stared out the window and imagined herself dancing among the wild mustard and bluebonnets; soaring with a flock of indigenous scissortails over the scrub oaks, mesquites, and cottonwoods; and possessing both the toughness of the ubiquitous cactus and the composure of the grazing cows that peppered the rolling Texas hills. But as soon as the low red-brick buildings and guard towers of the Gatesville prison compound came into view, the sinister six-stranded barbed wire on its double chain-link fences overwhelmed both nature's beauty and her imaginary courage. They were here. Ready or not, she had to do this.

"Don't worry," Regis said, reading her mind as usual. "No way I was going to let you do this alone."

She smiled at him. She thought she had been prepared to come without him, but now that they were here, she couldn't imagine confronting Raelynn Blackwell again without Regis by her side. The rules didn't allow it anyway; that had been made very clear to her.

"Did anyone from the trauma team call you?" he asked. "Amy Whitehall, maybe?"

"I don't know why she would."

"They want to make sure witnesses don't experience any problems after an execution—any physical or mental reactions."

"But there wasn't an execution, was there?" Her face burned with guilt and not a little embarrassment for snapping at him again. Even though she'd apologized several times, she still felt bad about how she'd treated him the night everything fell apart.

"You've had a lot to absorb in such a short period of time." He smiled his forgiveness. Then he paused and, keeping his eyes on the road, asked, "You sure about this meeting?"

"I need to know why she didn't tell me about that letter."

"What if she didn't know about it?"

"Impossible."

"What would it mean to you," he asked, "whether she did or didn't know?"

She repositioned herself on the seat. Her cotton dress was twisted into a knot under her, the edge of it stuck in a tear in the plastic seat cover. She yanked it loose. The first time Regis had asked her that question, she'd responded without hesitation, said that she was prepared to deal with Raelynn Blackwell's answer, whatever it was. Such bravado. The truth that she'd kept not only from him but also from herself was that she wasn't sure. Wasn't sure about anything except her need to know. So what if Raelynn Blackwell said she didn't know about the letter? Would Bernadette believe her? She didn't know that, either. Her stomach did a flip-flop—a warning that she might not be ready for this confrontation after all, that maybe she should have taken Marty's advice and waited a few more days.

At the red brick Texas Department of Criminal Justice sign, Regis turned left onto the asphalt road leading into the compound. In the adjacent field, a line of white-clad women marched in single file under the watchful guard of several gray-uniformed men on horseback. The threatening way the guards fingered their rifles made beads of sweat break through the surface of Bernadette's skin—on first her forehead, then her arms, and then the small of her back.

A burning sensation worked its way up her nostrils and down her throat when she saw that the temperature gauge duct-taped to the cracked dashboard of Regis's ancient Toyota registered over one hundred brutal degrees. She grabbed her trusty battery-powered spray water bottle and misted her face, then held the bottle up to Regis. He shook his head. She misted her face again.

"There's no shade out there," she said. "Even farmers provide shelter for their animals on days like this."

Even as the words were coming out of her mouth, Bernadette recognized the old dilemma for what it was. She sighed. It was a familiar conflict, her struggle between believing there should be consequences for bad behavior and the difficulty of determining what the appropriate punishment should be. She thought about all the times she had reduced her kids' timeouts or the number of days they were grounded. Following her heart is what Marty called it. Annamaria called it leading with her chin. And now it seemed she was in the same weightless position again, supporting Raelynn

Blackwell's execution while simultaneously troubled by it.

"We can come back next week," Regis said.

"No. I have my questions ready."

"But are you ready for the answers?"

THIRTEEN

The visiting room was hot, the air stuffy. Bernadette pressed her hand down on the family photo album that she'd brought along and willed her racing heart into submission. Raelynn Blackwell was on the other side of the Plexiglas divider, her sagging shoulders swallowed up in the starkness of her white prison uniform. Her hands, fingernails chewed down to the quick, rested on the table, almost touching the wire mesh at the bottom of the window. With each hammer-like tick of the big round clock on the wall, she seemed to wince, which made her look worried. Or maybe she was scared.

Regis handed Bernadette a glass of ice water. When she saw a drop of sweat making its way down the side of Raelynn Blackwell's elfin nose, she pushed the glass toward the window, only to be stopped by the wire mesh. Why did she do that? What was she thinking anyway? No one was allowed to pass anything to prisoners on the other side. There were no exceptions. That was the deal. That's what Raelynn Blackwell wanted. Bernadette pushed the glass off to the side.

"Both of you know," Regis said, "but just to remind you, we'll follow the same process and rules as before. Do either of you have any questions?"

Neither of them did.

"Whenever you're ready, then." He nodded at Bernadette.

She wiped her sweaty hands on her skirt. She closed her eyes and took three deep breaths, letting each one out as slowly as she could. And when she opened her eyes, the scared rabbit eyes of Raelynn Blackwell told her everything she needed to know. The woman knew the jig was up.

"Why didn't you tell me?" Bernadette asked.

"What?"

"About the letter. You know, the letter?"

"I didn't know about it, Mrs. Baker."

"You smiled."

"I didn't know. Honest."

"You *smiled*."

"I was glad you was there. I wanted you to know it was okay."

"Your attorney told you he wrote that letter."

"No. Mr. Pearl never did tell me."

"My daughter is a lawyer, and she says lawyers tell their clients everything."

"But Mr. Pearl didn't. Swear to God. He didn't want me to get my hopes up and then be all disappointed."

Bernadette's face flushed. So there it was. Raelynn Blackwell wanted to live. And if she wanted to live, how could she have smiled in the face of death the way she had? It wasn't possible to want to live and still be at peace with dying.

"You said you deserved to die," Bernadette said.

"I do deserve to die."

"But you don't *want* to, do you?"

Raelynn Blackwell's eyes shifted to the side, then flashed toward Regis. In spite of the room's harsh artificial light and Raelynn Blackwell's obvious panic, Bernadette could see there was a natural beauty to the woman, and with her hair down instead of pulled back in a ponytail, her face looked softer than before. There was something about her—the way her feathery blonde curls grazed her pink cheeks; the innocent way she tilted her head and arched her eyebrow.

"It would of messed me up to know. Mr. Pearl was right about that."

Bernadette squirmed in her chair, and its metal legs squealed in protest. She fidgeted with a piece of invisible dust on the photo album. Then she clenched her fists; opened her hands, palms up, on the table; clenched her fists again. Could it be that Raelynn Blackwell was telling the truth about the letter?

"If you did know, would you have told me?"

"Jesus tells us always to say the truth." Raelynn Blackwell fingered the silver cross hanging from her neck. There were tears in her eyes. "Are you mad at me?"

"I would be mad if you knew and didn't tell me."

"Nobody told me nothing. Honest. I know I don't deserve for you to believe me."

The sound of her voice, so childlike and innocent, broke straight through to Bernadette's heart. She reached for the glass of water, took a sip. Sat back in her chair with a sigh.

"Fin wondered what it must have been like," she said after a few minutes of silence.

"What?"

"To come so close to dying."

"Jesus was holding my hand."

Bernadette frowned, sat up straight. "Does Jesus want you to live?"

"I can't pretend to know his ways."

At that, Bernadette's body went rigid. "Does Jesus think you deserve to die for what you did?" she asked.

"I *do* deserve to die for what I done."

"Then why file so many appeals?"

"I'm done with them. I weren't lying to you about that, Mrs. Baker, honest. I never asked to *ever* get out of here. *Never.* Just for some time to try to make up for what I done. Some of them in here are pretty messed up. Some had it worse than me coming up."

When Raelynn Blackwell's voice trailed off, Bernadette wondered if she was aware that no matter how many good works she performed, it would never make up for what she did.

"You don't want to die," Bernadette said again, this time in a whisper.

"It don't matter what I want. Whatever happens is Jesus's will. "

Bernadette tightened her jaw. "Was it Jesus's will for you to murder Veronica?" she asked. "Was it his will for you to pump your body with so much junk that you didn't even know what you were doing?"

Agonizing minutes passed as Bernadette tried to calm herself. It didn't matter if she thought Raelynn Blackwell's faith was childish and illogical. What mattered was whether her remorse was real—whether it came from the core of her, from a place as deep inside as her faith.

"You say you're sorry," she said, "but you don't know what it did to us."

"I can't pretend to know what it was like, Mrs. Baker."

"What it *is* like. Don't even think it's over. Annamaria is consumed with rage. And my granddaughter, Patty—she's the same age Veronica was when you killed her—has to live under that cloud every day. Fin keeps trying to make up for Veronica's death. He thought what you did was his fault. Can you imagine? *His* fault? He still blames himself, deep down. I can tell. And Veronica's friend, Natalie, the poor girl she was helping the night you killed her? She'll never stop blaming herself for making Veronica miss that bus."

Raelynn Blackwell's hands covered her mouth, muffling her voice so much that it was impossible for Bernadette to tell what she was saying, if she was saying anything at all.

"I brought pictures." Bernadette opened the photo album and propped it up so that it was facing the Plexiglas window. "This was at Disneyland. Veronica was ten. That's her father with his arm around her. He doesn't look like this anymore. When you killed Veronica, you sucked the life out of him."

She turned the page and pointed to another picture. "This was our last Thanksgiving together. No one smiles like that anymore. See how relaxed I look here? I used to love the mess of the holidays. The dirty dishes, the leftovers, the chaos. But you killed that. You about killed me, too. I was out of my mind for a while. All I could do was clean and clean and clean. I couldn't help myself. I still don't do any of the things I used to do, except shop for food and cook. We still have dinner together every Friday, but it's not the same without Veronica. It never will be. See the smiling faces in this picture? Look at this one, too. And that one. Those faces don't exist anymore. Do you understand? Those happy faces are gone. My family is being eaten alive by grief, and you want to know what I do?"

She stopped, out of breath. Regis handed her a wad of Kleenex. She wiped her eyes and blew her nose. "I pick up," she said with a sigh, "that's what I do. I pick up."

Bernadette thought about how just this morning she'd kept Regis waiting because she couldn't leave the house until she picked up Marty's empty coffee cup from the table next to his recliner by the fireplace, put his philosophy journal in the magazine rack, fluffed up the pillows on the leather couch and put them in color-coded order, straightened the slightly askew candle on the dining room table. Then she'd had to check one more time to be sure everything was in its place. Just thinking about it was exhausting.

"I want my life back," she said. "I want myself back. I want my family back. Don't you see? It's about more than what you did to Veronica. It's what you're doing to us. Every day."

Raelynn Blackwell's face was a blotchy red, twisted beyond recognition, as if the words she was hearing were cutting so deep that they threatened her very existence.

"Guard," Bernadette called out to the man standing by the door on the other side of the window, "please get her some Kleenex."

The round-faced guard jumped, then nodded and stepped forward. He slipped his hand into the front pocket of his gray uniform slacks, pulled out a clean, pressed handkerchief, and placed it in Raelynn Blackwell's cuffed hands. She wiped her eyes and blew her nose and, with an apologetic look, handed the soiled handkerchief back to him with a whispered "thank you." The guard stepped back to his place by the door and resumed his stoic position.

"I won't never stop being sorry for what I done to you and your family," Raelynn Blackwell said. "Even when I'm dead, I won't stop." Her voice was hoarse.

Bernadette sighed, let out her breath. She believed her.

"I know I can't never make it right, Mrs. Baker."

During the silence that followed, Bernadette felt her heart stop as she went into a place deep inside that, while devoid of any hope that she could change the past, contained profound hope for the future.

"I forgive you, Raelynn Blackwell," she said.

A high-pitched gasp, almost a scream, came from the other side of the window as Raelynn Blackwell's face fell onto the table. Bernadette pushed against the Plexiglas with her hands. She looked to Regis for help and saw that he was struggling to hold back tears. The guard shuffled his feet and stared down at the floor with wetness on his cheeks, and Bernadette felt his tenderness merge with her own.

After what seemed like a very long time, Raelynn Blackwell, choking on a sob, lifted her head. "I wish you was my ma," she whispered. "I'm sorry, I know it's not my place to say that."

"I'm sorry about your mother," Bernadette said.

"If you can forgive me, maybe I can forgive her, too."

"Do you know where she is?"

Raelynn Blackwell shook her head and bit her lip. "The welfare split us all up when I was eleven," she said. "Timmy was six and Anthony was five. My sister Jenny, poor baby, she was just three. I never seen any of them again after that."

"There were four of you."

"Five, counting my baby brother. I never did know him. Never seen him. One day Ma went to the hospital pregnant, and when she got home she weren't pregnant no more. I asked where was the baby, and she said to forget about any baby. I never knowed what happened. Maybe he was sick. Maybe he died. I never even knowed his name. It was all my fault."

"Your fault?"

"It was me that told. I was scared Ma would do to Jenny and maybe even my brothers what she done to me. I didn't know what else to do. But I never should have called the police. That's when the welfare came."

"What about your father?"

"There was as many daddies as there was us, but we didn't know none of them. It was just us and Ma. And most of the time she was drunk or asleep or gone."

"How did you manage?"

Splotches of pink sprang up on Raelynn Blackwell's neck and spread up to her cheeks. "I ain't proud of what I done sometimes," she said. "I never was right in the head. Ma said it was because I was born with the cord tight around my neck. I tried to be good. In school I stuck up for the little kids when they were being bullied, and when I got teased about being slow at learning I didn't even fight back. But it don't matter. I think Ma was right, I was just born wrong."

"No one is born wrong." Bernadette ached to reach across the table and hold Raelynn's hands in hers.

"I just hope they was all adopted. My baby brother, too."

"You don't know what happened to them."

Raelynn shook her head. "It would be selfish of me to stir things up for them now. I just pray everything turned out good for them."

Tears stung Bernadette's eyes. She couldn't imagine what it would have been like to care for her brothers and sisters, like she did after her own mother died, and then have them snatched away, never to be seen again. Regis had already told her what happened to Raelynn after protective services intervened—how she escaped the sexual abuse of her mother's boyfriends only to be sexually abused by the father in one foster home and the teenage son in another, how she kept running away, trying to find her siblings, until she finally gave up and escaped into alcohol and drugs, somehow managing to avoid the juvenile justice system, probably because no one cared enough to look for her—but the reality of it hadn't hit her until now.

"What about your mother?"

"I asked Jesus, if he wants me to see her before I die, to bring her to me."

Raelynn Blackwell was a woman of faith, all right—in spite of a lifetime of evidence that would have convinced anyone else that a God of any kind had abandoned her. Bernadette, who had never seen such faith before, found herself in awe of it.

"I'm sure he will," she said in a soft voice. "I'm sure he will."

FOURTEEN

The back of Marty's head tapped against the rocking chair's undulating pinewood carving, keeping time with the antique winged-back's rhythmic creaking. He gripped the scratched and worn armrests upon which Bernie's much-beloved Swedish-Norwegian grandmother had once rested her hands and tried his best to pay attention to what Bernie was saying. But his mind kept alternating between guilt—he should have told her his news long ago, but since it was too late for that, he should have at least told her as soon as she got home today—and exoneration—she had too much on her plate already, she was working so hard and was close, very close, to figuring it all out, so it wouldn't be right to distract her now. He concluded that he should listen to her tell him what happened at Gatesville today, and then he would give her his news. He couldn't live with himself any longer if he didn't. It had to be done today, no matter what.

"You should have seen the guard," he heard her say. "He was this big, burly round-faced guy, don't you know, just like you expect prison guards to look. He handed Raelynn his own handkerchief, and I swear I could see these big tears in his eyes. Like she was his friend or something. And just when I was thinking how this same man was going to put her back in a tiny cell and strip-search her after we left, Raelynn said, out of the blue—almost like she knew what I was thinking—'they're good, hardworking people, Mrs. Baker, they're just doing their jobs.'"

That caught Marty's attention. It was just the diversion he needed. He stopped rocking and leaned forward, following the familiar and comfortable road to intellectualizing that lay in front of him.

"Interesting question," he said, "whether good people can participate in bad things and still remain good."

"You mean like me still thinking this is the right punishment?"

"No, actually," he said. "I was associating the death-row guard with Hitler's Gestapo."

"Come *on,* Marty."

"Hear me out," he said, allowing his thoughts a mind of their own, gladly succumbing to their demand for expression. "The comparison isn't so far-fetched. As I tell my students, we can begin to fathom how good people can participate in bad deeds when we understand that Hitler's soldiers who did their jobs by day were still loving fathers and husbands by night. Institutionalized evil relies on the cooperation and support of good people… or on good people turning a blind eye and doing nothing. Like the guard."

"This is different, Marty. The guard seemed to *care* for Raelynn. All I'm saying is that it seems like his job would be a lot easier if he didn't."

He heard the irritation in her voice, and even though he felt bad about once again retreating into philosophy and leaving her to carry the emotional load for both of them, maybe today such avoidance could reasonably be justified.

"Makes sense," he agreed, but only half-heartedly.

She nodded and he resumed his rocking, resigned to wait until she told him everything, determined not to interrupt anymore, not to spoil things for her.

"Don't tell Annamaria I said this," she went on, "but I think Raelynn is a good person. She took good care of her younger brothers and sister."

"Like you." He rubbed his chin and refrained from saying what he was thinking, that he was reminded of how crime victims sometimes identified with the aggressor as a way to cope with trauma. But of course he wasn't suggesting anything like that about Bernie. She was his wife, not a mental-health case.

"Sort of," she said, "but when Mom died, I still had Dad. And the rest of us had each other. Raelynn lost her whole family."

The sad look on Bernie's face made Marty wonder if she had crossed a threshold, had now moved to a place that was beyond his capacity to understand, much less to go to himself.

"You've forgiven her," he said. At least that much he could understand, or he thought he could.

Bernie nodded. He leaned toward her and ran his fingers along the top of her hand, glad he'd heard her out. Now that she'd gotten to the place she'd worked so hard to get to, his news wouldn't be a distraction.

"So, that's it," he said.

Bernie laid her hand on top of his. She looked thoughtful, as if there was more to be said. "I'm not sure. Regis keeps saying it's a process. He says this work I'm doing is sloppy, sometimes very sloppy."

Marty felt deflated. What was she saying? Was she going back to Gatesville again? "So… what does that mean?" he asked.

She shrugged. "I don't know," she said. "I just want to be done with death."

Marty's chest collapsed. "If only we could be," he said. "If only we could be."

He grabbed the armrests of the rocking chair and pushed himself up, doing everything in his power to feign casualness so as not to expose the creeping panic he felt inside. He mumbled reassuring things: He had to go to the bathroom. He was going downstairs to get them something to eat. He'd be back in a few minutes. And then, with labored steps, he fled the room.

***

Bernadette switched on the nightstand lamp and lay on the double bed. No wonder Marty needed a break. No doubt everything she'd told him about her meeting with Raelynn Blackwell had been a lot for him to absorb. She breathed in the pungent lemony smell of furniture polish and thought about how she always kept this room in pristine condition, even though it had yet to host a single guest. It had been a breakthrough for her to suggest that they talk in here today—so big a one, in fact, that she hadn't stopped to consider how hard it might be for Marty to be in the room that used to be Veronica's bedroom; as far as she knew, he'd never set foot in it since it had been redecorated. That was probably another reason he needed a break.

She glanced at the green and tan striped bedspread. It matched the rest of the color scheme so perfectly that even Annamaria had commented on how sophisticated a guest room they had created. But never once had Bernadette ever considered it anyone's room but Veronica's. It didn't matter that the once-purple ceiling with glow-in-the-dark stars was now a neutral off-white. Or that the hot pink walls Veronica had loved—the hotter the better—were now a stylish pale green. Or that her posters—Madonna with flying red corkscrew curls, the Spice Girls in hot and energetic poses, and Ricky Martin dressed all in black in what Veronica called his "most extreme to-die-for-sexy attitude"—had long ago been replaced by scenes of the Texas Hill Country.

Veronica's antique cedar chest stood in the corner shimmering like a living thing now in the last rays of the day's sun. Nine years ago they'd locked their dead daughter's most precious things in the chest, where they had remained locked up ever since. The chest evoked Veronica's presence for Bernadette—just what she needed today.

"I think I've forgiven her now," she whispered.

For a fleeting second, she saw the glow-in-the-dark stars back on the ceiling, twinkling down at her. But when she blinked, they were gone, replaced by a sense of uneasiness about something Raelynn had said that day: "If Jesus wants me to see Ma before I die, he will bring her to me."

But if Raelynn's mother had made no attempt to contact her daughter before, why would she do so now? Raelynn was bound to be disappointed, and what would happen to her faith then? The question had barely formed in Bernadette's mind when she knew what had to be done—and that she was the only one who would do it.

***

Marty pressed his back against the kitchen counter. He'd meant to tell Bernie before, and now he would. He had to. Even if it placed an added burden on her. Even though it seemed like she was at some new critical juncture with Raelynn Blackwell. He'd withheld the news for far too long already. He knew Bernie wouldn't take it well. And not just because what he had to tell her was difficult or she didn't need more to worry about right now, but because the two of them had promised never to keep secrets from each other, and yet that's just what he had done.

He gave himself a few more minutes to think, to prepare, before going back upstairs. He told himself to be sure to give her time to react, to not expect her to understand or forgive him right away just because he felt bad about not telling her. But she would understand. Eventually, she would. She always did. Mostly, he told himself not to worry that she would fall apart again. Hadn't she proven once and for all how strong she was by pulling herself together and finding the bravery and muscular courage to see things through with Raelynn Blackwell? He retrieved a couple of sodas from the refrigerator and put some snacks—slices of apple and pieces of sharp cheddar cheese, a cup of cashews—on a tray. He was ready, as ready as he was ever going to be.

"There you are," Bernie said as he walked back into the guest room.

She threw her legs over the side of the bed and sat up. He shifted his weight from one foot to the other, pausing to give himself a few minutes more to gather his courage.

"So," he said as he lowered himself into the rocking chair.

"I know what to do next," she said.

To his dismay, Marty realized that Bernie had interpreted his hesitation as an invitation for her to continue with her story. He sat back in the chair and started rocking, not sure if he was glad for or dismayed by the delay, whether waiting a while longer would make it easier or harder for him to tell her.

***

"I have to help Rae now," Bernadette said.

"Rae?"

She smiled and nodded. "I'm going to find her mother."

"You *what?*"

"So Rae can make peace with her."

When Marty reached for her hands and pressed them to his lips as if they were precious jewels, Bernadette sensed a desperation in him that made her stop talking and pay attention. In the soft glow of the lamp, his cheeks looked sunken and the flecks of gray in his thinning hair much more pronounced than usual. And yet, in the dusk-filled room, the calf muscles in his long, lean legs still looked strong, his body still athletic from years of jogging. Her face flushed with love for him. He was sweet and caring no matter how hard he tried to hide it under all those layers of rationalizing and intellectualizing. There was no one more loyal and devoted than her Marty. He always stood by her side, no matter what. She was sure he would be willing to help her find Rae's mother now. All she had to do was ask.

"Bernie," he said, "you know I love you, don't you?"

What an absurd question. She was about to protest that she had never doubted his love, not even for a second, but something in his face made her hang back. Maybe it was the shadows in the room that made his eyes look haunted. But why was his jaw set so tight? She noted the slowness of his motions when he rubbed his eyes, the way his shoulders sagged. Even though the polo shirt and drawstring shorts he was wearing usually gave him a noticeably youthful appearance, right now he looked every one of his sixty years and more, as if the life had been sucked out of him, just like she'd described him to Rae.

"You're upset with me," she said.

"Not at all."

"You think I shouldn't try to help her."

"You need to do what you need to do."

"So you don't think I'm crazy."

"I think you're courageous."

"You'll help me, then?"

"I don't want to be a burden," he said.

"You a burden? But I'm the one who …" Something in his eyes, something she'd never seen before, made her stop again. He bowed his head and pressed his hands together, then brushed his lips with his fingertips the way he used to at Mass when walking down the aisle to take Holy Communion.

"I'm sorry, Bernie. I know this isn't a good time. You have enough to…" His voice trailed off, and he looked up at the ceiling.

"What is it, Marty?"

A string of scenarios flashed through her head, each one she discarded immediately replaced by an even more frightening one. Maybe he had something more to say about Rae, but what could cause him this much distress? Maybe state budget cuts threatened his position at the university. But that was impossible. He was a full professor. With tenure. And if something had happened to one of the kids or Patty, how would that make *him* a burden?

She frowned and leaned forward, hands on her knees. "Look at me, Marty," she said, her eyes flashing. "I'm not getting up until you tell me why you said you don't want to be a burden."

"I didn't mean that the way it sounded."

"Then why has all the blood drained from your face?"

He bit his lower lip. His shoulders rose and then fell. "I don't want you to worry."

"Okay, Marty." She slapped her knees with the heels of her hands. "How about I promise not to worry? Honest. No matter what it is, I will not worry. Just tell me."

"I know you," he said, brushing a tear from his cheek with the back of his hand. "You'll worry even if I tell you the treatment is successful over ninety percent of the time."

"What treatment? For who, Marty? You? Or one of the kids?"

"Prostate cancer is common for men my age."

Cancer? What was he saying? How could she not have known? She twisted a clump of her hair so hard that her scalp stung and the blood throbbed in her head.

"I'm sorry," he said.

She took a deep breath. "How? When?"

"I should have told you."

When Marty hung his head and his shoulders slumped forward, it was more than Bernadette could bear, and she flew across the space between them and threw her arms around his neck. She felt him stiffen.

"Don't shut me out, Marty."

But wasn't she the one who had shut him out? Hadn't she been so obsessed with Rae that she had neglected this beautiful man who loved her and who she loved more than life itself? No wonder he hadn't told her he was sick. No wonder he didn't want to burden her. She had made him feel that way.

"I'm here," she said. "I'm here now."

His trembling fingers gripped her hair and he collapsed against her, clinging to her as if his life depended on it. She felt the beating of his heart next to hers, heard his halting breath in her ear. Then he gasped and, like the sudden bursting of a dam, began to sob, sounding just the way he had at Veronica's funeral.

FIFTEEN

Annamaria tapped her fingers on the steering wheel and her foot on the floor. Here they were, stuck on MoPac—a virtual parking lot as far as the eye could see—and no one to blame but herself. Whatever had possessed her to think that rush-hour traffic would be any less of a nightmare than it was every other Friday? How could she have made such a mistake tonight of all nights, after she'd already had to wait a week for this chance to talk to Mom because she'd apparently been so mad about the governor's stupid decision that she couldn't even talk about it on the phone. Now that Mom had finally seen the light, Annamaria didn't want to wait another minute to see her anger for herself. Whoever would have guessed?

"Everyone gets to go but me, Mom." Patty looked up from her iPhone with a scowl.

"I said no and I mean no."

"But, why Mom?"

"Stop whining. You know why. A sleepover at Kitty's house is just an excuse for boys to sneak over in the middle of the night. You know I'm right."

"You think you're right about everything."

"I usually am. And don't go dragging Gran into this. Not tonight."

Patty threw her body against the passenger-side door and hid her face behind her long hair. Annamaria clicked on the door's safety lock switch.

Just then, a car behind them set off a cacophony of honking. "What the hell?" Annamaria yelled as she leaned on her horn with one hand and shook her other hand, middle finger extended upward, out the window. Patty looked over at her, grinning.

"Never mind," she said. "And don't you be doing that, young lady."

"Like I'm fixin' to."

"Stop it with the language, already. I won't have you talking like a Texan."

"But I am a Texan. Weren't you the one that born me here?"

"You could at least act like an educated one." Annamaria rolled her eyes, thanking her lucky stars that even though she'd lived in Austin most of her life, she had been born in the Midwest thanks to her dad's early academic career and therefore would never be considered a real Texan.

"Whatever," Patty said.

People started driving their cars over the grassy strip between the freeway lanes and heading back in the opposite direction. "See that?" she said. "Another example of Texans' *aint nobody gone tell me what to do* attitude right there. Don't ever let me see you crossing the median like that."

"So, like, I should just drive in the ditch like you?"

Annamaria jutted her chin out, just like Patty's, and kept

driving on the shoulder until she reached the next exit, where she escaped the freeway and took West Thirty-Fifth Street the rest of the way to her folks' house. It had taken forty-five minutes to drive a measly five miles. How ridiculous was that? Well, better late than never. She'd waited years to connect with her mom; she guessed she could wait a few minutes longer.

***

"Glad you could make it," Fin said as he climbed into Chuck's car. "Thanks for picking me up."

"Your folks know I'm coming, right?"

"I left a message. Besides, you're like family."

"Has your mom calmed down after what happened?"

"I hope so. She did apologize on my voice mail."

"So," Chuck said with a knowing smile, "I'm your buffer in case she's still mad."

Fin smiled back. How handsome Chuck looked in that short-sleeved magenta button-down shirt and those tan slacks; what a contrast to his own faded Save the Planet tee shirt and worn jeans. Mom would be glad to see Chuck tonight. She always was. Of all his friends, Chuck was by far her favorite. He thought about the time she went on and on about what a handsome couple they would make. Those were her exact words. At least she never did that again.

Annamaria, on the other hand, had on more than one occasion come right out and asked them what were they waiting for, why not admit they were a couple. Chuck thought it was hilarious. But Fin felt a twinge of sadness whenever his sister said that, which he hid by laughing and telling her to stop worrying about his love life and think about her own—to which she countered that she did not have one of her own and had no intention of looking for one. Which, of course, made him feel sad all over again, this time for her.

When they got to his folks' house, his mom greeted them both with warm hugs. "I'm sorry again, sweetie," she said, giving Fin an extra squeeze. "I shouldn't have taken my anger out on you like that."

"I understand, Mom. We're cool. No problem." He kissed her cheek and ruffled her hair, feeling the coarseness of it on his fingers. She laughed and slapped his hand away good-naturedly, then patted the short strands back into place. Things were right between them again. If only he could convince her now, with the governor's reprieve, to help him get Raelynn Blackwell's death sentence commuted altogether.

"Annamaria's stuck on MoPac," his mom said, "but she said to go ahead, and dinner is ready."

"Uh-oh," Fin whispered to Chuck as they walked, arm in arm, to the dining room, "I have a feeling we better watch out for my sister tonight."

SIXTEEN

The car screeched to a stop at the curb. Annamaria turned off the ignition and yanked the door open.

"Put that phone away," she said, "and no texting at the dinner table."

Patty ambled out of the car as if she actually might get a move on, but no, there she was, down on the ground picking up God knows what.

"Look at all these pecans, Mom. The squirrels gone get 'em for sure."

"Stop dawdling." Annamaria motioned with a flick of her hand for her daughter to hurry up as she rushed up the long walk leading to the familiar reddish-brown brick house.

"It's all yellow." Patty ran her hand over the parched grass.

"No excuse for it. They have a perfectly good sprinkler system."

"Gran says water's for the fishes."

It was just like Mom to see it that way instead of admitting how pathetic the lawn looked next to the lush green of all the others on the quiet tree-lined street. She wondered if her mom even appreciated what a delight it had been for them as kids to play in the soft, thick grass, to feel it tickle their bare toes. But, irritated as she was, Annamaria brushed aside her irritation because tonight was going to be different.

Patty ran up to the porch and, without knocking or ringing the doorbell, pushed open the heavy mahogany door. Everyone was in the dining room already.

"Hey, like the black polish," Fin said with a wink as his niece sat down at her usual place across from him at the table. "Did you do your toes, too?"

"Don't encourage her." Annamaria rolled her eyes.

With a goofy grin, Patty fluttered her fingers in the air, obviously enjoying her uncle's approval. Annamaria shook her head; so much for her assiduous attempt to pretend she hadn't noticed the black nails. Well, her kid had attitude. She had to give her that.

"Here you go, everyone."

Bernadette walked in with an oversized pan of homemade lasagna that filled the room with the spicy smell of garlic, oregano, beef, and tomato blended to luscious perfection. To a chorus of oohs and aahs, she lowered the pan onto a cast-iron trivet without spilling a single drop of the bubbling sauce onto the bouquet of red carnations or the red and white-checkered tablecloth.

"Look! Gran made all your favorites, Mom," Patty said. "Good thing we got here in time."

"We're not *that* late."

"Like, look at your watch, Mom."

Annamaria was too busy ruminating over why her mom had made lasagna to argue with Patty. It wasn't a summertime dish, and it was so labor-intensive that Mom only made it once a year—on Annamaria's birthday, come to think of it. And today wasn't anywhere near her birthday. Could this be her mom's way of apologizing, her way of saying she wished she'd listened to Annamaria's warning not to trust Raelynn Blackwell? Was she admitting that she'd been conned? But an apology wasn't necessary; it was enough to know that her mom was furious, that she now understood what she'd gotten herself into. But why, if her mom was upset, was she working so hard to make things pleasant? She must be trying to cover up or contain her simmering rage, probably didn't want to upset the others. Well, not to worry. Her anger would show itself soon enough. Everyone knew she was incapable of masking her feelings for long.

"You didn't have to do all this, Mom," Annamaria said with a significant smile and nod meant to let Bernadette know that she understood.

To Annamaria's consternation, Patty reached for the wooden salad bowl and plopped a big helping of lettuce, tomatoes, radishes, and cucumbers onto her plate. What the hell? No matter how much she nagged at her about eating vegetables, why was it that her daughter would only eat the ones grown in her gran's garden? Fin reached for the spatula then—a signal for them all to pass their plates over to him, his chest puffed up like he was special because Mom had placed the pan closest to him. *Well, enjoy the moment,* Annamaria said to him in her head. *It won't be long now before you and everyone else will see that Mom has finally come to her senses, that she now sees what I saw all along.*

***

The pleasing sounds brought a smile to Bernadette's face: the clink of forks on plates—sounds of chewing, swallowing—random utterances of satisfaction—soft shuffling of feet—Patty licking the butter from the garlic bread off her fingers. They were the sounds of appreciation she always relished, and tonight they had the added effect of lessening her apprehension, if only for a bit, about the dinner conversation they were about to have. She couldn't believe so much had happened in such a short period of time. There was a lot to tell the kids. She pretty much knew what to expect; Fin would be pleased to hear about what happened with Rae, Annamaria would be angry, and Patty would be curious. Everyone would be upset about Marty's news.

Lines pierced Annamaria's forehead as she leaned forward, her hands resting on each side of her plate, like a cat ready to pounce. Bernadette wondered if it was her imagination or if her daughter was actually sitting there scrutinizing her every move instead of eating. When Marty coughed and cleared his throat, she turned away from Annamaria to give him a smile of encouragement. He was nervous, she could tell. She nodded at him, a silent message that it was okay, that they were in this together. He tapped his glass with a spoon and cleared his throat again.

"Your mom and I have something to tell you," he said.

"First, I want to apologize," Bernadette said. When she saw a smile widen on Annamaria's face, she had the crazy idea that maybe her daughter had been anticipating this moment, that she might already know what was coming. But, of course, that was impossible.

"I should have talked to you before now," she continued. "At least on the phone. I'm sure you're wondering what's going on."

"Hey, no problem," Annamaria said. "I totally understand. I

was just as pissed off as you, Mom. Still am. I can't believe what Governor Kopecky did. And that old Judge Groundtree, well…"

"Let me finish, Annie," Bernadette said.

"Of course. I just want you to know it's okay, Mom."

Bernadette raised her hand and blurted out her news. "I went back to Gatesville." Her tone carried the implicit warning that if anyone objected, they shouldn't even try to go there.

Annamaria's mouth fell open. Obviously, this was not what she expected to hear.

"What happened?" Fin sprang up in his seat, all excited.

"It was good I went," Bernadette said.

Annamaria slumped back in her chair.

"Rae and I talked for a long time."

"Rae? Did you say *Rae*?" Annamaria shot up, lurched forward.

"She didn't know about the letter."

"Oh, and I suppose she told you that." Annamaria snorted.

"I believe her."

"Big surprise." Annamaria said with a grunt. She gritted her teeth, covered her ears with her hands, and shot daggers at Fin. She wanted to wipe the crooked grin off his face.

Bernadette, anticipating that Annamaria was about to make a scene, decided that ignoring her would be the best way to head it off. She turned to face the others, leaving Annamaria to quietly sulk as she filled in the details of her meeting with Rae.

"I was wrong about her," she finally concluded with a sigh.

"What happens now, Gran?" Patty asked.

"They should let her spend the rest of her life in prison," Fin said. "Give her a chance to atone for what she did."

"Right." Annamaria muttered and rolled her eyes. She shoved her plate of untouched lasagna toward the middle of the table.

"I feel different about Rae now," Bernadette said.

"Could you please stop calling her that?" Annamaria pushed her fingers into her temples hard enough, it seemed, to bore a hole in her head.

"No child should be treated the way Rae was."

"Yeah, yeah. We know all her excuses, Mom. Abuse. Neglect. Yadda, yadda, yadda."

"Why didn't she run away?" Patty said. "Like, that's what I'd do."

"She wouldn't leave her brothers and sister. She ran away from several foster homes later."

"Why?"

"Enough with the questions, Patty." Annamaria dismissed her daughter with a wave of her hand.

"It's a sad story," Bernadette said. "She was sexually abused in two foster homes. After that, no matter where they placed her, she ran."

"Everyone failed her," Fin said. "Everyone."

Bernadette shook her head as Annamaria slammed her fists on the table and stalked out of the room. It was just the reaction she'd expected.

***

Unable to listen to them anymore, Annamaria stumbled from the dining room, her head spinning and her breath coming in short spurts. In the front hallway, she fell back against the closet door. Her legs were shaking. Was she the only one who could see how

Mom had been totally taken in by that monster, to the point that she'd even given her a nickname? What the hell? Did she think they were good friends now or something? Why couldn't she see that sympathizing with Veronica's murderer was the same as excusing her?

An army of goose bumps attacked her bare arms and made her shiver. She rummaged through the hall closet, slapping aside the winter coats and jackets, wanting to punish them for being so crammed together. Her fingers landed on the soft angora of what was once Veronica's favorite cardigan. She couldn't believe her mom had left it in the closet all these years. With trembling fingers, she slipped the sweater from the hanger and buried her face in its light-blue folds. She inserted one hand into one sleeve and the other hand into the other sleeve, then pulled the sweater on, held it tight against her body with her eyes closed, and breathed in her sister's essence.

***

Bernadette started to stand up but then seemed to change her mind. Fin figured she must have decided to wait for Annamaria to come back to the table on her own, so he decided that he, too, should wait. But as the minutes ticked away, he worried that his sister might not come back at all, that maybe she'd even left the house.

"Sit tight," he said as he picked up the lasagna pan. "Chuck and I will clear the table and get the dessert." He kissed his mom on her cheek—his way of letting her know he was glad she'd come around about Raelynn Blackwell, that he always knew she would.

On his way to the kitchen, he caught a glimpse of Annamaria out in the hallway. She looked like she was crying. He put the pan on the counter and went to her.

"You okay, sis?"

"I'm tired is all. I was up until three o'clock this morning working, okay?"

"Right."

"Mom's too naïve for Patty's good, Fin. I have to protect her."

He knew she was scared that what happened to Veronica could happen to Patty, too, but there was no point in telling her he understood that. She would deny it, wouldn't even listen to him.

"Come on, let's clean up," he said as he steered her back toward the dining room.

Annamaria picked up the empty salad bowl and breadbasket as *if* she was trying to pull herself together. It pained Fin to see the way she avoided looking at their mom.

"I know you don't agree with her," he said once they were in the kitchen, "but you've got to admit what Mom's doing is pretty darn amazing."

"Getting all buddy-buddy with that monster is just plain wrong, Fin. It's crazy. And downright disrespectful to Veronica."

"Au contraire, mon amour. Mom is doing just what Veronica would want her to do." He handed a plate to Chuck, who set about loading the dishwasher with self-conscious deliberation.

"So now you think you have the inside track on Veronica's wishes."

"Ah, but I do. Believe me, Veronica is very happy with Mom right now." Fin knew he sounded flippant, but he didn't mean to be. He was just trying to lighten Annamaria's spirits. He felt sorry for her.

"Can you imagine what other people would think if they heard

Mom talking like this?" she said. "I can sure tell you what people at my office would think."

"That's what you're worried about? What other people think about Mom?"

"The governor should reconsider."

"She made the right decision," he said, "just maybe not for the right reason. Come on, let's not argue. What's done is done."

"It should be done. But it's not, is it?"

Fin took a deep breath. What his sister needed right now was a hug, not a fight. He put his hand on her shoulder, and when she didn't flinch or turn away he moved closer. But then he felt the soft angora of Veronica's familiar sweater, and it drove him to his knees.

"Please try to understand," he whispered as he grabbed onto the counter to pull himself up. "I promised Veronica."

***

While the others were cleaning up in the kitchen, Marty instigated a debate with Patty about the quality of education today while Bernie silently observed.

"You have to admit," Marty said, "the system has improved considerably in both technology and sophistication."

"School is for shit, Grandpa," Patty said. "You're just too old and out of touch to know it."

He smiled, captivated by Patty's spunk, so much like Veronica. He lobbed one question after another at her, sticking to his original position not because he thought it was the correct one but as a way to help his granddaughter hone her critical thinking skills—and, he had to admit, to keep himself from worrying about what the rest of the evening might have in store for all of them.

When Annamaria, Fin, and Chuck came back into the dining room, Bernie started talking as if there had been no break between dinner and dessert. Marty didn't object, grateful for a reprieve before it was his turn.

"Rae wants to see her mother before she dies," Bernie said. "I'm going to help find her."

"What the hell!" Annamaria's eyes flashed. "This is just unbelievable… un–be–lieve–able!" Her hand flew up and almost tipped over a water glass.

Marty held his breath. No matter how many times he'd witnessed Annamaria's anger before, he'd never seen her this livid. He withdrew the bowl of spumoni ice cream he had been just about to pass to her out of fear that she might throw it back at him or onto the floor.

"It *is* pretty unbelievable," Bernie said, "and it's the right thing to do."

"You're something else, Mom." Marty thought Fin's smile was almost wide enough to swallow up his ears.

"Do you think you will, Gran? Find her, I mean?"

"I hope so, Patty. But then I'll have to convince her to go see Rae."

"Fuck that!" Annamaria's mouth fell open like a door with a broken hinge. Her eyes bulged as if they were about to pop out of her face.

"Watch your language, young lady," Marty said. "It won't do anybody any good, including you, to get so worked up." He saw everyone look at him, shocked by his outburst. He was shocked by it himself.

Annamaria's eyes were fixed on Bernie in that *I dare you* way usually characteristic of a teenager in full-blown sulk mode. A standoff was in the offing, and Marty knew what would happen if he let it deteriorate into one of their classic mother-daughter showdowns. They were too much alike, those two. That had been obvious to him ever since Annamaria was a toddler.

"It's useless," he said, "when you both dig in your heels like this."

Bernie opened her mouth, and he shot her a warning look. *Don't make it any worse.* Looking nonplussed, she sat back in her chair. Good. Message received.

"I have something else to tell you," he said, glancing at his watch, "but first let's finish our dessert and then go into the living room."

SEVENTEEN

Bernadette closed her eyes and rested her head on the back of her chair by the fireplace. As she waited for her family to reconvene, her mind wandered back to decades earlier.

"How's it going?" she remembered asking Marty when he was writing his philosophy dissertation.

"How do you eat an elephant?" That was always his response.

"One bite at a time," they would say in unison.

Well, she thought now, Fin and Annamaria had digested their first bite of the elephant—the news about her intentions to help Rae—pretty much as she'd expected. Fin was happy, Annamaria upset. But of course she hadn't told them everything. She hadn't told Marty everything at first, either, until he'd caught her talking on the phone the other day.

"Who was that?" he'd asked after she hung up.

"Some clerk at the Lubbock City Hall," she said.

"What?"

"You wouldn't believe how many women there are in Texas named Maxine Blackwell or something similar."

"How do you know that?"

"Internet searches. Phone calls. I only have a few left."

She didn't tell Marty right away how many long-distance calls she'd made to city halls and other government agencies in Texas and the surrounding states. In fact, it wasn't until hours later, after she'd finished her search, that she told him everything. But she wasn't ready to tell the others yet. If Annamaria knew about all the time and effort Bernadette had already put into searching for Maxine Blackwell, she would either be out the door or planning to have her mom committed to a mental hospital.

It was best not to reveal her plan to drive to Killeen, either. No, if she told Annamaria she was going to go to the last known address for the woman who best fit the description of Rae's mother, well, that just might be one bite of elephant too much for her to handle. Besides, there was no need to disclose anything else until she found Rae's mother. If she found her.

At the sound of Marty walking in front of her, Bernadette opened her eyes and watched him sit down in his chair on the other side of the fireplace. He wiped his brow with the back of his hand. He started tapping his foot.

"Don't you think they've had enough to deal with tonight?" he asked in a low voice.

"It'll be all right," she said.

She didn't say that just to reassure him about the kids. After going with Marty to the doctor, she had no doubt that he was going to be okay. Everyone at the medical center had been so pleasant, so positive. Especially Dr. Sortiev. When she whipped out her list of questions, Marty's oncologist had calmly answered every one of them without a single blink of an eye—and with an encouraging smile, to boot. Even when she let him know in no uncertain terms that some of his answers were insufficient, the man—how old was he, about seventy, maybe?—peered over the wire-rimmed glasses perched on the end of his long nose and let her know, without the slightest hint of impatience or arrogance, that he knew what he was doing. By the time she and Marty had left the clinic, she had been convinced that this cancer thing was just a bump in the road, one they would drive over and then be done with. She held onto that now. She had to. Not just for the kids but for her, too.

Soon the others were in the living room, huddled together on the leather couch. Fin's right arm was around Patty's shoulder, her head resting on his chest. Fin's other hand was placed on Chuck's knee in a protective way, as if to reassure him that he belonged with the family, while Chuck, his back erect and hands folded in his lap, looked as if he was being held hostage. Annamaria sat on the other side of Patty with her arms crossed and her lips pursed, her face a frozen scowl. Bernadette wondered how long it would take her to get over the shock and disappointment of hearing about her plan to help Rae. It was something she obviously had not expected to hear.

With everyone's attention now turned toward Marty, Bernadette could tell he was clearly wavering. *This isn't the most propitious time to tell them*, she imagined him saying to her with his eyes. When he looked over at the door as if he was plotting his escape, she got up and walked over to his chair.

"I'll help if you get stuck," she whispered in his ear. Four pairs of worried eyes watched her kiss his forehead and then followed her back to her chair.

"Go ahead, Marty," she said as she sat down.

He coughed. Took a breath. "It's nothing to worry about." He took out his handkerchief and blew his nose. He shrugged his shoulders at Bernadette as if to say this was the best he could do; at least it was a start.

"Your dad's right," she said. "Everything is going to be okay."

Annamaria unfolded her arms and leaned forward, her elbows on her knees, chin resting in her hands.

"Come on, what is it, Dad? Mom?" Fin asked. "*What's* going to be okay?"

"Prostate cancer treatments are very successful."

Bernadette breathed a sigh of relief. There, it was out. But the stunned silence that followed worried her. Maybe Marty had blurted the news out too fast? She wondered if it had sounded garbled to them. Why didn't anyone say anything? Then she saw Fin and Annamaria exchange worried looks. Next, Patty burst into tears, and Annamaria put her arm around her daughter and pulled her close. Chuck grabbed Fin's hand. It appeared that they got the part of the message about Marty having cancer, but not the other part—not the part about it being common and curable, not the part about everything was going to be all right.

"I have a good doctor," Marty said. "I'm fine."

"How long have you known?" Annamaria asked.

When Marty winced at the accusation, Bernadette could tell he still felt guilty about sneaking off to the doctor without her knowledge and keeping the test results a secret for so long.

"That's not important," she said.

A look of relief crossed Marty's face—the same look he'd had right after he'd confessed the news to her. Just before he'd broken down and cried.

"Your mom's taking good care of me," he said, "and my oncologist is most reassuring. I'm in good hands."

"What's the prognosis, Daddy?" Annamaria's voice, no longer angry, sounded the way it had when she was a little girl.

"It's not like I'm going to die," Marty said. "Not that I'm afraid of death, you understand. Don't get me wrong. I don't want to die. But we all know that life in this world is limited. Some even maintain that death just might be our highest fulfillment, the crown of our existence."

Bernadette raised her palms and shot him her sternest look, the one that warned *do not go there*.

"All I'm saying is that none of us gets guarantees," he said. "We all die sooner or later. It's the way things are."

Bernadette shook her head. She understood that pontificating about death was Marty's misguided way of trying to reassure everyone. She also knew that what he said was a simple statement of reality, *his* reality, and a source of considerable comfort for him. The truth for him, or at least what he liked to believe was the truth, was that society created an irrational fear that made death almost impossible for people to face it as a natural part of life. But even though she knew this was how Marty thought, it was not helpful, considering the circumstances, for him to impose it on his family right now.

"Dad just doesn't want you to worry," she said.

Marty sighed and looked at her, sheepish. She gave him a warm smile that she hoped would comfort him more than any philosophical treatise ever could. She thought again about how, in spite of—or maybe because of—their differences, the two of them made a good team, how together they were whole.

***

Annamaria was taken aback, not only by what she'd just heard, but also by Fin's response. It wasn't like him to be this angry, much less at Dad and at something as serious as this.

"Why didn't you tell us before?" he asked with lips pursed as if he was about to spit. "And how can you expect us not to worry when we know nothing about your condition? Mom? Dad?"

Fin fell back onto the couch then, with his chin tucked in and his arms crossed over his chest, which made Annamaria wonder if that's what she looked like when she was angry. She reached across Patty and laid her hand on Fin's knee to calm him down, but he ignored her.

"Come on, Dad," he said, "could you stop tiptoeing around the tough stuff just this once?"

"Like I said, the doctor is optimistic," Marty said. "There's no need to worry."

"You can't know that," Fin shot back.

Patty poked Annamaria in the side with her elbow, and Annamaria saw that her daughter's eyes were filled with a kind of terror that she'd never seen in them before. She was obviously begging her to do something, to take charge, to fix things.

"Let's step back and look at this," Annamaria said in a tone deliberately calibrated to let Patty know that she was in charge, that she would keep Fin under control. "What stage is it, Dad?"

"It's curable."

"What *stage*, Dad?" Fin's voice was tight, impatient.

"What … what's most important for you to know is that the success rate is very good."

Annamaria took a deep breath. "How good, Dad?" she asked.

"Dr. Sortiev says each case is different, but he's very positive about mine. So, that's it."

"Dad. Stop it," Fin barked.

"The surgery your dad will have is done all the time," Bernadette said.

"You can't tell us you're not worried, Mom," Fin said.

"Of course I'm worried. But it's going to be all right."

Annamaria knew the tone in her mom's voice signaled that she meant for the conversation to be over, but Fin's jagged breathing next to her told her he was having none of that. "And then treatments?" she said, keeping her voice steady, the conversation rational and factual. "How many?"

"We've got it covered," Marty said.

"We have a right to know more, Dad." Fin's anger was now tinged with worry. "Are we at risk? Is it genetic?"

"No, no," Marty said. "You're all healthy. This just happens sometimes."

"Is there anything we can do to help, Dad?" Annamaria asked.

"Well, there is something."

"Anything, Dad."

"You can help your mom."

"Sure. How?" Annamaria was quick to answer, eager to have the conversation shift from fear to action. But she couldn't imagine what kind of help Mom could need. No one doubted for a minute her capability to handle things; in fact, she would end up taking over like she always did. Maybe the folks needed help drawing up their wills, something she'd been trying to get them to do for ages.

"You can support what your mom's doing with Raelynn Blackwell."

Annamaria bit her tongue. How dare Dad use his cancer to manipulate her like this? She looked at her mom, and when she saw the anticipation on her face, it was too much. "How the hell," she said, shooting daggers at her mom, "when Dad needs you, can you even consider wasting your time on Raelynn Blackwell? Is this why you've been calling me Annie all night, to get me on your side? Is that why you made lasagna?"

"Enough," Marty said. "Support your mom and you help me. That's the way it is."

Annamaria squeezed her eyes tight to keep the tears at bay. Here was Dad acting like cancer was nothing to worry about and her easygoing brother a ticking time bomb, ready to explode any minute. And, as if that weren't enough, in the midst of it all, Mom seemed even more determined than ever to jump off a cliff into who knows what, to go on yet another wild goose chase. But the worst part was that Mom and Dad had conspired to use his life-threatening illness to hold her captive to a murderer. This wasn't like them. This wasn't like them at all. They must be desperate. This had to be their way of coping.

"I'll try," she mumbled. "I'll try." What else could she say?

EIGHTEEN

A quick glance at the odometer and the MapQuest directions indicated that Bernadette had twenty more miles to go on I-35 before turning onto Highway 195 North. After that it was only thirty-four miles to Killeen. She should be there by one thirty and back home before dark—if all went well, that is. Butterflies started flapping in her stomach as she anticipated finding Maxine Blackwell. She speculated about what she might encounter once she got there: run-down conditions, for sure, most likely a trailer. But what if Rae's mother refused to talk to her? What if she was drunk, incoherent? Best to be prepared for anything. Above all, she needed to be or at least appear to be composed, to remember to breathe before reacting; then she'd be okay, no matter what happened.

She still wasn't sure, even after staring up at the ceiling and thinking about it most of last night, what would be the best way to introduce herself to Rae's mother. *Hello, I'm Bernadette Baker; your daughter killed my daughter.* That would be the most direct approach but also a surefire way to get the door slammed in her face. *Hello, I'm Bernadette Baker, and I'd like to talk to you about your daughter Raelynn.* Maybe. *Hello, I'm Bernadette Baker. Do you*

have a few minutes? No, too vague. It hadn't occurred to her before
now that someone else might answer the door. She decided the
first thing she should do was ask for Mrs. Blackwell. Or should it
be Ms.? Or maybe she should call her by her first name. She tried
it out. *Hello, are you Maxine Blackwell? I'm Bernadette Baker. May I
come in and talk to you?*

A few more tries and she settled on *Hello, are you Maxine
Blackwell? I'm Bernadette Baker and I'm here about your daughter,
Raelynn. May I come in, please?* That was probably the best she
could do. She rehearsed it out loud, making sure to speak in a calm,
matter-of-fact voice so as not to cause alarm or raise suspicion. She
expected getting Rae's mother to talk to her to be the most difficult
part, but she shouldn't have to worry too much after that. She had
her arguments ready: seeing Rae would give Maxine a chance to
come to terms with her relationship with her daughter—it was
Rae's last wish to see her—it was the right thing to do—Gatesville
was less than an hour's drive from Killeen—she could take Maxine
there if she wanted, help get a visit approved with the prison
authorities, make all the arrangements.

She drove past a billboard announcing last year's Belton Fourth
of July Rodeo with a cowboy on a bucking Longhorn bursting
through a blur of red, white, and blue U.S. and Texas flags. That
meant she was getting close now. Sure enough, a few miles later she
saw a small sign that said Killeen, Texas, Population 116,934.

She propped the directions on the dashboard, noting that
she was on course when she passed the Hallmark Lanes Bowling
Alley set back from a large parking lot filled with cars and trucks.
When she passed a strip mall with a McDonald's and a Red Robin

restaurant, she decided that after she'd seen Maxine Blackwell she would reward herself with a burger and fries. For now, a few bites of her energy bar would have to do. At an intersection at the edge of town, where the directions said to turn onto a backcountry dirt road, there were items for sale on the porch of a sagging house—an old refrigerator, an easy chair with fluffy white stuffing peeking through holes in the seat, a metal cabinet, a Formica table and chairs, an assortment of small household items. She slowed down, mostly out of curiosity, saw nothing worth stopping for on the way back.

As she drove on through rolling hills dotted with Texas Ash, red oaks, and scrub brush, a cloud of dust from a Fort Hood helicopter suddenly disturbed the quiet setting, scattering a herd of cows just before a camouflage-covered Humvee whipped by in the opposite direction. She looked at the odometer and saw that she'd gone two and three-tenths miles since the turn, which meant she should have arrived at her destination, so she pulled over. But there was no mailbox or address sign, only a narrow path made by truck-tire tracks off to the right that she decided to follow. But the front tire of her old station wagon dove into a hole right away, and the car lurched to a stop. She rocked it back and forth—a trick she'd learned from driving in Minnesota blizzards years ago—and after several tries was able to free the wheel. Not about to take any more chances, she backed up and parked her car on the side of the road. She would have to walk in.

It didn't take her long to realize she shouldn't have worn sandals, as scrub brush started poking through the spaces between her toes. But irritating as that was, it was nothing compared to the tiny fire ants biting her ankles. She slapped at them while at the same time dodging their anthills as best she could. She heard something scurrying through the woods, at which point she considered turning back; who knew what hidden dangers lurked behind the trees in rural Texas. Then she told herself she was being silly, that it was just a raccoon or some other innocuous creature going about its business and she should go about hers as well.

She took a deep breath and resumed walking until she came to a clearing. A footpath through knee-high weeds led to a ramshackle house with an unpainted exterior and a cracked roller-coaster foundation that had to be a feast for termites. Pieces of tattered cardboard fluttered over shattered windows, shingles were missing from large sections of the roof, and the screens on the sagging front porch were pretty much ripped to shreds.

She stumbled up the crumbling steps toward the lopsided screen door that was stuck partway open, leaving a space just wide enough for her to squeeze through. Rusty nails stuck up through the floorboards; with each cautious step she took, she was afraid that she'd either step on one of them or that the sagging porch would collapse under her weight and take her with it. With a sigh of relief, she reached the front door and knocked on it. No answer.

"Hello, is anybody home?"

She knocked again, louder. Still no answer.

"Hello? Hello?" She pressed her ear against the door. Nothing. She reached for the doorknob but then pulled her hand back. Wasn't she trespassing? What if the person with the truck came back and found her here? But wasn't the house too dilapidated for human habitation? Wasn't it most likely abandoned? Maybe teenagers used it as a hangout. But that wouldn't explain the clean rag rug in front of the door, the way the porch floor looked recently swept. She decided to take a quick peek inside. If it looked like people lived there, she would either wait for them to come home or she'd come back later, maybe leave a note. She tried to turn the doorknob and it spun around in her hand. She pushed on it, and the door creaked open a crack.

"Who is it?" The voice on the other side of the door was low and hoarse, almost inaudible.

"Hello?"

Before Bernadette could say anything else, the door swung open. The first thing she saw was a rifle pointed right at her face. Then she saw the wisp of a woman holding the rifle, her trembling finger perilously close to the trigger. Finally, she saw that the rifle was scratched and rusted, which gave her hope that it might not work. But she wasn't about to take any chances. She raised her palms in a gesture of surrender and, being careful not to lose her balance, lifted one foot up and placed it down behind her, then the other. As she backed away she reminded herself to breathe, to stay calm.

"I'm so sorry," she said in the most natural tone of voice she could summon. "I didn't think anyone was here."

"Who are you? What do you want?"

"My name is Bernadette. I have a message from Raelynn Blackwell for her mother."

The rifle crashed to the floor, and the woman's body slumped over.

Bernadette took a step toward her, still keeping her hands in the air as a precaution. "Are you Maxine Blackwell?"

"I'm Raelynn's mother."

Maxine Blackwell didn't look anything like Bernadette had imagined she would. Her eighty-pound frame—if she even weighed that much—seemed to be drowning inside a crisp white blouse and white slacks; there was a sheer red scarf tied around her neck, and red loop earrings dangled from pierced ears. It was obvious right away that she was not well. Not well at all. First, there was her hair: colorless, almost transparent, with bald patches exposing blue veins on her scalp. Her face and eyes were yellow, her cheeks skeletal like those of someone exhumed from the grave.

"May I come in?"

Rae's mother tipped her head to the side and Bernadette, taking the gesture as an invitation, stepped into the room. Given the decrepit exterior of the house, she wasn't at all surprised by the bare, rotting wood walls; faded patches of wallpaper with pink roses; crumbled ceiling tiles dangling over a mattress on the floor in the corner. In the middle of the room, a lumpy overstuffed chair faced an ancient television set that was balanced on a much-too-small wooden crate. A brown refrigerator at the far end of the room was so lopsided, it seemed on the verge of toppling over. What did surprise Bernadette was how clean everything was, how orderly. Even the yellow and red polka-dotted bedspread, though faded and torn, was tucked with square corners over the sides of the mattress.

Maxine Blackwell hobbled over to a slab of wood held up by two wooden crates and motioned for Bernadette to sit on a flimsy metal chair at the makeshift kitchen table. Then she lowered her own frail body onto a lopsided stool across from her. The kitchen counter was uncluttered, the sink and stove a gleaming white. Not a single dust particle floated in the ray of sunlight streaming through the cracked window.

"You know my daughter?" Maxine Blackwell said. "You saw her?"

"Yes. I saw her this week. Tuesday."

"My Raelee will be gone soon. It was on the news." The woman's voice shook, and she twisted her mouth the way people do to keep from crying when she called her daughter Raelee.

"Yes."

"Who are you again? How do you know Raelee?"

"My name is Bernadette Baker. Your daughter killed my daughter."

Silence. They stared at each other. Bernadette didn't know what to say next. She hadn't meant to blurt it out like that.

Rae's mother shook her head with a vehemence that didn't seem possible from someone so frail. "My Raelee was a *good* girl," she said with a weak yet unmistakable huff in her voice. Her thin chest rose up in a challenge.

"Yes," Bernadette said.

"It weren't her fault she had a bad mother." Maxine Blackwell shrank forward with her chest curved inward.

"Your daughter wants to see you."

"Is Raelee…? I mean, how is she?" Maxine's hand flew up to her mouth just as a sob escaped from her lips, making her sound as if she was choking.

"They say she does a lot to help others there."

"That would be like her. That would be just like my Raelee."

Maxine Blackwell twisted her scarf around her neck, tighter and tighter, until her face turned almost as red as her scarf and she started to cough. She fumbled in the pocket of her slacks for a handkerchief, and when the coughing fit ended, Bernadette saw that it was covered with bloody splotches. She looked away.

"She wants to make peace with you."

Rae's mother shook her head. Tears filled the cracks in her hollow cheeks.

"It's something good you can do for her before she dies."

"The only good I can do for my Raelee now is keep my bad self away. I ain't never been nothing but a curse to her. I weren't never a mother to her. Not to none of my kids."

"You sound like a mother when you call her *my Raelee* and insist that she was a good girl. That's what mothers do. They defend their kids."

Maxine Blackwell looked at her sideways and shook her head.

"Believe me," Bernadette said, "I know. If anyone ever dared to say anything bad about my kids, I would defend them to the death." She stopped and scolded herself for such a poor choice of words. "I hear that protective tone in your voice. That's what a mother sounds like."

"My Raelee was the real mother. She protected the others. It done broke that girl's heart when they was all taken away. It's my fault what happened."

"It sounds like it broke your heart, too."

The look of pain on Maxine Blackwell's face at that moment plunged so deep into Bernadette's heart it made her wonder if this was what a heart attack felt like.

"I don't deserve to live," Maxine said. "Your daughter is dead because of me. And now my daughter is going to die because of me. I'm the one should be dead by now."

"Are you sick?"

"It don't matter that I am. That don't make for no excuse."

Bernadette was momentarily stunned to hear her say almost the exact same words Rae had said. "No one should be defined just by the bad things they've done," she said.

"I done nothing but bad by my Raelee. I won't do no more wrong."

"No one is all bad, and wrongs can be made right," Bernadette said, even as Rae's words rang in her head: *Ma was right, I was born wrong. I was just born wrong.*

Maxine Blackwell squinted as if searching deep inside for something, anything, that might not be bad about herself. It took a long time before she spoke again.

"The only mother thing I ever did was birth my kids," she finally said. "My Raelee was born March 3, 1972; Timmy was June 16, 1977; Anthony was September 8, 1978; Jenny was January 20, 1980."

"See," Bernadette said, "no one but a mother could rattle off her kids' birthdates like that."

"...and the baby was born in 1985."

Bernadette looked down at the table, thinking what a coincidence it was that Veronica would be the same age as Rae's baby brother. In an ordinary situation, she would say that out loud, the way people do when they meet for the first time and discover they have something in common. But she didn't. Not this time.

Somehow it wasn't right.

"My Raelee never gave me no trouble."

"Veronica was a good girl, too. I always thought it was because she was my youngest, but then, Rae was your oldest, wasn't she? My oldest, she's a girl too; we don't get along very well. My husband says it's because we're too much alike, but I don't think we're alike at all. My son Fin is most like me. I'm closest to him."

Bernadette watched Maxine Blackwell drop her head down onto the table. *What am I doing,* she asked herself. Here she was acting as if they were two normal mothers talking about their kids over coffee. She should have had the sense to keep her mouth shut. Wasn't Rae's mother having enough trouble holding herself together as it was? It was one thing to lose a child, as they both had, but a different thing altogether to know you were responsible. She couldn't imagine what it would be like to carry such a heavy burden of guilt and think there was no way to make it right. But it wasn't too late. Rae and her mother could still come to terms with the past. They could at least try. But how was she to convince Maxine of that? Maybe a more indirect approach would work.

"Tell me about your other children," she said.

Maxine Blackwell shook her head. "I don't know what happened to them."

"Do you want to know?"

"How can you even ask me that? I was promised they would be taken care of when I gave them up. Don't you think I want to know they was?"

"You gave them up to protect them."

Maxine Blackwell shrugged. Then, after a few minutes of

silence, her eyes opened wider and her eyebrows arched up as if something had just occurred to her. "Does my Raelee want to see them?"

"No. She doesn't want to hurt them. She thinks they would have visited her by now if they wanted to see her."

"Do you think it would help her if she knowed they were okay?"

"I think it might help both of you to know that. If you write down their birthdates, I can try to find out."

Bernadette thought about what a strange twist of fate it was that had brought the two of them together, two mothers bonded by a desire to protect their children. Yet both of them had failed, hadn't they? Her Veronica was dead, and Maxine's Raelee would soon be dead, too. But there was one big difference: while she had Marty, Fin, Patty, and even Annamaria to help her cope with Veronica's death, Maxine Blackwell had no one to help her. No one at all.

"My mother overdosed," Bernadette said, "pain pills. Her father, my grandfather, died an alcoholic."

"My mama never could stop drinking," Maxine said. "I never knew my papa."

"I never drank," Bernadette said. "I was afraid if I started I wouldn't be able to stop."

"I done stopped just a short time ago."

"Rae would be glad to hear that. I know someone who could get the warden's approval for you to visit. I could drive you there. It's not far."

Maxine shook her head.

"Give her a chance to forgive you."

"No forgiveness for me." Maxine slapped the table with her fragile hands, then doubled over in pain.

"It's not for you. It's for her. Think of her."

Maxine looked her in the eye without blinking and with great effort lifted her body back to an upright position. "Don't you know that's what I'm doing?"

Bernadette lifted her hands in the air, then dropped them onto her lap. So that was it. Maxine Blackwell thought she was protecting her daughter by not going to see her. There would be no convincing her otherwise.

"What should I tell Rae?" she asked with a sigh.

"Tell her I'm dead."

"I won't lie to her."

"My liver's shot." Maxine shook her head. She looked exhausted.

"My husband has cancer." Bernadette saw Maxine Blackwell start to reach across the table, seem to think better of it, and withdraw her hand. Why hadn't she just said she was sorry? After all, Marty was not dying, but the woman sitting across from her right now clearly was. But who was she to feel sorry for her? It was obvious that the world had been a cruel, hard place for Maxine Blackwell, so who was she to think it was sad that the poor woman might soon get to leave it?

At a loss for what to say or whether to say anything at all, Bernadette looked at Rae's mother and saw that with her eyes closed, her face seemed to disappear into her grief. There would be no atonement for her. There was nothing more to be said. They would both have to come to terms with having failed, her for not convincing Maxine to go see her daughter and Maxine for failing as a mother. But, she wondered, would Rae be able to come to terms with the truth about her mother?

NINETEEN

When she got back from Killeen, Marty was so intrigued by Bernie's detailed account of her trip—what Maxine Blackwell and her house looked like, how their conversation went—that he only once felt compelled to interrupt her. It was when she said, "She's dying. Cirrhosis of the liver is my guess."

"My cancer is different," he said.

"Oh, I know. Believe me, Marty, I know."

He went back to listening, particularly captivated not only by Bernie's compassion for Raelynn Blackwell's mother, which he expected, but also by the way she didn't seem distressed about failing to convince the woman to visit her daughter before it was too late. There was something different about Bernie; he sensed it. But he couldn't put his finger on what it was except that it seemed to have something to do with her being so accepting of Maxine Blackwell's refusal.

"We think alike," she said, "like mothers, you know what I mean?"

His eyebrows shot up toward his receding hairline, and he scratched the side of his head. No, he didn't know what she meant.

He didn't know what she meant at all. From everything he knew, Maxine Blackwell had been a very inadequate mother, to say the least. How could Bernie, the best mother in the whole world as far as he was concerned, compare herself to an abusive and neglectful mother like her?

"Her kids' birthdates are engraved in her brain," she continued, "like mine are. She may not have been able to act like a mother, but she thinks like one. She cares about her children. It's sad."

He rubbed his chin, trying to figure out why it made such a difference to Bernie whether Maxine Blackwell cared about her children when her behavior had been so hurtful and destructive to them. He was pretty sure she wasn't implying that caring was enough. Maybe, as usual, she was just looking for the good in people. He loved that about her.

"Well, you tried," he said with a smile.

"But there's still Rae's siblings. I have to find out what happened to them."

So that was it. That's what was going on. Bernie had a new mission.

"I'm calling Annamaria," she said, reaching for the phone. "She can help me."

He put his hand on her arm. "How about a walk first? Town Lake?"

"Good idea," she said.

He laughed out loud then, not only because he was surprised at himself for making the suggestion, but also because he was even more surprised and delighted when she agreed so readily. He had missed their regular early-evening walks but had given up asking her to go with him a long time ago.

As they strolled the gravel-covered Lady Bird Trail together, the views of the lake and the Austin skyline seemed much more stunning than usual, and he knew it was because he was with Bernie. They stopped for a few minutes at Deep Eddy, silently appreciating the huge treasure of a pool right in the middle of the city. He squeezed her hand, then put his arm around her shoulder and pressed his cheek against the top of her head as together they remembered how their kids used to love swimming in that pool. She leaned into him, and they walked on in silence.

But once they were home and Bernie headed for the phone, Marty started to feel anxious. "You sure you're ready for her reaction?" he asked.

She placed her forefinger on his lips to shush him. "Annie, this is Mom," she said into Annamaria's answering machine. "Call me, okay? It's important."

"You know how stubborn she is," Marty said after Bernie put the receiver down. He stuck his hands under his armpits and poked his chin out. "Remember how she'd curl up her tiny fists, like this, whenever she pouted? No one could ever talk her out of trying to get what she wanted until she was ready to let it go herself. Not even you. I've never known another two-year-old who could hang onto her anger as long as she could."

"Stubborn, yes," Bernie said, "but not hateful. Not our Annie."

He nodded as if he agreed—unable to admit, even to Bernie, his fear that, if Annamaria stayed stuck in her rage, it could, in the end, make her hateful.

"She won't help," he said.

"Then I'll figure out a way to find out what happened to Rae's siblings without her."

"Amazing," he said.

"What?"

"You."

"Why? Because I'm stubborn? Like Annamaria?"

"Because you're persistent." Marty dug around in his brain for a possible answer in case Bernie asked him—he hoped she wouldn't—how he defined persistence, how it was different from stubbornness. The closest he could come to understanding it himself was that being stubborn seemed more about being right while being persistent seemed more about caring enough or maybe being desperate enough to hang in there no matter what. He saw Annamaria as stubborn, but not Bernie. Bernie was persistent.

She smiled at him then, a crooked, almost teasing smile that aroused in him a longing, a desire to wrap his arms around her and feel the softness of her breasts. Maybe later, when they were in bed, she wouldn't pull away when he pressed his chest against her back. Maybe she would let him draw her warmth into him, and they would fall asleep in each other's arms the way they used to.

TWENTY

Annamaria liked going to the office on Saturdays, when, uninterrupted by colleagues or clients, she was able to fully employ her considerable powers of concentration and get tons of work done. But today was different. The stack of files on her massive mahogany desk seemed insurmountable as her mind kept jumping from one thought to another. Not only that, everything from the late-afternoon view of the Hill Country outside her twenty-third-floor picture window to the sunny yellow walls and the red, blue, and purple area rug in her expansive corner office seemed downright gloomy. Even the coffee she'd just brewed tasted bitter on her tongue.

She fidgeted with the edges of the folder on top of the stack, then opened it. It was a corporate fraud case involving a well-known Austin investment banker-turned-politician. It wouldn't be long before the media were all over this one. Well, if anyone was up for the challenge, she was. At least, that's what she'd thought when she accepted the case. But now, as she read more of the details, hints of her client's duplicity—even outright dishonesty—began to emerge. The legal jargon blurred on the page, and she squinted to catch the words.

I can't do this. She could hear herself moaning in her head. What she needed was a good, stiff drink. She walked over to her office bar and fixed herself a gin and tonic, heavy on the gin. Back at her desk, she took a big gulp and tried once again to read the case file. But the words swam across the page like a school of fish adept at avoiding detection. She slammed the folder shut, slid it into the top desk drawer, and locked the drawer.

She swiveled her chair around so that she was facing the computer table behind her. If anyone in the family was going to do this, it would have to be her. She was the only one with her feet grounded in facts, not in fantasy like Mom or deep philosophical concepts like Dad or raw emotions like Fin. If anyone was going to find out what the hell was really going on, it would be her. Her fingers trembled as she typed the dreaded words—prostate cancer— in the Google search engine on her computer. She clicked on the Mayo Clinic website, took a deep breath, and read about Stage IV of the disease.

> *At this stage the cancer would have spread not only to tissues next to the prostate, but to lymph nodes or other more distant sites in the body such as the bones as well.*

Metastatic prostate cancer, it was called. A tear splashed onto the keyboard, and she swiped it away with her fingers. Why hadn't her folks used that term? Were they sugarcoating the truth, or were they in denial? Or could it be that they didn't know how serious Dad's condition was?

> *The average survival for men at Stage IV is usually one to five years.*

Her throat tightened and she turned her chair back to the desk, gulped down the rest of her gin and tonic. Dad couldn't be that sick. He looked good. A little tired is all. Maybe she should call him, ask more questions. But just then, her phone rang. She wiped her eyes and took a deep breath to pull herself together before answering.

"Pizza and a movie, okay, Mom?"

The eagerness in Patty's voice reverberated through her ear and tumbled straight down to the core of her. "I'll pick up the pizza on my way home," she said. "You find a movie on cable."

***

It was rare to spend a Saturday evening at home, just the two of them. More unusual still was Patty's chattiness about who was dating whom, who had broken up with whom, and the new boy in school. The innocence of a child in the body of a woman, Annamaria thought with a shudder.

"Mom? Are you even listening?"

"You think the new boy is cute."

"And?"

"He asked you out."

"I said, like, I *want* him to ask me out. Oh, never mind."

"Sorry. I guess I'm worried about your grandpa."

Patty's half-eaten piece of pepperoni pizza dropped onto her plate. She wiped the grease from the corners of her mouth with a napkin, her eyes filling with tears.

"I know you're worried about him, too," Annamaria said. "So is Gran, no matter how much she tried to cover it up last night."

Just then, her cell phone rang. "That's her now," she said as she turned on the speakerphone.

"Hey Gran," Patty called out, "we're having girls' night in."

"Mom?" Annamaria said, "are you calling about Dad? Is he okay?"

"Oh, Annie, I knew you'd worry yourself to death all day."

"How could I not?"

"Your dad's going to beat this thing. And it's not just me who thinks so. The doctor does, too."

"I don't think you know enough about the kind of cancer he has to be so sure, Mom."

"Trust me. My instincts tell me everything's going to be all right."

Of course, Annamaria thought. Mom's instincts always ruled, didn't they? Never mind the facts.

"Listen, Annie, I called you about something else. I need your help finding someone who was adopted."

Annamaria stiffened. What now?

"There are ways to find people who were adopted after they've grown up, right?"

"Who do you want to find, Mom?"

"If you knew someone's birthday and you thought he was adopted when he was little and now he's an adult, how would you go about finding him?"

"It depends on who's doing the looking."

"What do you mean?"

"The person looking has to have good cause."

"What counts as good cause?" her mom asked.

"Does this have anything to do with Veronica?"

"No. I mean, not directly."

"What are you up to, Mom?" Annamaria slouched back onto the couch, shaking her head.

Silence.

"Talk to me or I'm going to hang up, I swear." She sat up straight, moved to the edge of her seat.

"Don't worry, Gran, she won't hang up," Patty called out. "I won't let her."

"I have to find out what happened to Rae's siblings."

"You what?" Annamaria and Patty stared at each other, their mouths open.

"I found Rae's mother yesterday. She's dying."

Annamaria was too flabbergasted to do anything but listen as her mom came clean about going to Killeen—*all alone, for God's sake*—about feeling sorry for Maxine Blackwell—*no surprise there*—and about wanting to help find out, of all things, what happened to her other children.

"Why, Mom? For God's sake, why?"

"I want to find out if they were adopted so I can tell Rae before she dies. Her mother, too. Will you help me, Annie?"

Annamaria gritted her teeth. Her head throbbed. How many times did she have to say that she detested being called Annie? Come to think of it, her mom always called Fin and Veronica "sweetie"—so why not call her that?

"Promise you'll at least sleep on it, Annie."

"I'll call you in the morning."

"'Night, Gran," Patty called out. "Don't worry, she'll help you."

With a sigh, Annamaria snapped her phone shut.

"You will, won't you?" Patty threw her body back into the beanbag chair in front of the television.

"Such nonsense. Gran should be taking care of Grandpa now."

"Why do you have to be so stubborn?" Patty's lips tightened into a thin line of disapproval.

"Because enough is enough."

"So, like, you always know better than Gran."

"She doesn't know when to quit. Pretty soon she'll be adopting that whole damn family. Who knows what the hell she'll do next."

"You think you know, but you don't." Patty glared at her, a dare.

"It's movie time," Annamaria said with a sigh.

"If Gran says it's the right thing to do, then it is."

"Okay, okay. I said I'd sleep on it, didn't I?"

"You'll feel better if you help, Mom. I know you will."

TWENTY-ONE

It was well past dusk and the dinner dishes washed, dried and put away as Bernadette and Marty lingered over cups of decaf coffee at the kitchen table.

"Annie took it pretty well," Bernadette said.

"That doesn't mean anything," Marty said.

"Don't worry, I'm not counting on her help."

He stood up and pushed in his chair. Then he leaned down behind her and nuzzled his nose into the curve of her neck. "Come to bed," he whispered.

"I want to do a few things first," she said as she stood up. "You go on ahead."

The crestfallen look on Marty's face compounded the guilt already churning inside her. She pushed it aside and kissed him full on the lips, then strode over to the kitchen sink, turned the water on, and set about rinsing out their cups. "I won't be long," she called over her shoulder.

She waited until she heard his footsteps in the bedroom above the kitchen and then slid open the drawer to retrieve the piece of paper on which Maxine Blackwell had written the names and birthdates of her children. She brought her laptop to the table and clicked on the web browser icon. For good luck, she lit a candle.

"Damn it," she said when she realized she couldn't decipher Maxine's writing. Thinking that having more light might help, she brought a reading lamp over from the counter and plugged it in. She squinted at the little squiggles of handwriting, her fingers positioned on the keyboard like swimmers ready to dive into a pool. When the Google search space flashed on the screen, she typed in *Timmy Blackwell, DOB June 16, 1977.* She hit the return key and a daunting 300,000 results popped up.

She scrolled down the list until she came to one that said *We found Timmy Blackwell, current phone, address, age and more.* She clicked on it. The People Search site had found Timmy Blackwell, all right, eighteen of them, but only one was even close to the age Rae's brother Timmy would be now, and that one had never lived in Texas.

"Not likely," she muttered as she forged ahead anyway, charging $14.95 to her credit card for an in-depth follow-up search. It confirmed that this was not the Timmy Blackwell she was looking for, just as she'd suspected.

She repeated the process for Anthony and Jenny Blackwell, plodding through exhaustive lists of names and charging over a hundred dollars to her credit card for in-depth searches that resulted in only one dubious possibility—and even that one turned out to be a dead end. Since Maxine had given Rae's youngest brother up at birth without naming him, she knew it was hopeless to even try to search for the baby.

Fighting exhaustion, she rolled her head around and stretched her neck from side to side. She looked at her watch. It was two o'clock. She grabbed a can of Diet Coke from the refrigerator and gulped it down while staring at the computer screen and wondering what to do next. A long, drawn out burp moved up her windpipe and out of her mouth, along with the realization of what she had been doing wrong.

"Good lord!" She slapped her forehead. What had she been thinking? If Rae's siblings were adopted, they would no longer be named Blackwell. They would have been issued new birth certificates showing the adoptive parents' names as their mothers and fathers. Like when they had adopted Veronica. Had she become so obsessed with all this that she'd lost her ability to think straight?

She dropped her head onto the table and moaned. All that time and energy. Wasted. For nothing. She went over to the sink and splashed cold water on her face, then stepped out onto the deck and breathed in the fresh night air. That's when it occurred to her that not finding Rae's siblings under the name of Blackwell might actually be good news. It could mean that they *had* been adopted. But without knowing their new names, how could she ever hope to find them?

She went back into the kitchen, sat down at the computer, and typed in *How to find an adoptee when all the information you have is a birth date?* She scrolled down the first ten pages of 48,000 results until she came to the one that seemed to be the most promising: How to Find Someone Who was Adopted (An Adoptee) with Limited Information. She clicked on it twice for good measure.

In order to find an adoptee, the text at the top of the web page said, *there are three things you will need: persistence, a bit of luck, and stubbornness.*

She grinned—so far, so good—and read on.

If you know only the birthdate and the state in which the adoptee was adopted, don't be discouraged.

Even better.

Most people stay in the same state and can be found by acquiring a birth date search by sex for that particular state.

Okay then, all she had to do was find the birth date search engines. There were several such websites for Texas, some free, some not. She tried all of them, entering over and over again each child's name, gender, birth date, mother's name, and birthplace—Austin being her best guess since she hadn't thought to ask Maxine Blackwell that question.

She didn't know how much time it took, but it must have been a lot because when she finally stopped and moved her neck, it sounded like walnuts cracking. She walked stiff-legged over to the counter, reached up into the cupboard for a glass, and popped a couple of Advil. Back at the table, she picked up the box of matches and passed it from hand to hand, then slowly opened it. She took out a match and held it between her thumb and index finger. She stared at it, imagined lighting a cigarette, inhaling, and blowing out smoke rings in a string of perfection the way she used to when she was a chain smoker, back in her college days. Good lord. She hadn't had the slightest craving for a cigarette since she quit in her mid-twenties, but right now the idea of smoking sounded awfully good to her, too good.

She touched the match head against the striking surface on the side of the box and moved it briskly across the surface until it ignited. The flame beckoned to her. With one hand cupped around it, she watched it flicker until it burned her fingers. She blew it out and let the charred remains of the match drop onto the table.

The instructions about how to find an adoptee with limited information called out to her from the computer screen. What could she do but follow?

What you need is a search angel, someone experienced in looking for adoptees in your state.

She leaned forward. This just might be the answer. The instructions referred her to another site, and then another, and yet another, until she came to a website for a search angel in northeast Texas. Plump babies bounced across the screen on pastel pink and blue clouds while rescue angels played harps and sang for them. In the foreground flashed the words

Hello, my name is Hannah Newcastle and I am an adoption search angel and an adoptee myself.

This was followed by a story about how Hannah had helped a man in his seventies with terminal cancer find his two sisters before he died. Even though it turned out that her angel experience was limited to that one case in one small town, Bernadette nonetheless composed and sent a lengthy email to Hannah Newcastle asking for her help.

By the time she finished, streaks of pale blue, white and pink bands were brightening the sky outside the kitchen window. She felt her anxiety rise along with the rising sun.

"Just one more," she whispered as she clicked on the website for another adoption registry service. How could she quit now?

Just fill out a search form and it is forwarded to a team of search angels who are very generous and helpful people with a lot of skills and experience in conducting adoptee and birth-parent searches in your state.

Her heart beat faster. Maybe this was it. She typed in all the information she had about Rae's siblings on the form and clicked the Send button.

"Bernie, what are you doing?" The strands of baby hair poking out from the top of Marty's head didn't match the scolding-parent look on his face.

Like a child caught with her hand in the cookie jar, Bernadette slapped the lid of the laptop down.

"Were you up all night?"

"I didn't mean to be."

"You need to stop this, Bernie."

She stared at the lump of wax that was once a candle in the middle of the table, realizing she knew nothing more now than when she had lit it. She dropped her head into her hands. What was she doing? Why was she being so obsessive about this? But even as she asked herself that question, she knew the reason she couldn't stop: because she had to do something, and this was the only thing left to do.

TWENTY-TWO

The title of what promised to be an inane teen movie scrolled across the flat TV screen as Annamaria snuggled closer to Patty on the couch and thought about what her daughter had just said, that she would feel better if she helped her mom. Maybe she could at least give her some legal information related to searching for adoptees. What could it hurt? Nothing was going to stop her, anyway, why not humor her? And it would be something she could do for Dad. Besides, with the execution now rescheduled, this whole nightmare was soon going to be over for good.

Annamaria tried to get into the movie, but she found the star—an insipid girl who fell in love with a bad boy who, of course, was incapable of loving anyone—to be as tiresome as the plot. Still, when the movie reached its predictable tearjerker ending, Annamaria savored the way Patty laid her head on her breast for comfort.

Much later, she crept into her daughter's room and sat down on the chair next to her bed. Patty was sound asleep, her fingers curling into the palm of her hand next to her face, her thumb forming a dimple in her cheek. Patty's soft, gentle breath tickled Annamaria's ear when she leaned over to kiss the knuckles on her daughter's hand. She kissed Patty's upturned nose before tiptoeing from the room, careful to dodge the items of clothing scattered across the polished hardwood floor.

Across the hall, her own spacious white bedroom—which she usually considered well suited to her proclivity for order over chaos—seemed sterile tonight compared to the cluttered energy of Patty's cozy and colorful room. As Annamaria undressed and washed up, she realized that her evening with Patty must have softened her toward her mom, because right now she felt more of a need to understand her than to fix her. If she could figure out the motivation for her mom's latest antics, then maybe she could make some sense out of helping her. Doing it for Dad wasn't enough of a reason unless, of course, it would make his cancer go away. But unlike Fin, she had never cottoned to that kind of magical thinking.

Annamaria believed there was always a logical reason for one's behavior. There had to be. In fact, the essence of what made her a good lawyer was her ability to figure out why people did what they did. She got into bed, asking herself why her mom had such an urgent need to search for the offspring of the idiot who spawned Veronica's murderer, knowing that sleep would elude her until she found a satisfying answer to that question. It was tempting to throw up her hands and write her mom off as crazy, but she couldn't do that. Her mom might be a lot of things when she set her mind on something—more loving than God and clever as a fox were the first two that came to mind—but crazy was not one of them.

There were times, of course, when her mom seemed insane, like when she tried to fix things she had no business or hope of fixing. But her motivation, once you understood it, had never been crazy. So could it be that all her mom was trying to do was somehow atone for the rough life Veronica's murderer had had by helping her before she died? No, that would imply that people committed murder because life had been unfair to them, and her mom would never, ever accept excuses for bad behavior like that. No one knew that as well as Annamaria did from her own experiences as a teenager. She remembered one time in particular when she had been grounded.

"It's not fair!" she had screamed.

"The punishment fits the crime, young lady," her mom had answered.

"But Bill asked me to the dance a long time ago."

"You should have thought of that before."

"He'll never ask me out again. I just know it."

"If he likes you, one dance won't change that."

"So what do I say when he shows up tonight?"

"You haven't told him?"

"I can't."

"Well, young lady, you need to call him right now and tell him you're grounded. Go ahead and blame it on me."

Annamaria remembered how hopeful she had been when she saw the pained look in her mom's eyes then, the way her hand had trembled as she handed her daughter the telephone.

"Please, Mom."

But she hadn't backed down. Not even when Annamaria ran to her room, threw herself on her bed, and let out the loudest, highest-pitched wail she could muster. Later that night, though, her mom had come back to Annamaria's bedroom with an apologetic look on her face and a bowl of popcorn, asking if she wanted to watch a late-night movie on TV with her.

So that was it. That was the answer. *Mom felt guilty then, and she feels guilty now.* If her mom was still opposed to the death penalty, like she said she was, then she'd have to feel guilty about supporting it in Raelynn Blackwell's case, wouldn't she? It all made sense now. That's why she searched for Maxine Blackwell and, after that, for information about her children. She was just trying to find a way to live with herself. Who could blame her for that?

Something new came over Annamaria then, almost a sense of admiration for her mom. In spite of her moral opposition to the death penalty, Bernadette was being true to her principle that the punishment should fit the crime. And in the case of Raelynn Blackwell, she was absolutely right that it did. Annamaria yawned, pulled the covers up to her chin, and fell asleep.

TWENTY-THREE

The bedroom was cool, almost chilly, a sure sign that Marty had readjusted the temperature on the air-conditioner again. The next-door children were screaming outside the window, squirting each other with the hose, a signal that it was way past time for her to get out of bed. But Bernadette was glad she'd slept longer than she meant to because the more rested she was, the more clearly she could think. She threw on an old tee shirt and jean shorts with an elastic waistband and hurried downstairs.

Things on the kitchen table were just as she'd left them: her laptop, the slip of paper with the names and birthdates of Rae's siblings, the lump of wax, the opened box of matches. A message on a three-by-five card, in Marty's almost illegible handwriting, was perched on top of the computer. "Went to the mall," it said. "Need new running shoes."

Bernadette looked out the window at the bright crimson hibiscus flowers in the back yard. The flawless blue sky beckoned to her, and she decided to fix a bowl of yogurt with granola, raisins, apples, and brown sugar and take it and her coffee out on the deck. But just then the telephone rang and she saw the number on the caller ID. It was Annamaria.

She was careful to answer in a calm voice, to not sound too pushy or eager. If Annamaria had decided to help her, Bernadette didn't want to give her any excuse to change her mind by saying something to set her off.

"I did some research, Mom."

Bernadette grabbed the pad of paper that said *Proud Grandmother of Patty* across the top and searched for a pen in the drawer.

"Here's the problem," Annamaria said. "All protective services and adoption records are confidential."

"I *know* that." Is that why Annamaria called, just to tell her what she already knew? Was it too much to hope that she had new information?

"So you need a court order to get any records released."

"Okay. So I get one."

"You can't."

"Come on, Annie."

"You don't have good cause."

"Yes, I do."

"Good luck getting any court to agree. You're not even related by birth."

"What if I were?"

"Don't be silly. You're not."

"What if the biological mother requests the information?"

"She'd have to have good cause, too."

"Good Lord, the woman is dying. Doesn't she have the right to at least know whether her own children were adopted or not?"

"Not if her parental rights were terminated, she doesn't."

Bernadette wished she knew if that's what Maxine Blackwell meant when she said she had given up her children. She bit her bottom lip, kicking herself for not asking more questions when she was in Killeen. "What if her rights weren't terminated?" she asked.

"Then her children couldn't have been put up for adoption."

"How do I find out?"

"Well, if it was an involuntary termination, there would be court records. And before an adoption can be finalized, there should be a notice in the newspaper searching for the birth father. But just so you know: I'm not going to go looking for either of those, and neither should you."

"Come on, Annie, stay with me, okay?"

"I'm trying."

"Just tell me what a birth mother has to do if she wants to find out what happened to her children."

"Look, Mom, that's all on the Internet. But the best thing you can do is just tell Maxine Blackwell you couldn't find any information."

"So your lawyerly advice is that I should lie." Bernadette knew that sounded sarcastic, but she didn't care. She was beginning to wonder if Annamaria had done any research at all.

"I'm saying you should tell her you tried."

"I guess my search angel team will have to help me. I've already requested one."

"Good luck with that." Annamaria went on to tell her it was ridiculous to think that strangers could just walk in off the street and get confidential information. She persisted in throwing out one more piece of discouraging information after another until Bernadette had no choice but to think she had called to dissuade her rather than to help.

"You tried, Mom," Annamaria finally concluded. "You can quit now."

Not if I can help it, Bernadette thought, but she kept it to herself because she didn't want to end the conversation on a sour note. No matter how useless the information Annamaria gave her was, at least she'd bothered to call. She guessed she could thank her daughter for that.

"How's Dad?" Annamaria asked after an awkward silence.

"Your dad's going to be fine, Annie."

"You better be right about that."

"Aren't I always right?"

"Your granddaughter sure thinks so."

"Then it must be true."

With some goodwill restored, Bernadette said goodbye— making sure to say "I love you, Annie" before hanging up. She slid open the sliding glass door and stepped outside. She settled down in a shaded deck chair to review what Annamaria had told her and was happy to discover that her lawyer daughter had given her some new leads in spite of herself.

TWENTY-FOUR

Fin reached for the remote control on the coffee table and clicked on the public television channel. He took a sip of his espresso and waited for Kevin Madderhorn to light up the television screen. The host's brilliance, combined with his luminous smile and striking good looks, made watching *Issues of the Day* one of Fin's favorite Sunday rituals.

But today he was troubled, distracted. He kept thinking about Dad's cancer, about Mom's determination to find Raelynn Blackwell's mother, about how Annamaria was more distressed about both those things than he'd ever seen her. He hadn't talked to anybody in the family since Friday night, and he wondered how they were doing. He couldn't imagine Annamaria agreeing to support Mom, but he thought she should at least try, for Dad's sake if nothing else. He started to reach for his cell phone but then stopped. What made him think his sister would listen to him, anyway? If only she weren't so stubborn. If only Dad weren't sick. If only Veronica hadn't been murdered. If only Raelynn Blackwell... if only, if only, if only.

Fin was relieved when the sound of Kevin Madderhorn's voice

interrupted his spiraling negativity. "This week," the TV host said, "the Supreme Court will decide the fate of convicted murderer Jonathan Lowgren. With us today is legal expert Lisa Hammer. Welcome, Ms. Hammer. Summarize this case for us, if you would."

Fin leaned forward, his eyes drilling into the TV screen.

"It's a significant case with broad implications for the death penalty," the lawyer said with an unambiguous air of confidence that reminded him of Annamaria.

Fin scooted onto the edge of the couch and turned the volume up.

"The case revolves around a growing shortage of one of the drugs used in lethal injections," Lisa Hammer explained. "When the one U.S. manufacturer of sodium thiopental suspended production, Arizona officials obtained the drug from a British company in order to carry out Lowgren's execution as scheduled. Right away, his lawyers questioned the safety of the drug because it was obtained from a foreign source. They argued that if the drug didn't render him unconscious as intended, Lowgren could suffocate painfully. Both a federal judge in Phoenix and the U.S. 9th Circuit Court of Appeals in San Francisco found in Lowgren's favor. Now the Supreme Court's decision will determine his fate and possibly the fate of death-row inmates in several other states, as well, where executions have already been delayed due to shortages of the drug."

Fin felt as if he was going to jump out of his skin. Was Texas running short of the drug, too? Could this be the solution? He turned up the volume some more.

"The last time the Supreme Court ruled that capital

punishment was cruel and unusual was in 1972," Lisa Hammer
said. "That decision, as we all know, resulted in death sentences
across the country being commuted to life in prison. In effect, there
were no more death rows."

"Do you think the court will uphold the lower-court decisions
in this case?" Kevin Madderhorn asked.

Fin nodded, anticipating the legal expert's affirmative answer.

"It's not likely," Ms. Hammer said.

"Come on, Kevin!" he shouted at the TV. "She's wrong,
challenge her. Ask her about Justice John Paul Stevens. Didn't
he change his position on the death penalty just last year? Ask
her about Justices Blackmun and Marshall. Didn't they declare
that they would no longer support capital punishment? Ask her
about the moratorium in Illinois. What about all the evidence
that support for the death penalty is dwindling? Come on, Kevin.
Challenge her. Do your job, man."

But that segment of the show was over. Fin seized the remote
control and clicked off the TV, then slumped back on the couch.
What did it matter, anyway, if a purported legal expert predicted
the Supreme Court's decision? It was just one person's opinion.
Besides, whatever the court's decision, the fact remained that a
shortage was a shortage. It was a disruption. An opportunity. Yes,
that's what it was: an opportunity. He jumped from the couch and
grabbed his cell phone from the coffee table. *I have to talk to Mom.
Now.*

He tapped his foot on the hardwood floor and counted the
number of times the phone rang. Where was she, anyway?

"Mom," he said into the answering machine, "call me as soon

as you get this message."

"Fin?"

"Mom, you there?"

"Just a minute, let me turn this thing off."

"Did you watch *Issues of the Day?*" He blurted the question out even before he heard her answering machine click off.

"What is it? What's wrong?"

"We need to find out if there's a shortage of sodium thiopental in Texas."

"Slow down. I don't know what you're talking about."

"I know how we can stop the execution."

"Fin..." she said, stretching his name out the way she always did when she thought he was being overly emotional or unrealistic.

"There's a case before the Supreme Court right now that could change everything."

Hearing the long, weary sigh on the other end of the line irritated him at first, but then he thought about his dad, and his stomach knotted up. He wished he could hold onto his anger at him for not telling them about his cancer, for expecting them not to worry, for being sick in the first place. But he knew better, knew that the anger was just a cover for his fear.

"Is Dad okay?" he asked.

"Sure. He's not home. I just got up."

"Are you sick?"

Fin listened as his mom confessed that she'd been up all night. She told him she'd found Raelynn's mother in Killeen and that now she was trying to find out what happened to her other children.

"I haven't had much luck so far," she concluded, "except for some leads I got from Annamaria."

Fin was speechless. With so much to digest about what his mom had been up to, it took him a few minutes to realize what Annamaria had gone and done. For the first time ever, she surprised him. *Well,* he told himself, *if my sister is able to help Mom with this, then anything is possible. Anything.*

"We can save her, Mom."

"No, we can't."

"One thing's for sure," he said, "finding out what happened to the other children isn't going to keep her alive."

"It's all I can do, Fin."

"Just so you know: I'm not giving up, Mom. Not like you."

There was that long sigh of hers again. He clenched his jaw and pursed his lips at the sound of it. Then he did something he'd never done before. He hung up on her.

TWENTY-FIVE

Bernadette checked the folder's contents one more time before starting the car. The last thing she needed was to forget something. The letter she'd typed from Maxine Blackwell to the Texas Department of Family and Protective Services was there. So was the DFPS contact-consent form she'd found, thanks to Annamaria, on the Internet, all completed and lacking only Maxine's signature. Then there was the note reminding her to make sure Maxine brought some form of identification when they went into town to get everything notarized and, finally, the names, locations, and hours of operation for notary publics in Killeen. She opened her wallet. Good. She had enough cash to pay the notary fee—about six dollars per stamp—and to buy lunch for Maxine and herself.

"All set then." She turned the key in the ignition and drove away from the curb.

Once on the freeway, she looked at her watch and did quick calculations. She should get to Killeen by ten o'clock and be back in Austin to hand deliver the signed and notarized documents to the DFPS office before it closed for the day. She was confident that all would go as planned, in spite of Marty's skepticism.

"Are you sure about this?" he had asked when he saw her typing the letter.

"There's a better chance of getting the information if the request comes from the birth mother."

"I mean, will Maxine Blackwell be okay with this?"

Bernadette had been irritated by his question. "If she had a phone I'd call and ask," she said, "but I don't have time to go to see her first and then write the letter."

"What if she won't sign it?"

"She'll do it for Rae."

But will she? she wondered now. Was she being presumptuous? She asked herself how she would like it if someone took charge of her like this. She didn't have to think twice about her answer. She wouldn't like it one bit. Until now, she hadn't considered the possibility that Maxine Blackwell might be insulted. If anything, Bernadette had assumed she would be grateful.

Maybe Marty was right. She went back to the drawing board, just in case, and by the time she reached Killeen she had a revised plan in her head about how to approach Maxine Blackwell, one that was more sensitive to her feelings and needs and thus more apt to be successful. It might take longer than she'd anticipated, but that was okay. If she didn't make it to the DFPS office by the end of the day, she could deliver the documents first thing tomorrow morning. No harm done.

Fresh tire tracks on the narrow path leading to Maxine Blackwell's house emboldened her to drive in this time instead of walking. Her Volvo heaved from side to side as she navigated the maze of bumps, holes, and ditches, yet she somehow managed to make it to the clearing unscathed. Seeing no other vehicle there, she parked up close to the house and, clutching the folder under her arm, headed up the porch steps.

The screen door was still dangling on one hinge, but this time the inside door was wide open. Probably Maxine's attempt to capture a bit of the morning breeze before the noonday heat became intolerable.

"Hello," Bernadette called out as she squeezed sideways through the screen door. "Hello? Is anybody home?"

The room looked pretty much as it had when she was there before, except that the bed was unmade and there were dirty dishes on the counter, a coffee cup on the table. She tiptoed inside and saw that the stool by the makeshift kitchen table was lying on its side, as if someone had left in a hurry and knocked it over. When she went over to pick it up, she spotted a red puddle that looked like blood on the floor. She jumped back. Had Maxine Blackwell fallen and hit her head? Worse yet, had someone attacked her? Where was she?

She stumbled from the house and jumped into her car. The tires squealed as she headed back on the treacherous path, holding her breath all the way until she reached the main road. Then she turned off the ignition and told herself to stop and think, to pull herself together. If something dreadful had happened, the police should know. She reached for her cell phone to call 911.

"Sorry, ma'am," the voice on the other end of the line said. "We've received no reports of any trouble at that location. Maybe your friend had an accident. Have you checked the hospital?"

"What hospital? I don't think she has health insurance."

"In that case, ma'am, try the urgent-care hospital center. That's where the indigents go."

"Can you give me their phone number? I'm out in the middle of nowhere."

Her hand shook as she wrote the number on the folder, and she had to repeat it to make sure she'd gotten it right. She called the hospital, and an-eager-to-please receptionist with a drawl that made her sound like Dolly Parton answered the phone on the first ring.

"I'm looking for Maxine Blackwell," Bernadette said. "I think she might be a patient there."

"I'm sorry, ma'am," the receptionist said after a few minutes. "There has been no one by that name in this hospital."

"Could she have been taken some place else?"

"There are several hospitals in Killeen."

"I have to see her today. I have to find her."

"Hold on, ma'am, I'll see what I can do."

The instrumental music in the background grated on Bernadette's nerves, and the wait for the receptionist seemed interminable. What if she didn't find Maxine Blackwell? Or what if she found her but she was too sick or, God forbid, too injured, to talk? Where was that receptionist? Maybe she should just hang up and drive over to the hospital. But which hospital?

"Are you still there, ma'am?" the receptionist said. "I've never used this newfangled thang we have to communicate with other hospitals before just now. I'm sorry, but no one has any record of your friend."

"I know she's hurt," Bernadette said. "I saw the blood."

"Well, ma'am, I hate to worry you, but might I suggest you

check the funeral homes?"

"Good lord." Bernadette dropped her cell phone onto the car seat and held her head in her hands. Could Maxine Blackwell be dead? With the air-conditioning on full blast and her mind in a muddle, she headed back toward Killeen. Near town, she spotted a Starbucks and drove into the parking lot, thinking a strong cup of coffee and some sugar would help her decide what to do next.

"A tall double nonfat latté," she said to the young barista as she handed him her Starbucks card, "extra hot. And one of those raspberry scones, please."

"For here, ma'am?"

"To go," she said. "Well… no… for here. And a phone book, please."

She patted her upper lip in time with the tapping of her foot as she scanned the place for a quiet spot to sit down and think. A teenage couple sat at a table in the middle of the room, the girl rolling her eyes at her boyfriend as if her being braless had nothing at all to do with the way he ogled her apple-sized breasts instead of listening to what she was saying. Bernadette shook her head. She never would have allowed her girls out of the house dressed like that, and she knew Annamaria would never let Patty be seen like that in public, either. Over by the window, a middle-aged man in faded blue jeans was engrossed in a thick hardcover book. The only other customers in the place were a bickering couple with a toddler in full meltdown. Bernadette chose a table back in the corner, as far away from them as possible.

She nibbled on bite-size pieces of her scone between sips of coffee and wondered if she should call Marty and tell him what was going on. But no doubt he would have a number of logical explanations for the blood and tell her there was nothing else she could do but come home now, so she decided against it. She opened the phone book instead and wrote the numbers of all the funeral homes in Killeen on a napkin. Then she threw away her cup, gave the phone book back to the barista, rushed out to her car, and started making the calls.

With each call she made, she held her breath. After the last one, she let out one big sigh of relief. None of the mortuaries had heard of anyone by the name of Maxine Blackwell. But now what? She had no idea. She put the car in gear and headed toward the highway and home.

TWENTY-SIX

By midafternoon Bernadette was back in Austin, bereft and empty-handed, feeling as stuck and motionless as the blistering Texas air. She exited the freeway but instead of going home found herself at Central Market, clinging to a flickering hope that being there might help her figure out what to do. The smell of hot peppers on a grill out front made her tongue water and her eyes run. That and a sign announcing the annual arrival of New Mexico's prized pepper crop inspired her to make an apple-jicama salad with Hatch Chile dressing for dinner. She told herself this was a good sign that new ideas were coming to her already.

Cool, almost frigid, air blasted into her face as she pushed her shopping cart into the market's sprawling produce section. She shivered as she wandered from bin to bin, checking out one piece of fruit after another, all the while urging herself to be open to new possibilities: a new recipe, a solution that had eluded her. An imperfect piece of fruit or vegetable at Central Market was as rare as finding a needle in a haystack, so when she spotted an apple with a small black blemish on it, she felt strangely compelled to place it in her cart. The luscious smell of organic peaches in the next bin brought with it an image of two-and-a-half-year-old Veronica, standing on a chair with juicy, sweet syrup running down her chin, her tiny fingers oozing with warm peaches from a pie that had been cooling on the kitchen counter. Bernadette brushed a tear from her cheek and placed two perfect peaches in her cart.

"How about a hug for your old buddy?"

Bernadette would have recognized that Texas drawl anywhere. Clarissa hadn't changed one bit in the almost ten years since she'd last seen her. Her peroxide-blonde pageboy was still perfect, her skin still wrinkle-free, and her cheeks still a natural blush. What a contrast the two of them made. Even though they were the same age, Clarissa didn't look a day over forty-five in skintight blue jeans and a brightly embroidered Mexican-style blouse, while Bernadette looked every bit her sixty years in sensible wash-and-wear slacks with an elastic waistband to accommodate her thick midsection.

"Good lord… it's been… well, you know." Bernadette's eyes welled with tears as she reached out to hug her old friend.

"I know what it's been, girl," Clarissa said. "It's been way too long, that's what it's been. I'll meet you over in the café for coffee, and I will not be taking no for an answer. First one there grabs a table."

"And we both know who that will be," Bernadette said with a laugh.

***

Even though the Central Market café was crowded, as usual, Bernadette was still able to secure the table back in the corner that used to be their favorite spot. She left the cloth shopping bag that contained everything she needed for dinner—a plump organic chicken, a large jicama, some hot peppers and apples for the salad, and the two peaches for dessert—on the chair while she went to get something to eat.

After returning to the table with a cup of coffee and piece of chocolate cheesecake, she tried to keep her imagination in check while she waited for Clarissa. She told herself that not finding Maxine Blackwell at any of the hospitals or funeral homes had to be good news, that if she went back to Killeen tomorrow or the next day, she would find her back at home. But what if she didn't? What if she never found her? How could she hope to find out what happened to Rae's siblings without her?

"I know, I know, late as usual." Clarissa pushed a shopping cart up to the table with one hand while balancing her tray with the other.

Bernadette glanced at the pile of plastic grocery bags in her friend's cart and the cup of tortilla soup, the Southwestern chicken Caesar wrap, and the sweet-potato pie on her tray; she guessed some people must just be born with the skinny gene.

"So what are you sitting here thinking on so hard?" Clarissa said. "You and me got a lot of catching up to do. So start talking, girl."

Clarissa had never been one for idle chitchat. She laughed now, the same throaty laugh Bernadette had been drawn to when the two of them bumped into each other at the crowded Pecan Street Festival way back when she and Marty first moved to Austin. It hadn't been long before the two of them were sharing confidences as if they'd known each other all their lives.

Now, just as then, once Bernadette started talking, she couldn't stop. She told Clarissa everything: how she had died inside when Veronica was murdered—how hard it had been to work with Regis but how he had helped her move through her grief like no priest ever could, that was for sure—her first confrontation with Raelynn Blackwell—how the aborted execution shattered her trust and how it was restored when she met with Raelynn the second time— Marty's cancer, which, thank God, wasn't serious and he was going to be fine—how Annamaria was trapped in her own anger and rage while Fin had a polyannish notion that somehow it was still possible to get Rae's death sentence commuted—how she found Rae's mother, Maxine, a few days ago but she was nowhere to be found this morning, and how she hoped the poor thing was okay but now she was stuck and didn't know what to do next.

Clarissa didn't say anything, which was not like her at all; she just nodded and looked sympathetic. At times, she got teary-eyed. At other times, her eyes got really big, especially when Bernadette told her about her quest to find out what happened to Rae's siblings.

"You *what?*" she said. "I just gotta say, honey, no one else on this entire planet would go out of their way like that for the murderer of their child."

"I have to do what's right, that's all," Bernadette said.

Clarissa plopped back in her chair with a belly laugh. "Please be my friend again, Bernie. I need a saint in my life, heaven knows."

"Your friend, yes, but a saint, no." Bernadette laughed along with her but then turned serious. "Sometimes I still want her to pay for what she did. Other times, well, other times I'm not sure."

"So why help her? What's that about?"

Bernadette looked down at her hands, unable to even try to explain. "Good lord," she said, "where are my manners? Tell me about you. What are you doing these days? Are you and Hal still together?"

"I broke up with that boy a few years back, or maybe he broke up with me. Whatever. No way that dog was going to hunt, nohow. I'm still working at the bank, putting in my time until Social Security clicks in so I can live the life of leisure I was meant to live. My love life's another kettle of fish. I'm built for living alone, but everyone needs a little roll in the hay once in a while, don't you think, and half a loaf is better than none, as they say. Genealogy's my big thing these days. I tell you, girl, digging into your family ancestry makes you think you're related to everyone in the entire universe. You wouldn't believe what I'm finding. Some people you're connected to, I tell you, you don't want to know. Oh, yes, and I'm fixing to trade in my old clunker soon and buy me a new car. I'll get around to it one of these days. Yup, that's me in a nutshell. So why are you sitting there looking so anxious?"

"What do I do if I can't find Maxine Blackwell?"

"Maybe you could ask your old adoption worker for advice."

That was it. That was the answer. Bernadette leaped from her chair, cupped Clarissa's cheeks in her palms, and kissed each one in turn.

"You're a genius, Clar," she said, "an absolute genius. I'm on it."

"Like smell on skunk," she heard Clarissa say as she hurried away.

TWENTY-SEVEN

Talk about missing the obvious even when it's right in your face, forest for the trees and all that, Bernadette thought as she rushed away from Central Market. She headed north on MoPac without paying any attention to the speed limit, without giving a thought to how out of character that was for her. Her car squealed onto the freeway and from there seemed to know the way by itself as it turned onto Wells Branch Parkway and then onto Summit Drive. She found a parking space right in front of the Travis County Health and Human Services Department building and ran toward the entrance, pushing against the stream of staff and clients going in the opposite direction. She reached the main intake area just as the receptionist was turning off her computer for the day.

"I need to see Mary Jane Crenshaw," Bernadette said, out of breath.

"Sorry, ma'am, we're closed."

Bernadette frowned and pointed to the clock on the wall. "In five minutes," she said. "Is Mary Jane here?"

The receptionist's nails bobbed up and down like ripe red tomatoes on the ends of her arthritically misshapen fingers as she patted her puffed up and obviously dyed black hair as if she was considering whether or not to answer the question.

"Please." Bernadette would have gotten down on her knees if she'd had to. "It's important."

With a roll of her eyes, the receptionist picked up the phone. "There's someone here to see Mary Jane. Just a minute." She paused and held her hand over the phone. "And you are?"

"Mrs. Baker. Bernadette." She rocked back and forth on the balls of her feet as the receptionist repeated her name into the phone.

"Please, tell her all I need is one minute. That's all. Just one minute."

The receptionist mumbled something into the phone that Bernadette couldn't hear. Then she hung up with a disconcerting nonchalance, locked her desk drawer, and dropped the key into a bulky leather purse draped over her bony shoulder. She opened her mouth to say something, then seemed to think better of it.

"What?"

"I don't want to say anything, ma'am."

"Will she see me or not?"

"Maybe you can catch her on her way out," the receptionist said with a shrug.

Bernadette wondered if Mary Jane had refused to see her. Maybe she didn't even remember who she was. And it was, after all, the end of a long day, so she would be tired. Bernadette turned to leave, thinking it might be best to come back first thing in the morning.

"Hello? Bernadette?"

Mary Jane Crenshaw's hair was white now, a perfect match for her stylish linen suit. Her blouse, a pale pink, was the same color as the one she wore twenty-six years ago when she placed Veronica in Bernadette's arms for the first time. How pink everything had been that day: Veronica's scrunched up face—those tiny fists, fingers, and fingernails—miniature feet and toes—the soft blanket—Mary Jane's pink lipstick and rouge, a perfect match with her blouse. Even the clouds in the sky had been tinged with pink.

She gripped Mary Jane's hand. "I have something to ask you," she said. "It's important."

Mary Jane Crenshaw's face blanched. She glanced down at the floor, and when she looked back up, her eyebrows were knit together in a tight worry frown and she was biting at her bottom lip.

"Please."

Mary Jane tipped her head, a gesture so tentative as to be almost imperceptible. Bernadette chose to accept it as an invitation to come with her.

They walked in silence down the familiar hallway, its institutional gray walls covered with black-and-white glossy pictures of smiling children. Bernadette's eyes filled with tears as she remembered the last time she and Marty were here. At the end of the long hall, a plaque on the door said Adoptions Supervisor. So, Mary Jane Crenshaw had been promoted, which meant she was in a perfect position to help. Her bright, sunny office was meticulous and efficient, further confirmation to Bernadette that she had come to the right place.

They sat down at a round table with a bamboo plant in the

middle. When Mary Jane pushed the plant to the side, her hands shook so hard that the vase filled with water and stones almost slipped onto the floor. Bernadette glanced at the stack of boxes in the corner.

"Friday is my last day."

"But you don't..." Bernadette stopped, thinking it might be rude to ask why Mary Jane was leaving. She wasn't old enough to retire, so maybe she was going to a new job. Or maybe she was ill.

After an awkward silence, Mary Jane said, "I feel horrible about Veronica." Her face crumbled as she spoke, and her voice quivered. "I didn't know how to... what to tell you."

"There was nothing you could have said that would have helped back then," Bernadette said. "But you can help me now. I have to find out what happened to the siblings of the woman who killed Veronica."

Mary Jane's eyes widened and her mouth opened, then closed. She looked frightened.

"It's a long story, but I think you'll understand once you hear it," Bernadette said, wanting to reassure her.

When Mary Jane neither encouraged nor discouraged her, Bernadette launched into her story, going into much more detail than she'd intended about what it had been like for her, how she'd found Regis, what it had been like to work with him.

"And then, when I met Raelynn Blackwell," she said, "I felt sorry for her."

Mary Jane's eyes opened wider.

"It surprised me, too," Bernadette said. " I was convinced she had conned me, but it turns out she was telling the truth. And there was something about her. I don't know what it was."

Mary Jane's cheeks reddened. She covered her mouth with her hand, but a gasp or a muffled moan—Bernadette couldn't tell which—escaped nonetheless.

"I know, it amazed me, too," she said. "I'm sure that's why I felt I had to help her find her mother." She went on to describe her visit with Maxine Blackwell and how she was unable to convince her to go see her daughter. As she spoke, Mary Jane seemed to regain some of her composure.

When Bernadette said, "I guess I felt sorry for her mother, too," she interpreted Mary Jane's frown as disapproval. "I know she wasn't a good mother, but she's still a mother. Here are her children's birthdates." She slid the letter and form containing Maxine Blackwell's request for information about her children across the table. "There was a baby boy, too, that she gave up at birth."

"These aren't signed," Mary Jane said, after a quick glance at the documents. "They need to be signed." She shoved them back across the table. She looked as if she was about to faint.

"That's the problem," Bernadette said. "You see, Maxine Blackwell is very sick. And there's not enough time left."

Mary Jane Crenshaw expelled a long breath through her open mouth. "What if things didn't turn out well?" she asked. "What if you found out something you'd rather not know?"

"I have to find out. It's for Rae."

In the silence that followed, Mary Jane stared out the window with an anguished look on her face. Then, with a quick nod of her head, she said, "Come back in a couple of days."

"I knew you'd help."

"I'm not promising anything, okay?"

"I can't tell you how much I appreciate this, Mary Jane."

"I feel horrible about what happened to Veronica."

"I know. I know you do."

TWENTY-EIGHT

Fin had to talk to his mom in person. This was too good to tell her on the phone. He was sure she'd be as surprised as he was by what he'd found out today, although he doubted that she would be as happy, or as hopeful, about it as he was. He got on the #20 bus and paid his fare, wondering if the day would ever come when he didn't think that if this same bus were always on time, then Veronica would still be alive today. He found a seat by a window and closed his eyes, turned his thoughts away from the past and toward what was possible.

At his folks' house, his stomach knotted up when he found his dad out back on the deck, sitting in a lounge chair, sipping a Coke. But when Marty looked up from his book and broke out in a normal smile, looking the way he always did—meaning not sick—Fin let out a sigh of relief.

"Well, I didn't expect to see you today," Marty said.

"Hey, you look good, Dad."

"I'm feeling fine. Why are you here?"

"I have something important to tell you and Mom."

"So your phone doesn't work now? Your mom went to Killeen

this morning to see Maxine Blackwell again."

"Shouldn't she be home by now? It's after six."

"Like a dog with a bone, that's your mom when she's on a mission, you know. So what's so important for you to take the bus over here during rush hour?"

"I know how to stop the execution."

"Now, Fin…"

"Come on, Dad. You'll feel different when you hear what I have to say."

"Hello? Anybody home? Oh, here you are. What a day! I . . ." Bernadette's outstretched arms halted in midair when she saw Fin leaning against the railing. She rushed over to hug him.

"Sorry I'm so late," she said, kissing Marty on the cheek. "Maxine Blackwell seems to have disappeared without a trace. But on my way home, I stopped at Central Market. Oh dear, I forgot the groceries in the car. Anyway, I ran into my old friend Clarissa, remember her, Marty? She looks the same. She suggested I talk to our adoption worker. I don't know why I never thought about that before. So I drove out there. Talk about timing. Mary Jane Crenshaw is leaving her job at the end of this week, but she's going to help me. So why are you here, Fin? I'm glad to see you, but it's a bit unusual for a workday, isn't it?"

"He thinks he can stop the execution again." Marty nodded toward Bernadette with a knowing glance that didn't escape Fin's notice.

"Fin…"

"Just hear me out, Mom. You won't believe it. Remember what I told you about the sodium thiopental shortage? Well, guess what?

Texas only has *two* doses left, and they're about to expire."

"They'll get more from another state," Bernadette said, "or they'll use a different drug."

"I figured you'd say that, but this is where it gets even better." The words gushed out of Fin's mouth now like water pumped from a well. "Over thirty other states are running short of the drug, too, and that's not even the best part. Other countries are refusing to sell *any* drug to the United States if it's used for executions. Italy was the first. Then Germany, the United Kingdom, Denmark. Even India. Who knows what other countries will follow?"

"But Texas still has it," Bernadette said, "and in time for Rae."

"Not if there's another delay. Not if the governor stops it again."

"Fin—"

"We can make a direct appeal to her. Come on, it's worth a try, Mom. If the Supreme Court delays its decision in the Arizona case, that could be grounds for an appeal, too. And it wouldn't hurt to contact the Innocence Project. You know better than anyone how many convictions they've gotten overturned."

"Rae is not innocent."

"She didn't mean to do what she did. She didn't even know what she was doing."

"That doesn't make her any less responsible."

"Come on, you're the one who always says all you have to do is scratch the surface to get at the reasons people do things."

"There's no excuse for choosing to murder someone."

"Was it really a choice for her? Why isn't the state responsible? If someone had protected her, she wouldn't have ended up like she did."

"Haven't we had this conversation enough times already?" Bernadette said with a sigh. "Life isn't fair, Fin. It just isn't."

"I *hate* it when you say that." The childlike whine in Fin's voice made him think about when he stopped believing in Santa Claus, who up until then had been the ultimate arbiter of justice, back when life was simple. If you were good, you got presents; if you were bad, you didn't. He'd never forget the day he found out that Santa Claus didn't bring presents to some children.

"Those children are *not* bad," his mom had said, much to his surprise. "They're just poor."

"No," he had insisted, "they did something bad. They had to."

"Sweetie," she'd said as she folded him into her arms, "those children deserve presents just as much as you do."

"We have to tell Santa Claus they're poor, then," he had wailed, "so he'll bring them even *more* presents."

At least, he thought now, something good had come out of that childhood trauma. It shaped the belief he held to this day that those who had less should receive more. But the real reason he hated it when his mom said life was unfair was because he hated that it was true.

"The point isn't to claim that the world is just," Bernadette said now. "The point is to help make it so."

Fin rolled his eyes at his mom's standard line and felt his body stiffen. "Being able to tell Raelynn Blackwell what became of her family isn't going to do anything but make *you* feel better."

"We do what we can do," Bernadette said.

"It's the way things are," Marty said.

"Don't you care? Don't either of you care?" Fin's voice cracked. The whine was back.

Bernadette took both of his hands in hers and kissed away a tear that fell onto the tip of one of her fingers. "It's time to move on, Fin," she said. "Sometimes we just have to accept life on life's terms."

"I can't," he said, jerking his hands away from her with a sharp shake of his head, "and neither can you, Mom. Neither can you."

TWENTY-NINE

Bernadette pulled off the highway and parked on the shoulder. A torrential downpour had hit full force, without warning, and the wind gusts shaking the car and the jagged lightning were way too close for comfort. She turned on the radio.

"The storm is moving southeast at ten miles an hour," a crackling voice reported, "with a flash flood warning along Shoal Creek until nine a.m."

So much for being on time. She rummaged through her purse and then dumped the contents onto the passenger seat in frustration when she realized she had forgotten her cell phone. She told herself to calm down. MoPac wasn't going to flood. It wouldn't be the end of the world if she was late. And fretting was not going to make the storm pass any faster.

She rested her head against the back of the seat and tried to hold onto the cautious optimism she'd had before she left home. Though she didn't dare to be too hopeful, one thing did seem clear: if Mary Jane Crenshaw had no intention of helping, she would have canceled their appointment today. But what if she said she would help, but only if the request came from Maxine Blackwell?

Well, then, tomorrow was another day. She would have to go back to Killeen again and try to find her, that's all. At the very least, she hoped Mary Jane would be able to cut through some of the red tape in the short time that was left.

She thought about the advice she'd given Fin about accepting life on life's terms, advice that she would be wise to take as well. But there was a big difference between what she was trying to do and what Fin wanted; Fin's quest was hopeless, while hers at least had a chance of being successful. Nonetheless, just as Fin was going to do what Fin was going to do, whatever happened with Mary Jane today was going to happen, and all the worrying in the world wouldn't make one iota of difference.

Bernadette listened to the rain pelting the roof of the car, pouring down so fast and furious that it rendered anything beyond the windshield invisible. And then, in a flash, the car turned silent. The storm was over. It made her dizzy how like life the storm was, how it could change in an instant. She pulled back onto the highway. She might get to her appointment with Mary Jane Crenshaw on time, after all.

When she arrived, the Health and Human Services department's parking lot was packed, so she had to park two blocks away and then navigate around all the puddles to get to the main entrance. Once she was inside the imposing building, her eyes blinked at the glaring florescent lights and her nostrils burned from the smell of sweat, soiled diapers, and disinfectant. Her soaked sandals sucked at the linoleum floor as she walked past three rows of plastic chairs on which dozens of weary women sat, anxiety and defeat written all over their faces as they shushed crying babies and squealing toddlers.

"I see you're back," the receptionist said as Bernadette approached the desk.

"This time I have an appointment."

"You're lucky Crenshaw is still here."

"She got another job, I guess."

"Not after the trouble she got herself into, I wouldn't think."

"Oh?"

"People have to follow the rules."

"What did she do?"

"Uh-uh, I'm not one to gossip," the receptionist said with a wag of her bony, misshapen finger. "The waiting room is down the hall to your right. I'll tell them you're here."

***

Compared to the chaos and sadness of the reception area, the adoptions waiting room was upbeat, with pictures of fat, happy children on the walls; and it was comfortable, too, with a thick-cushioned dark blue sofa and two matching oak-framed chairs. Bernadette sat down and reached for the current edition of *Parenting* magazine on the coffee table. Then she peeled off her wet sandals and tucked her feet under her on the couch.

"Mrs. Baker?"

She unfolded her legs and scrambled to put her sandals back on. A young woman stood before her, chunky and not pretty in the traditional sense, more like cute in a ruffled red blouse and short denim skirt. She kept tucking her hair behind her ears the way Veronica always had, which endeared her to Bernadette immediately.

"I'm Briony Reid," the young woman said. "I'm an intern here."

"Nice to meet you, Briony. What high school do you go to?"

"I'm a senior at UT. It's okay," she said with a wave of her hand, "Everyone says I look younger than I am."

Briony's upturned nose and the smattering of freckles on her round, rosy cheeks didn't only make her look young; in Bernadette's opinion, she looked way too innocent and vulnerable to be working at a place like this.

"Ms. Crenshaw's running late," Briony said. "Is there anything I can get you?"

"I'm fine. I don't mind waiting."

But, of course, she really did mind. She opened the magazine, pretending to read, and speculated about what Mary Jane might have to tell her and whether there was any hidden meaning to her tardiness.

Bernadette glanced up at the clock on the wall. Marty would be at the doctor's office about now.

"I'll be okay," he'd said when he kissed her goodbye that morning.

"I should be going with you," she'd said.

"I don't plan on dying soon."

"You'd better not be." She'd forced a smile, tried to make it sound like a joke.

But in spite of Marty's reassurances, she knew she was letting him down, and it made her feel guilty to imagine him sitting there all alone at the doctor's office. She tried turning her mind to other things, like how much longer she would have to wait, what kind of trouble Mary Jane Crenshaw might have gotten herself into, the blood on the floor in Maxine Blackwell's house, how everything was going to be over after Raelynn's execution in a couple of weeks. But no matter how hard she tried, her thoughts kept returning to Marty and what she'd said to Fin about acceptance. Well, some things in life were too unacceptable to be considered even remotely possible. Losing Marty was one of those things. *That,* she could never accept. And wasn't she here instead of with him at the clinic right now because she knew he was *not* going to die, but Raelynn Blackwell was? She stood up and stretched, then sat back down and reached into her purse for the list of questions she had brought along.

Just as she was checking the list to be sure she wouldn't forget anything, Mary Jane Crenshaw was ready to see her. The first thing Bernadette noticed was that Mary Jane didn't seem on edge as she had on Monday. In fact, she appeared quite confident—or was it determined? Her office, on the other hand, no longer felt warm and welcoming. With the pictures, plants, and most of the books gone, it now had a stark, almost desolate feel about it. One lone box remained in the corner, waiting to be filled with last-minute personal items. There was a folder on the table that was about three inches thick and frayed around the edges, bulging—Bernadette hoped—with all the information she was looking for. Her heartbeat sped up in anticipation of such good fortune as she squinted, stretched her neck, and tried to read the name on the tab without being too obvious about it.

Mary Jane nodded at the folder and motioned for her to sit down. "It was in the archives," she said. "Nowadays, of course, everything's computerized."

Briony came into the office and sat behind them on a chair by the wall and a look of irritation flashed across Mary Jane's face. She leaned over the folder as if protecting its contents from the young intern.

"You understand that I'm only allowed to give you general information," Mary Jane said with a surreptitious glance in Briony's direction.

"Yes."

"But there is one thing I can tell you." Mary Jane slapped her hand on the folder. "The Blackwell children had to be better off anywhere other than in that home situation."

"Even Rae? What about what happened to her in foster care?"

Briony leaned forward in her chair, her eyes watchful, and Mary Jane Crenshaw shrugged her off with a flick of her shoulder. "What happened to that girl should *never* have happened," she said, "but things did turn out better for the other children. At least it seems so."

"What can you tell me?"

"The two boys were placed in separate foster homes."

"Were they allowed to see each other?"

"That information would be in the foster care file, which I don't have. But after their mother terminated her parental rights, a middle-aged couple with no other children adopted both of them."

Bernadette smiled. This was far better news than she'd expected.

"Do you know what happened to them?"

"There was some suspicion that Timothy might have learning disabilities. Maybe fetal alcohol syndrome."

Briony coughed in the background, and Mary Jane shot her another irritated look.

"What about Raelynn's sister?"

"Jennifer was three years old when the children were removed from the home. Her foster parents ended up adopting her. They had three older children of their own and two other adopted children. I think you can assume things worked out okay for her."

"I can't tell you how much this means," Bernadette said with a smile.

Mary Jane Crenshaw did not smile back but instead held Bernadette's gaze as if she were turning something over in her head. Then she glanced at her watch and started to talk faster.

"The baby, of course, was adopted at birth. I'm sorry, Bernadette. Right now I have to leave to get some papers signed. It shouldn't take long. Fifteen minutes, max."

She stood up, patted the cover of the folder with her open hand, and took a step toward the door. But then she hesitated and came back. "Sometimes," she said, touching Bernadette's shoulder, "it's better not to dig too deep."

Mary Jane motioned to Briony with a brusque flick of her finger. The intern, looking confused, followed her out of the room, leaving Bernadette to wonder if something more happened to Rae's siblings than Mary Jane had told her. She decided that, even if there was more to the story, she already had all the information she needed. Or did she? She averted her eyes from the folder and looked out the window to see that the sky was darkening and another storm was rolling in.

THIRTY

Marty stopped at BookPeople on his way home from the clinic, where he and Dr. Sortiev had finalized plans for his surgery. It was his favorite place to linger over a latté and a good book, although this morning he felt a bit too squeamish for the latté part. Just inside the bookstore's front entrance, he spotted *The Book of Dead Philosophers*, which he'd wanted to buy ever since he'd read a review in the *New York Times*. He picked up a copy and, with a reverence usually reserved for sacred texts like the Bible or the Koran, carried it to the checkout counter along with his credit card.

Back home, he settled in with the book in the living room, reading for a while and then closing his eyes with a satisfied smile, at times even laughing out loud. How peculiar, it seemed, that reading about death made him feel so alive. The time passed quite pleasantly as he savored each word as if it were his own, from time to time stopping to appreciate the author's deft prose style by re-reading a phrase. The book made him think about the positive attitude he presented to his family about having cancer even as he kept the source of his optimism—his acceptance of death—to himself. Like Bernie, he believed things were going to be okay; yet, unlike her, he left room for the possibility that they might not be. But he never said any of that aloud, out of a desire to protect his family and because he didn't want to sound pessimistic, which he wasn't.

He looked forward to telling Bernie about the book, hoped that she would find it as amusing as he did. He wanted her to know how reading it gave him the strength to look death in the face and see that it was nothing more than a part of life. But, of course, the first thing he would tell her was that the doctor had said everything was going as expected and that Marty had gotten the distinct impression that meant he was going to lick this thing.

When he heard the sound of rolling thunder, Marty put the book down and looked out the window. New storm clouds churned across the darkening sky, and winds whipped the branches of the pecan tree from side to side in the front yard. Bernie should be home by now, but there was no need to worry; if she was still meeting with the adoption worker, that must mean she was getting lots of information.

A flash of lightning slit the sky, and he hoped she hadn't gotten caught in the storm on her way home. He considered calling her but then remembered what she told him about the dangers of talking on the phone during a lightning storm. Knowing Bernie, she was probably waiting out the storm somewhere. He could see her sitting in Starbucks right now, drinking coffee and going over her notes from her meeting, planning her next move. He turned back to the comfort of his book, secure in the knowledge that if anyone knew what to do when caught in a storm—or anything else, for that matter—it was his Bernie.

THIRTY-ONE

Bernadette stared down at the folder on the other side of the table. Mary Jane Crenshaw's words still rang in her ears. *Sometimes it's better not to dig too deep.* If that was supposed to be some kind of warning, then why did Mary Jane leave her here all alone with the damn case file sitting on the table like this? She resisted the temptation to look. It wouldn't be right. But the harder she fought off the urge to sneak just a little peek, the stronger her desire became. Finally it took hold of her. What would it hurt? If something jumped out at her, wouldn't that mean she was supposed to see it?

She slid her clammy fingers across the table. She only had fifteen minutes. Well, less than that now, though she wasn't sure how much less. She had to act fast. Just as she pulled the folder closer, she heard someone out in the hall and shoved the case file away with such force that it landed right on the edge of the table, poised to tip onto the floor. She stared at the doorknob, waited for it to turn, her chest about to explode. Time stood still. Maybe Mary Jane had realized she shouldn't have left Bernadette alone with the folder and had come back to get it. Or maybe the intern had come back to keep watch over her. The silence in the room was as piercing as a scream in her head. Unable to bear it any longer, she crept over to the door and put her ear against it. Hearing nothing, she opened it a crack, just enough to see that no one was there. She closed the door and collapsed with her back against it, silently releasing the air she'd held captive in her lungs until then.

She sat back down and took three deep breaths. Then, with trembling fingers, she pulled the folder toward her again. It was close enough for her to make out the words on the tab—*Blackwell, Maxine, PS #6875413*—when she snatched her hand back. What was she thinking? It wasn't right to mess with people's lives, without their permission, like this. It just wasn't right.

But she couldn't help herself. She caressed the cover of the folder with her fingertips. She knew she was playing with fire, but she meant no harm. Still, what if she got caught? What would Mary Jane say if she came back now? Bernadette removed her hand from the folder and wiped away the moisture that had gathered above her upper lip.

Still, the folder was relentless in calling to her, and soon she found its tantalizing edge between her thumb and forefinger. She was meant to read it. Why else was it staring at her? With a defiance that matched the way Mary Jane Crenshaw had looked at the watchful intern earlier, she flipped open the case file. All she wanted was peace of mind for Raelynn Blackwell. How could that be a bad thing?

In the end, she came up with a compromise. When she came across any names or other identifying information, she would cover them up, erase them from her mind. She did glance at Maxine

Blackwell's name and the names and birthdates of her children on the brittle and yellowing cover page, but that didn't count because she already had that information. As soon as she turned the page, though, the disapproving side of her kicked in again. She imagined the newspaper headlines, the shame brought down on her family if she were found to have violated the law. It sent shivers through her.

It wasn't too late to close the folder and do the right thing, but then, wasn't it the spirit of the law that mattered? Didn't the situation require her to consider one good over another? She looked at her watch. If she hurried, she could go to just the most relevant parts. She flipped through the pages, stopping at a child protection worker's report written around the time Rae and her siblings were first placed in foster care.

> *Based on a phone call from the oldest daughter, an investigation was conducted to determine the safety of the Blackwell children. During a home visit on December 22, 1983, it was determined that Maxine Blackwell, almost eight months pregnant, was despondent to the point of being incapable of caring for her children or herself. The mother had left Raelynn, the oldest, in charge and the girl seemed overwhelmed and frightened. The only food in the house was an almost empty bottle of ketchup in the refrigerator and a piece of moldy cheese; empty alcohol bottles were broken and scattered everywhere, including on the floor; the children and their clothes were filthy and there was clutter over every inch of surface. Due to the seriousness of the situation the children were removed and placed on a temporary basis in separate foster homes until*

one could be found to take all of them.

A tear slipped from Bernadette's eye and dropped onto the page. She read on, desperate for more reassuring information. She skipped over the names of the foster parents whenever she could and tried to delete any identifying information from her mind when she couldn't, until she came to an entry that stopped her in her tracks.

Maxine Blackwell had given birth to a healthy seven-pound girl.

So the baby was a girl, not a boy. And she was healthy. Bernadette read faster.

> *Maxine Blackwell voluntarily terminated her parental*
> *rights and a temporary six-month placement of the*
> *newborn was made after which…*

Just then there was the distinct sound of footsteps coming down the hall. Bernadette slammed the folder shut and slid it over to the other side of the table just as the footsteps stopped right outside the door. There was a rustling sound, followed by a loud knock, and then the door opened.

"I'm sorry, ma'am." A chubby man in a janitor's uniform stood in the doorway. "I was just fixing to see if Miz Crenshaw might be needing any more boxes."

Bernadette placed her chin in her open hand and tried to act nonchalant, but she must have looked guilty or something because the man's face turned red and he made a hasty retreat, mumbling something about coming back later. Only when she could no longer hear his footsteps was Bernadette able to breathe again. She looked askance at the folder and warned herself to stop, that the next time she might not be so lucky.

But then she thought more about what she'd read. Rae's baby sister was placed somewhere, but where? And why for just six months? She supposed she could ask Mary Jane those questions, but how could she do that without revealing that she'd opened the folder? More questions about the baby buzzed around her like fruit flies harassing a peach, refusing to leave until they landed on some answers. She grabbed the folder and opened it again, fumbling with the pages until she found the place where she'd left off.

> . . . *a temporary six-month placement of the newborn was made with the adoptive parents after which it is expected that the adoption will be finalized.*

Yes, yes, yes, Bernadette said to herself as she read on.

> *The adoptive parents have two children of their own, the older one a girl, the younger a boy.*

This was perfect. Rae would be so happy to know her baby sister had older siblings to look after her.

> *The adoptive mother, a devoted stay-at-home mom, is a former teacher with a college degree in special education.*

Excellent. If Rae's baby sister turned out to have fetal alcohol syndrome or other special needs like those her brother Timmy may have had—which would be no surprise given Maxine's history of drug and alcohol addiction—the adoptive mom would have known what to do.

> *The adoptive father is committed to his family and very involved with his children.*

Bernadette smiled. Reading the case file had been the right thing to do after all. Now she would be able to tell Rae what had happened to her siblings with much more satisfying detail than what Mary Jane had given her. She went back to the file.

When the adoption is finalized, a modified birth certificate will be issued to the adoptive parents.

Satisfied now that a nice family had adopted Rae's baby sister, Bernadette's thoughts turned back to the other siblings. She still might have time to get a few more details about them as well. She turned the page and saw the Application for a New Birth Certificate.

Name of Child Assigned at Birth: <u>Baby Girl Blackwell</u>
Date of Birth: <u>February 10, 1985</u> Place of Birth:
<u>Brackenridge Hospital, Austin, TX</u>

What a coincidence. Rae's baby sister was born on the same day as Veronica and at the same hospital. That settled it. She knew she'd crossed the line now, but she had to keep reading. Maybe she knew the adoptive parents. Maybe she even knew who Rae's baby sister was. Wouldn't it be something if Veronica had gone to school with her?

She looked back down at the file now without restraint, and what she saw made her face burn, her throat close up. She blinked at the blurry signatures at the bottom of the form. It couldn't be. She blinked again. There was no mistaking it. Something sharp stabbed her in the pit of her stomach. She doubled over. Her breath came in short spurts, and she was afraid she was going to pass out. She gripped the seat of her chair until her knuckles turned white and her hands went numb. She had to get out of there. She made it to the door and stumbled down the hall in a daze.

"Mrs. Baker?"

A voice screamed *no* in her head at the sound of the intern's voice. She walked faster, not daring to look back.

"Just a minute, Mrs. Baker."

No, no, no, no, no! The voice in her head screamed louder. She started to run, slower at first, then faster and faster. Blind to anyone or anything around her, she ran down the hall and through the main reception area. She slammed her shoulder into the heavy exit door, and it gave way, thrusting her out into the crashing thunder just as the skies opened in a torrential downpour. With the driving rain and wind bearing down on her, she ran as fast as her short legs would allow, not stopping or looking behind her until she was too out of breath to go any farther.

THIRTY-TWO

Marty was oblivious to the rain smashing against the windows
and the twisting tree branches almost touching the ground until a
sudden flash of lightning and sharp crack of thunder that made it
sound like the storm had moved right into the living room startled
him. He looked at his watch and was alarmed by the lateness of the
hour. Just then, much to his relief, the front door opened. Bernie
was home.

"I'm in here," he called out.

She stood in the dark hallway, staring at him with her mouth
open. Her hair was wet, plastered on her head like a doll's. Her eyes
looked as if she'd seen something she couldn't believe she'd seen—not
frightened-looking, but more dazed, the way he imagined the
survivor of a lightning strike might look, an incongruent coupling of
disorientation and heightened awareness. *The Book of Dead Philosophers*
hit the floor as he flew from his chair and rushed over to her.

"My god, Bernie," he said as she fell against him like a rag
doll. He helped her to her chair opposite his by the fireplace and
wrapped a soft wool throw around her shoulders. Then he knelt on
the floor in front of her.

"You didn't drive in this condition, did you?"

"The man warned me not to," she said with a vacant stare and shake of her head.

"What man?" He shuddered, gripped her knees. Something really terrible had to have happened to put her in such a state.

"I couldn't get my car door open. I don't know how he got my keys."

Marty grabbed each side of her waist, an awkward attempt to calm her and himself at the same time. A chill shot up his spine as he braced for the worst. "Did he hurt you?" It came out in a whisper.

She turned toward him, her eyes unfocused as if she didn't understand the question or maybe didn't hear him. He swallowed his growing panic.

"Tell me about the man, okay, Bernie?" His voice cracked.

"He helped me." She spoke in a disconnected voice that didn't sound like her. "He unlocked the door. He said I shouldn't drive. But I did. I don't know how I made it home."

"Did he hurt you?"

"No," she whispered, "he was very kind."

Tears sprang to his eyes as he felt the terror inside draining away. But when he laid his cheek on Bernie's thigh, he felt her body tremble, and it made him fearful all over again. He squeezed the outsides of her legs in a futile effort to stop the shaking. She gnawed at her hands, biting away at one patch of skin after another, her eyes darting back and forth, her face paler than white.

"Don't." He reached up and pulled her hands away from her mouth.

She shivered. Her eyes were wide, her gaze fixed on nothing.

"It can't be," she muttered.

"What?"

She closed her eyes and shook her head.

"What can't be, Bernie?"

Her head twisted from side to side in sharp, quick movements as if she'd developed a tic. Tears trickled down her cheeks. Then she started to sob. He jumped to his feet and pulled her up from the chair—he didn't know why, he just didn't know what else to do—and held her tight. She started to convulse and gasp for breath, just as she did the night the police officer came to the house to tell them Veronica was dead.

"My god, Bernie," he said. "We need to go to the hospital."

He felt a jolt of her body, heard a low moan.

"I'm calling 911," he said.

"No," she said pushing against his chest. "Don't."

With her hands covering her mouth, she fixed her red, swollen eyes on his face, as if seeing him for the first time since she'd come in the door. He grew wary, wanting to ask if she was ready to tell him what happened but afraid that if he did she might collapse again. She started biting the side of her thumb, and he grabbed her hands and pressed them against her abdomen. She pushed him away and took a step back.

"Marty!" It was a rasping sound, unlike anything he'd ever heard.

"What is it?"

She stared at him. And then, like water breaking full force through a broken dam, she screamed the words.

"Veronica and Rae are sisters."

His stomach caught in his throat and left him speechless. Nothing could have prepared him for this. He covered his eyes and waited for the arrow on the roulette wheel spinning in his head to land on something, anything that could help him understand what she'd just said, because it made no sense to him whatsoever. He felt her hand on his cheek, then her arms around his neck. He leaned into her trembling embrace, pressed his brow against her quivering neck. And just when he was sure the sharp mixture of pain and fear shooting through his heart was going to kill him, she pulled back and gripped his upper arms tight as a vise.

"Marty," she said, her eyes big and round, "this changes everything."

The hot iron touch of her hands made him flinch. What was she saying? What did she mean? It was all too much… too much. He twisted away from her, but she turned him around, forced him to face her. He wanted to resist, but he couldn't as she took his face in her hands.

"Look at me," he heard her say.

But he couldn't see her. Couldn't see anything. Everything had ceased to exist. Then she kissed his cheeks, each in turn, and he felt his arms collapse at his sides. He buried his face in her throat for protection from whatever it was that threatened to devour all meaning from his mind and life itself and thus destroy his sanity. Destroy him. She clutched his hair and pressed his face into her breasts, and a low guttural sound assailed him, so terrifying in intensity that it wasn't until later that he realized it had come from both of them.

THIRTY-THREE

Bernadette knew they were doing the right thing. Last night's dream, strange as it was, left her no doubt about that. In the dream, she was in bed with her children, only they had curiously long arms and legs that were wrapped around each other like soggy noodles. An arm reached out to pull someone else into the bed. Then a leg did the same. Again and again they pulled others in until the mass of twisted arms and legs turned into the world's largest ball of twine, like the one she'd seen during a third-grade field trip to Darwin, Minnesota. Only in the dream, the ball wasn't twine but a mass of living, breathing bodies. As soon as she woke up that morning, she had told Marty she knew what she had to do, and he had agreed. They had both acknowledged that it wouldn't be easy, especially for Annamaria, but there was no getting around that.

She called the kids right away and that very afternoon, at five o'clock sharp, Annamaria marched into the kitchen, followed by Fin and Patty, holding hands. Bernadette's stomach started doing flip-flops. She took in a mouthful of air, blew it back out and silently chanted *breathe in love, breathe out fear* before ushering her family into the living room.

Marty stood next to her in front of the fireplace, and together they watched everyone get settled. Annamaria's shoulders were pulled back and her head tipped up as she sat on the leather couch in a posture of self-assurance, but her eyes—a collage of anxiety, fear, and confusion—betrayed her. Patty plopped down next to Annamaria with a decisive thump, while Fin lowered himself into a lotus position on the Oriental rug in front of them. They all looked worried, and no wonder; they weren't used to being summoned to a family meeting about something so important that it couldn't wait until dinner, especially when Friday was just the next night.

Marty kissed Bernadette on the cheek. "You ready?" he asked.

She cleared her throat and opened her mouth to speak. But when she saw her children's upturned faces looking first at her and then at Marty, a wave of lightheadedness came over her and beads of sweat broke out on her forehead. She placed her wobbly legs a few feet apart to keep them from caving in and held onto Marty's arm for support. Then she took in a deep breath and let it out with a long whoosh.

"What's wrong?" Fin asked.

"Give me a minute." She held the palm of one hand up and pressed the forefinger of her other hand against her lips. It would be best to just get it all out at once, let them react in whatever way they had to. She opened her mouth again, only to find that all the words she'd so carefully rehearsed seemed to vanish.

Marty took her hand in his and nodded his encouragement. "Do you want me to start?" he whispered to her.

She shook her head, pulled her square shoulders back, and took in another deep breath. "There's something we..." She exhaled.

Three sets of eyes fixed on her. *Now. Tell them now.* She looked at Marty, and his smile made it possible for her to go on.

"It's about Rae and her mother." There was no turning back now. She had to keep going.

"I found out that Maxine Blackwell is... well, she's not only Rae's mother." She gulped in some more air, released it. "She's Veronica's *birth* mother, too."

There, she'd said it. She closed her eyes and waited, not knowing what to expect. No one said anything. Were they still there? Why not a sound? She opened her eyes and saw that Annamaria's eyebrows were a knot in the middle of her forehead, her lips a tight thin line.

"What the hell makes you think that?" Annamaria's voice, like shattering glass, broke the silence.

"I can't tell you how I know."

Annamaria tucked in her chin and glared upward like an animal ready to pounce. Bernadette braced herself. She'd expected anger to be Annie's first line of defense, knew it had shielded her from her pain for far too long not to protect her now. But just as anger served as a lifeline between Annie and Veronica, it kept her tied in a negative way to Rae as well. Asking her now to believe, without question, that Veronica was related to the very person she most detested—well, that would be asking too much. Annie would need a lot of time; there was no doubt about it.

No one said anything for what seemed like a very long time. They were in shock—traumatized, no doubt, as she and Marty had been just yesterday. How they'd gotten from the living room to the safety of their bedroom after she first broke the news to him was still a blur to Bernadette. They'd clung to each other for a long time—it seemed like forever—before they had been able to begin talking about it. Even hours later, when there was nothing more to say and Marty had fallen asleep from exhaustion, she'd stared up at the white blades of the ceiling fan flashing against the ghost-like shadows and prayed that he really did believe her, that he really was on her side. Well, she knew Marty was by her side now. And just as he'd come to believe her, so, too, would the others.

Bernadette saw that Patty's curious eyes, round and wide as spaceships, were almost glowing. "What does this mean, Gran?"

"Maybe my friend Clarissa's right," she said with a smile. "Maybe we're related to everyone on the planet."

"Six degrees of separation," Marty said with a shake of his head.

Fin, who had yet to utter a sound, sat in a meditative pose with his eyes closed, the palms of his hands face up on his knees. He was smiling.

"Veronica knows," he whispered to no one in particular.

"Yes," Bernadette said.

"I think your mom knew, too, without realizing it," Marty said. "I think that's why her heart went soft for Raelynn Blackwell right from the start."

***

That was it. Annamaria couldn't stand any more of this. She jumped up from the couch and stumbled out to the front hallway with her lower lip leading the way, her breath shooting out in flames. Then she stalked back to the couch and out to the hallway again, back and forth, back and forth, finally coming to an abrupt stop behind the couch. She dug her sharp fingernails into the soft leather.

"How can you expect us to believe this," she said with a squinty glare, "when we don't even know who told you?"

"I trust my source," she heard her mom say.

"Is there anyone you don't trust?"

"No need for that," her dad said. "I didn't believe it at first, either, if that's any help. It's a lot to take in."

"If I thought it would help, Annie, I'd tell you how I found out, but my source is in enough trouble as it is."

"So," Annamaria snorted, "sounds like we have some violation of Texas confidentiality laws or something going on here."

"Mom wouldn't have told us if she didn't know it was true," Fin retorted.

"But Mom hasn't told us how she knows it's true, have you, Mom?"

"It started when I found out that Rae's baby sister was born on the same day as Veronica... and at the same hospital, too."

"You're basing this on a coincidence?" Annamaria was flabbergasted. This was the extent of her mom's evidence?

"I thought it was just a coincidence at first, too."

Annamaria crossed her arms and glared at her mom. "Well, there you have it," she said, "all this grief and drama over nothing."

"But it turned out not to be. There was only one baby born at the hospital that day. That baby was our Veronica, and her mother was Maxine Blackwell."

Annamaria snorted and looked away.

"Knowing the details about how your mom made this discovery is not what's important," her dad said. "What's important is how we face this."

Annamaria couldn't believe it. Both her parents were against her. Again. She gripped the back of the couch to keep herself from sinking onto the floor. There was only one thing she knew how to do to stay in the fight, to inject reason into the craziness that had descended on her family. She tugged at the jacket of her red power suit and projected herself back to earlier that day when she was in court. She narrowed her eyes at her mom, a hostile witness. Then she looked at her dad and turned him and the others into members of the jury. It wouldn't do for her to seem shaky in front of any of them. She had to appear confident, in charge, no matter what she felt inside.

"Okay then," she said in the most professional tone of voice she could manage, "let's say it's possible that Veronica and that murderer were related somehow." She coughed into her hand to cover up the cracking in her voice.

". . . Which none of us should believe," she added, raising her voice, "without verification." She paused, sighed, gulped in some air.

"There is verification, Annie," her dad said. "It is what it is."

"Okay, for the sake of argument, let's say it's true. The question remains: what difference does it make? I'm not just asking you, Mom, Dad. I'm asking all of you. What the *hell* difference does it make?" She drew her lips together in a circle and released the air from her lungs with a loud puff.

"The answer to that question is in your heart, Annie," her mom said.

"You have the freedom, as do all of us, to choose how to respond," her dad said, "to decide what it means."

"It means," Fin said, "that Raelynn Blackwell is all that we have left of Veronica."

"No, Fin," Annamaria said. "The *correct* answer is that it doesn't mean anything."

"It doesn't mean anything to you that Veronica and Rae are sisters?" Fin said.

"*Nothing.*" Annamaria's eyes flashed, and her words scorched the air.

"Come on, they're blood," Fin said. "*Blood.*"

Annamaria felt rage building inside her. She gritted her teeth. "They are not alike in any way," she said. "Veronica was born good."

"And Raelynn Blackwell wasn't?" Fin said.

"Good, bad, blank slate," her dad said with a shrug.

"You know what I mean, Dad. Veronica was a good baby. We all know that."

"She was a happy baby," Fin said, "with Mom and Dad beside themselves with happiness at the smallest hint of a smile from her and an older sister, *you*, unable to resist her charms no matter how hard she tried and, of course, a brother who anticipated her every need. But what if she'd been neglected or mistreated instead of loved and cared for? If she cried then, would that mean she was a bad baby?"

Patty shuddered. "If you guys didn't adopt Veronica, she could have ended up like Rae."

"No, she couldn't have." It was Dad's voice, much louder than usual.

"I shudder to think about what she was spared." This was Mom.

Annamaria thought she was going to explode. She squeezed her eyes shut. Her hands shook. She slapped at her cheeks until they burned red. "No way, no way, no way. Veronica was *nothing* like her. Nothing at all." The words kept spitting out of her mouth until the pressure of her mom's hands on each side of her face made them stop.

"It's okay, Annie, it's okay."

Her dad's hands were on her arms now, guiding her to the front of the couch, urging her to sit down. Then Patty nestled in close, her arm around her, squeezing her shoulder.

"Why did you have to tell us?" Annamaria heard the distant wail of her voice sounding as if it was coming from someone other than herself, someone little and far away.

"We don't keep secrets in our family," her mom said.

"No, we don't." It was Dad.

"Gran? If Aunt Veronica and Rae were sisters… then… wouldn't…"

"Half," Bernadette said. "They're *half* sisters."

"So, like, that means my mom and Uncle Fin are Raelynn Blackwell's adoptive half-sister and half-brother or something?"

"Yes." It was Fin. Too loud.

Annamaria's eyes stung. Her stomach contracted. She bent forward with her face between her knees, her hands over her ears.

"So what are you going to do now, Gran?"

"I'm going to see Rae again."

"And do what?" Annamaria asked in a weak voice.

"Whatever I can. She's Veronica's sister."

Annamaria's stomach churned, and its contents started to heave up into her throat. Her eyes watered. "I need some air" was all she could manage to say. With one hand clutching her stomach and the other covering her mouth, she lurched out the front door and stumbled away from the house.

THIRTY-FOUR

A stream of light, on its way toward dusk but not quite dusk, moved across Annamaria's desk as she stood with her back against the sink, following the rays with her eyes. Nothing was real. Everything was upside down. She had no memory of how she had gotten to her office. All she knew what that she couldn't stay at her folks' house another minute, couldn't listen to them talk about it as if it mattered. As if it changed anything. Veronica was still dead, wasn't she, and all that talk about good babies and bad babies, about who's related to whom, didn't change a damn thing.

She wiped her face with a paper towel. Then she reached into the mini-refrigerator next to the sink and pulled out a bottle of white wine. With the bottle in one hand and a glass in the other, she walked over to her desk and filled the glass to the rim. After a couple of sips, she was calm enough to reach for the phone. Her mom answered right away.

"Are you all right, Annie?"

"I'm okay," she said, an automatic response. "Is Patty…?"

"She's fine, honey. We're making chocolate chip cookies. Let her stay the night. I'll bring her home first thing in the morning.

Where are you? We're worried about you."

"I'm at my office."

There was silence on the other end of the line. Then her mom said, "It might help to talk about it."

"Just tell Patty I love her. I'll be all right." She hung up the phone, fast, before her mom could ask any more questions.

She *would* be all right. All she needed was a glass of wine to cool her down and a legal brief to distract her. She reached into her desk drawer and grabbed a random folder, but the words inside bounced around on the page like Mexican jumping beans. She pinched her eyes, but still the words were nothing but a gray blur. She gave up and sat back, the only sound in the gloomy silence the squeaking of her chair whenever she moved to refill her wine glass. The next thing she knew, her office was dark and the bottle was empty.

Outside the window, lights shimmered here and there from houses tucked into the hillside as families prepared and ate dinners, watched television together, talked. She wondered what her family was doing now, whether Fin was still at her folks' house. Maybe they were talking about Dad's cancer; was she missing the most recent update? Maybe they were talking about how Mom was going to break the news to Raelynn Blackwell. Or maybe, just maybe, they were talking about her. She shouldn't have run out of the house like that. But then, no one had asked her to stay, had they?

A wave of loneliness hit her then with such force that it drove her back to the refrigerator for another bottle of wine. She switched on the floor lamp and flopped onto the couch.

"What the hell are you smiling about?" she said as she lifted the glass to her lips.

She shook her head. So now she was hallucinating? "Fin is not here," she said out loud. She was alone, in her office, with no one to talk to but herself. No one to see how upset she was at Mom for caring more about Veronica's murderer than about anyone else—no one to see how worried she was that Fin might cross over the line into insanity—no one to see what was happening to her—no one to hear her confess that, even though she said she didn't believe it, she knew Mom had told the truth.

"Why the hell don't you call Mom and tell her that?" she said out loud. But she made no move to do it. No, if she told her mom that she believed what she had said about Veronica and Raelynn Blackwell being sisters, her mom would want to know how she felt about it. And there was no way Annamaria could tell her it was triggering something inside that was so deep she couldn't reach it, so menacing that she was afraid to even try. No way she could talk about how it took her breath away to feel Patty's vulnerable body pressed against hers today when they were on the couch, to hear her daughter's sweet voice—her poor baby trying to reassure her that everything was going to be all right. No way she could admit how terrified she was. No, there was no way she could tell Mom any of that, no way she could understand. How could she, when she couldn't even understand that all Annamaria had ever wanted was justice for Veronica?

She poured herself another glass of wine and looked at a framed eight-by-ten family picture on the coffee table. The photo had been taken the last time they were all together for Christmas. Mom sat in the middle, with Dad to her right with one arm around her shoulder and the other around Veronica. Fin was next to Veronica, his arm around her, too, intersecting with Dad's. And there she was, on the other side of Mom, her arms wound around then-six-year-old Patty, who was sitting between her legs.

"I want us back," she whispered as she picked the picture up and looked into their laughing faces. "I just want us back."

She pressed her family to her breast with one hand, picked up the wine glass with the other, and stumbled over to her desk. She propped the picture up next to her computer and sat down. What she was about to do didn't make any sense. But it was the only thing she could think of doing, the one thing she knew how to do best. She turned on the computer and started to type.

THIRTY-FIVE

Fin hadn't spoken since Bernadette picked him up this morning, so all she could do was guess what he was thinking from the jumbo mustard-yellow letters on the cardinal-red tee shirt he was wearing—*Love* on the front and *is everything* on the back. It worried her, though not for the first time, that one of these days Fin's loving spirit was going to crush him. It's not that she thought he was too compassionate. Heavens no, she loved that about him. It's just that he had never learned to contain his caring. She tipped her head in the direction of a sign that said it was ten miles to Gatesville.

"Nervous?" she asked.

He sighed, and out of the corner of her eye she saw his head go up a little, then drop back down. She hoped the conditions in the women's prison wouldn't be too much for him, that he wouldn't get overwhelmed when he found himself face to face with Rae for the first time. She'd tried to talk him out of coming with her. When that had failed, she'd gone ahead and asked Regis to get him on the approved visitors list and then done her best to tell Fin what to expect. But there was no way anyone could ever be prepared for

Gatesville. She sure hadn't been.

"You can change your mind," she said.

He shook his head, kept staring straight ahead.

"It's okay. If you decide you don't want to do this."

"I have to," he said.

Bernadette couldn't help but smile. Even now, four days later, it warmed her heart to think about how well Fin had taken the news. She felt strangely grounded by Patty's curiosity, as if it normalized things somewhat, and she would be forever grateful for Marty's unconditional support. It was Annamaria who worried her.

"You're not going to tell her, are you?" Fin asked.

She squirmed at the intensity in his voice.

"You *are*, aren't you?" From the way his lips curled downward and his brow furrowed into a tangled mass on his forehead, it was clear to her that Fin was making an accusation, not asking a question.

"I want to do the right thing," she said. "I keep thinking she's entitled to know." She ran her hand through her short hair, and its coarse gray strands prickled her fingertips.

"Don't tell her, Mom."

One minute she agreed with him, but then the next minute she thought it was only right to tell the truth. She worried, though, that there might not be enough time left for Rae to come to terms with the fact that she'd killed her own sister. So maybe it was better if she never knew. Bernadette was glad she no longer believed in an afterlife; at least she didn't have to worry that Rae would find out that way. Still, afterlife or not, her motivation for telling the truth shouldn't be based on fear of being found out. It should be about doing the right thing. She hated not being sure, no matter how many times Regis told her that ambivalence was a natural part of the human condition.

"What does Dad think?" Fin asked.

"He says I'll know what to do when the time comes."

"What would he do?"

"You know your dad. He works things out in his head. He doesn't need to do things hands on like I do."

"How about Regis? I suppose being a preacher and all, he would say 'Thou shalt not lie' or something."

Bernadette ignored the snort at the end of his sentence. "Regis never tells me what to do," she said. "Except when I told him about Veronica and Rae being sisters, he right away said I was not to go to Gatesville without him and that he would rearrange his schedule and meet us there."

They drove for a while without talking, but the silence made Bernadette more nervous. "Rae cried when I told her I'd try to find her mother," she said.

"That's the point, Mom. You promised to look for her mother. You don't have to tell her anything else."

"We don't keep secrets in our family, Fin. You know that."

She saw the pink splotches spring up on his neck and didn't know if that meant he was hurt or angry. She used to be able to tell, but it was harder these days. She hadn't meant to scold him, didn't mean it to sound so harsh. But she did believe family secrets were harmful—at least as a general principle. Still, was it always wrong not to tell the truth? She patted Fin's hand, a half-hearted attempt at best to reassure him, not enough to drive the apprehension from his eyes. She wished she could tell him there was nothing to worry about, that his dad was right that she would know what to do. But that would be lying. The truth was, she wasn't at all sure that she would know what to do when the time came. In fact, right now, she wasn't sure about anything.

THIRTY-SIX

Not only was the wire mesh at the bottom of the Plexiglas divider abhorrent, the whole place was so revolting it made Fin want to puke. And if that wasn't bad enough, he had no idea what was going on with his mom, except that something changed as soon as they walked into the Mountain View unit. Her anxiety disappeared, and suddenly she was all composed. Could it be that Dad was right, that when the time had come, she knew what to do? But just what was she going to do? A tremor rippled up his arm, and his mom pushed her head against his neck as if trying to stop it from reaching his head and messing with his brain—a well-meaning gesture that wasn't helpful.

"Thirsty?"

Fin found it disconcerting, the way Regis didn't seem to mind being in this repugnant place at all, the way he was able to pour ice water from the pitcher into the three tall plastic glasses without spilling a single drop. It was almost as if he already knew what was going to happen. Fin lifted a glass to his lips, but his hand was shaking so hard that he spilled most of the water onto the table. He jumped back, his metal chair making a scraping sound on the concrete floor that hurt his teeth. He soaked up the spill with the bottom of his tee shirt, squeezed the water out, and let it drip onto the floor. Then he clasped his hands on the table, clenched his teeth, and tried not to look at his mom. It was his job to make sure she didn't tell Raelynn Blackwell that she had killed her own sister, and no matter how many worried looks his mom sent his way, nothing was going to deter him. Not spilled water. Not his mom's inexplicable composure. Not the ghastliness of inhumanity all around him. Nothing.

Several minutes passed before a wiry young guard with a kind face appeared on the other side of the Plexiglas window, cupping the elbow of a slight woman dressed in white prison garb. He pulled the chair out for the woman, removed her handcuffs, and patted her shoulder before retreating to his post by the door. Fin didn't realize at first that he was looking at Raelynn Blackwell. He didn't expect her to be so small.

"This is my son, Fin," he heard his mom say, "Veronica's brother."

Raelynn Blackwell lifted her hands up in a prayer-like gesture. Her fingertips brushed her lips like a kiss, and then she smiled at him, a shy kind of smile that reminded Fin so much of Veronica that he felt dizzy and had to grip the edge of the table. The big round clock on the wall ticked, each tick more deafening than the last, Raelynn Blackwell's smile fading a little bit more with each tick until her smile was gone. She chewed on her upper lip and looked down. It wasn't long before jagged slashes of tears were fracturing her cheeks.

"I will go to my grave sorry for what I did," she said.

Fin wanted to tell her he'd forgiven her a long time ago and
so had Veronica, but the tears in his throat kept swallowing the
words. He stood up, leaned across the table, and pressed his palms
against the Plexiglas. *Touch my hands,* he pleaded with his eyes. But
Raelynn Blackwell stared down at the table and turned away from
him in shame. The ticking clock drowned out the silence.

"Go ahead," Bernadette said to Raelynn. "It's okay."

Raelynn Blackwell looked at Fin then, and when he saw the
panic in her eyes, he tipped his head toward his hands, then nodded
to reinforce the invitation. She began to lift her hands from her
lap, and he moved his hands farther down the window so they were
closer to hers. With excruciating tentativeness, her hands moved
toward the window until her trembling fingers grazed the Plexiglas.
He tapped the window and nodded. She paused and looked at him,
her tear-filled eyes a question. He smiled and nodded again. Their
hands sought each other, fingers meeting first. He pressed his palms
against the glass. She pressed back. Through a blur of tears, he saw a
slight smile begin to form on her lips.

"I love you, Veronica." He mouthed the words as he slid his
hands, little by little, down the window. But when his fingers
touched the wire mesh at the bottom, they flew off as if they'd
touched a burning stove, and he fell into his mom's arms.

"Don't tell her," he whispered in her ear. "Don't do that to my
sister."

***

It took Bernadette's breath away to so clearly see it now:
Veronica's life connected in the flesh with the life of the woman
who murdered her. But even though her composure was shaken,

her conviction was not. She knew what to do. She ran her fingers through Fin's hair and pressed her palm against his cheek, knowing that he had been as stunned as she by the resemblance between Veronica and Rae.

"Please *don't*," he pleaded with her one last time.

"Trust me," she said.

Fin slumped back in his chair, but he wouldn't stop squeezing her hand as Rae watched from the other side of the barrier with a confused look.

"I saw your mother," Bernadette said.

"You did?" Rae's eyebrows shot up. "Disappearing was what Ma done best." She shook her head as if she couldn't believe what she was hearing, and her eyes were big with hope.

"I couldn't convince her."

"I knew she weren't coming." Rae's face fell and she slumped back in her chair, her face a mask suddenly devoid of any detectable emotion.

"She thinks it would make things harder for you," Bernadette said. "She doesn't want to hurt you any more than she already has. She says it's all her fault, what happened to you."

Rae stared at the floor.

"She called you 'my Raelee.' She said 'my Raelee is a *good* girl.'"

Bernadette cursed the wire mesh that kept her from wiping away the tear that she saw fall onto Rae's folded hands.

"Your ma stopped drinking."

"Really?" Rae's head came back up, but her eyebrows were squished together.

"She's very sick. I think it might be cirrhosis of the liver."

Rae sighed and then smiled, a sad smile. "I guess me and Ma will work things out in heaven, then."

Bernadette shrugged.

"I'll pray for her," Rae said. "Jesus is merciful."

How comforting it must be, Bernadette thought, *to have that kind of faith, the faith of a child.* But Rae's praying wouldn't make any difference if her mother was already dead, which she might be. And if Jesus really was merciful, Veronica would be alive and none of this would be happening.

"There's something else," Bernadette said.

"Mom, *don't.*" Fin gripped the edge of the table, his body back on hyper alert.

"It's okay, Fin." She looked him straight in the eye, willing him to believe her.

"Is it about Ma?" Rae's panicked eyes darted from Bernadette to Fin and back again.

Bernadette shook her head. "Your brothers and sisters," she said.

Rae, looking frightened, fell back in her chair. She looked like she was about to cry.

"It's good news."

"Really?" She leaned forward again.

"They were all adopted."

"*All* of them?"

Bernadette smiled and nodded. "Timothy and Anthony were adopted together."

"You seen them?" Rae's eyes were round saucers now.

"Good lord, no. I just found out what happened to them after you… after…"

"After I called the police."

"You did the right thing."

Rae's eyes filled with tears and she shook her head, obviously not believing that for a minute.

"It was for the best," Bernadette said. "The boys were able to stay together, and Jennifer was adopted by her foster parents. They had other children, so she wasn't alone, either."

"They ended up okay?"

"Yes."

Bernadette searched Rae's eyes for the signs of happiness, contentment, perhaps relief that she expected would come once Rae had time to absorb the news, but Rae looked puzzled instead, as if she was trying to figure something out.

"My baby brother," she said, rubbing her hands together.

"Your ma had a baby girl, not a boy."

Fin gasped and curled into himself with his hands over his head, his forehead pressed against the table. When he started keening—a soft wailing that deepened in both intensity and volume—Bernadette covered his body with hers as if it were possible to hold him together that way.

"Trust me, sweetie," she whispered in his ear. "Honest, it'll be okay."

That seemed to calm him, at least enough that he stopped moaning. Bernadette turned back toward Rae, feeling the need to take care of two children at the same time.

"Was she—? Did she—?" Rae's words were staccato blasts of raw fear, her eyes filled with panic.

"Your baby sister was adopted, too. She was very well cared for. She was very much loved." Bernadette's voice went up an octave with each word. *Adopted. Cared for. Loved.*

"What do you mean *was*?" Rae was staring at Fin's distraught face.

"I mean your baby sister had a *very* good life."

Rae fell quiet for a minute, thinking.

"I never even knowed her name," she finally said. "When I called the police that day I never thought anyone would come... but there were men... I mean, everyone was drunk... the house... we didn't have any food... I was so scared... I didn't know what else to do..."

"Your brothers and sisters lived because of what you did. You saved them."

Raelynn Blackwell grasped the chain around her neck, brought the silver cross up to her lips, and kissed it. Bernadette and Fin sat back in their chairs. They both sighed. Rae smiled—just a little at first—and then her smile grew bigger. Later, Bernadette would tell Marty that Rae's and Fin's smiles got so bright that she was sure everyone at Gatesville must have wondered what it was that all of a sudden made the entire prison compound light up that day.

THIRTY-SEVEN

Marty lay in the dark with his eyes open, listening to the cacophony of murmuring voices, laughter, and music that sounded as if the air filter by the bed was channeling it into their room from a neighbor's party or something. It was late and he was tired, but he couldn't sleep. He rested his cheek on Bernie's chest, and his head rose and fell with her ragged breathing—a sign that, even though she was asleep, it was a restless sleep. Sweat glued their bodies together, yet instead of making space for puffs of air from the ceiling fan to cool them, he burrowed even deeper into her skin, wanting to get inside her, make sense of her. He went back to the beginning again, one more time, to when she first got home that afternoon.

"So," he'd said as soon as she walked in the house.

"I didn't tell her."

"I expected you would." He remembered being surprised.

"I started to."

"And?"

"You should have seen the way she looked at Fin. How could I tell her she'd killed her own sister when she looked at him like that?"

"Truth or compassion," he'd said, nodding his head. "A fork in the road."

"What?"

"You chose compassion." He remembered being awestruck, once again, by Bernie's uncanny ability to come to right decisions through what, to him, seemed pure instinct.

"Fin thinks he can get her sentence commuted to life in prison."

"Not a chance," he'd said.

She'd looked irritated with him then, and he remembered wondering if that meant she now agreed with Fin. He moved away from her a bit now and studied her face in the dim glow of the night-light. There was a slight grimace on her lips and her cheek twitched, both of which made him think she was still bothered by what they had talked about just before she fell asleep.

"Fin cares too much," he'd said. "He always has."

"His caring is beautiful." There was that look of irritation again.

"But he gets over-involved."

"So do I," she'd said.

"So that's *it?*" he'd asked. It was hard for him to believe Bernie would leave Fin alone to pursue his futile quest without even trying to stop him, that she wouldn't want to at least try to spare him the inevitable disappointment he was setting himself up for.

"I love Fin," she'd said with a firm shake her head. "I love the sun in the morning, too, but I'm not *responsible* for making it rise."

"Be serious, Bernie." He remembered wondering at that point why he was starting to get irritated.

"I am. It might surprise you to know, Marty, that I'm not

responsible for this god-awful Texas heat, either, much as I hate it. Or, much as I love it, for the moon shining through our bedroom window right now. Oh, and for your information, I can't make it rain, either."

He turned onto his back and stared up at the ceiling now, trying to figure out what might have been behind that outburst of hers. It occurred to him that it might have been a sign that Bernie was shedding, or wanting to shed, the burden of excessive responsibility that had plagued her since childhood and that had been the source of most, if not all, of their disagreements over the years.

But if that was the case, he wondered why that didn't make him happy—why, instead, an inexplicable feeling of abandonment came over him at the thought of it. Maybe he was afraid of losing the positive side of Bernie's nature along with the negative, the side that meant he could always count on her, no matter what. And now, with Fin setting himself up for a bigger fall than usual from his Don Quixote horse, what if Marty couldn't count on Bernie to even *try* to rescue him? He shuddered at the prospect that it might be left up to him to intervene. That didn't sit well with him, didn't sit well with him at all. But then he thought about what had been the most revealing part of his earlier conversation with Bernie. He returned to it now.

"Just so you know, Marty, I am *not* going to let Rae die."

He'd stared at her, in that moment painfully aware that Bernie had become so obsessed with Raelynn Blackwell that she was now oblivious not only to Fin but to everything and everyone else, including him. Had she not even noticed what was happening to him, the changes in his appearance, how the skin on his back was pasty white instead of its usual tan, how his stomach was more sunken than toned? Did she even see him anymore?

"We're all dying, Bernie." He remembered saying it in a quiet voice. He'd tried hard to contain the intensity behind the words because he didn't want to say something he'd later regret.

"Good lord, Marty. *You're* not dying. I won't let you," she'd said with a stinging seriousness.

"So you can cure my cancer?"

"Oh, Marty, how I wish I could." He remembered how her eyes had filled with tears then, real tears, big tears, desperate tears.

"I bought new jogging shoes," he'd said.

"Who's into wishful thinking now?"

"It means I plan to live."

"You better." She'd kissed him and run her fingers down his cheeks, as if that settled it.

"But seriously, Bernie," he'd said, "Fin needs to accept the inevitable. Raelynn Blackwell *is* going to die."

Marty realized now that he should have left it at that. But instead, he'd gone on and said, "It isn't just her. We're all going to die. Raelynn gets to know when, that's the only difference."

That's when Bernie had started to cry, and right now he thought he finally understood why.

"I'm not going to die," he whispered to her as she tossed and turned next to him in the bed. She rolled over and moaned. He rubbed her back, her shoulders, her head.

"I'm not going to die," he said again. "I promise."

THIRTY-EIGHT

"Sorry I'm late," Bernadette said. "PoK-e-Jo's was packed. I got chicken and ribs, plus a bunch of sides. Why only three places at the table?"

"Patty's got a dance tonight, and Annamaria's working late," Marty said.

"Well, I'm glad you're here, sweetie," she said to Fin.

She watched Marty take the barbecue containers out of the bags. He placed them on the dining room table without putting anything under them to protect against spills, but she didn't care. Nor did it matter to her that there were no candles or fresh flowers on the table or that the silverware and glasses were incorrectly positioned on placemats that didn't match. The only thing that mattered were the amazing discoveries she'd made at the university law library this afternoon.

"Rae looks just like Veronica, Dad," Fin said, once they were settled at the table. He paused and then added, "We have to work fast. There's only ten days left."

"It's too late," Marty said.

"Maybe not," Bernadette said. "I read some court cases today that seemed more hopeless than Rae's where the sentences—and in some cases even the verdicts—were overturned, a couple of them at the very last minute."

"See, Dad," Fin said, "I have news, too."

Bernadette smiled at her son. She was aware that things had shifted between the two of them since their trip to Gatesville, but there was no need to speak of what they both instinctively knew.

"I don't know what you're doing, Fin," Marty said, "but trust me, whatever it is, it won't work. Just remember, 'if you beat your head against the wall, it is your head that breaks, not the wall.' That's a direct quote from the great philosopher Gramsci, by the way."

Bernadette frowned and shook her head at him.

"I just don't want Fin to get hurt," Marty said.

"I learned something else this week: that juries are rejecting capital punishment more now, fourteen times just in the past four years," Bernadette said.

Fin pulled his shoulders back, and his chest expanded. "And now we have this." He was almost giddy as he waved some legal-sized papers in the air.

"What is it?" Bernadette and Marty asked in unison.

"It's a petition to the governor for an act of clemency on Rae's behalf. It was delivered to my house this afternoon."

Marty leaned forward with a skeptical look and took the document from Fin's hand, set about studying it.

Bernadette sat on the edge of her seat. "Let me see it," she said with an impatient motion of her hand. Marty turned the petition over to her, and she started to read it out loud:

PETITION FOR AN ACT OF CLEMENCY

To the Governor of the State of Texas

On behalf of Raelynn Blackwell

> *A request that the sentence of death be commuted to life*
> *in prison without the possibility of parole for Raelynn*
> *Blackwell, whose execution is scheduled to take place on*
> *August 15, 2011.*

Stunned, she stopped reading and stared down at the petition. This just might be the answer. "Go on," she heard Fin say, "keep reading." So she did.

> *The decision about whether to impose the death penalty*
> *involves a determination as to whether the crime was*
> *heinous, atrocious or cruel as compared to other capital*
> *murder cases. There is no doubt that Raelynn Blackwell's*
> *murder of sixteen-year-old Veronica Baker was heinous in*
> *all respects. Nonetheless, there are three other compelling*
> *considerations in this case that argue for clemency:*
>
> *1) based on unforeseen circumstances, the victim's family*
> *is unanimous in its desire that Raelynn Blackwell be*
> *spared the death penalty;*
>
> *2) the mitigating factors of Raelynn Blackwell's life—*
> *including, but not limited to, the State's failure to protect*
> *her from a childhood of physical and sexual abuse and*
> *neglect, including sexual assault while in the foster care*
> *system—point to a case for clemency; and,*
>
> *3) there is overwhelming evidence that, since her*

incarceration, Raelynn Blackwell has been rehabilitated to
the point where her help of troubled prisoners has proven
to be an asset to prison personnel.

"I can't believe it." Bernadette put the legal paper on the table.

"Me either," Fin said. "There was a note with it saying it was for Rae's lawyer. I already called Mr. Pearl and left him a message."

"No, I mean, I can't believe she did this."

"Who?" Marty asked.

"Who else writes like this?" Bernadette said, still shaking her head in disbelief.

Just then, Fin's cell phone rang, and they all jumped.

"It's Jimmy Pearl," Fin said with a big smile when he saw the caller ID.

Bernadette's heart raced. She crossed her fingers under the table. This was a miracle, all right: a miracle for Annamaria, a miracle for Rae—for all of them. It wasn't too late after all. She was sure Mr. Pearl would be all over this. But then she saw Fin's smile vanish, his eyes turn fearful. His bottom lip quivered.

"No!" he yelled, dropping his cell phone onto the floor. He slumped forward, his cheek pressed against the table. Marty rushed over to him and, in a loving but awkward gesture, put his arms around Fin, tightening his embrace with each heave of his son's body and weeping along with him.

A thick rubber band squeezed Bernadette's chest as she waited for an answer to the question she didn't dare ask out loud. Time stood still. She couldn't move.

When Fin's sobbing subsided, he wiped his face with his napkin and blew his nose. Marty kissed the top of his head and returned to his place at the table.

"The execution is Monday." Fin tried to say something else but choked on a sob instead. Sweat and tears poured down his face.

Bernadette stared at him, her mouth open.

"The thiopental"—he clenched his fists and spit out the words—"it expires in three days."

Bernadette was confused. Fin must have misunderstood something.

"So the date was moved up so they can use the drug on her before it expires," Marty said. "Nothing more can be done now."

Fin nodded and fell back in his chair, his face crumpled in abject defeat. "She's at the Goree Unit now, and they're transferring her to The Walls," he said. "Jimmy Pearl is on his way to Huntsville now. It's over."

Bernadette straightened her back, jumped up from her chair, and pounded her fist on the table. "It is *not* over. We have to get this petition to Mr. Pearl right away. It's not too late."

"Bernie," Marty said, "Fin is right. You have to let it go now."

"Call Jimmy Pearl," she told Fin. "Tell him we'll meet him there in three hours. I'll get the car keys. We're going. *Now.*"

THIRTY-NINE

Fin gripped the door handle with one hand and his seat belt with the other, his eyes glued to the white line in the middle of road as the car lurched from side to side. Even though it wasn't raining, the windshield wipers hammered hard against the window.

"Slow down, Mom. Come on, now."

Bernadette rubbed at her eyes as if she was having trouble seeing and, much to Fin's dismay, pressed the pedal even harder. It was getting dark, that time of night when a deer was apt to dart across the highway without warning. The fear in Fin's legs and arms had made them go numb hours ago, and he was sure his knuckles had turned permanently white by now.

"This never would have happened if I had listened to you before," Bernadette mumbled. "It's all my fault. Call Jimmy Pearl again."

"We can call him when we get there," he said.

"Call now. Tell him we'll be there in five minutes." The car veered onto the shoulder, and its tires squealed when Bernadette made the sharp turn back onto the highway.

Fin gasped and grabbed at the steering wheel. "Let me drive the rest of the way. *Please.*"

"*Tell* him."

"Mr. Pearl already knows we're coming," he said, even as he reached into his jeans pocket for his cell phone. "He's going to think we're crazy if we keep calling like this."

"Tell him we want to see her." The car lurched ahead as she pressed her foot down yet again on the accelerator.

"Jesus," he said. "We'll be lucky to live long enough to see anyone."

"Tell him we'll meet him outside the Walls Unit."

"Not until you stop driving like a maniac."

"Call."

"No."

"Fin."

"Slow down."

When Bernadette lifted her foot a bit, Fin leaned across the seat with his eyes focused on the speedometer and gripped her shoulder until she slowed the car to sixty miles an hour. "Okay," he said, turning the windshield wipers off before sitting back to make the call.

"Mr. Pearl?" he said into the phone.

"Is he with her now? Can we see her? Here, give it to me." The car swerved as Bernadette tried to grab the cell phone from his hand.

"Come on, Mom! Watch what you're doing. Sorry, Mr. Pearl. We'll be there soon."

"Let me talk to him, Fin."

"Not while you're driving."

"Tell him about the court case I read about, the woman who was freed from death row even though she confessed."

"Sorry, Mr. Pearl. My mom's talking to me here."

"You folks just sit tight now," Fin heard Jimmy Pearl say. "I'm going to talk to Miss Blackwell first, okay?"

"Ask him if the governor has the right to cut short the thirty days. What about the investigation? Is there a report already? Oh, never mind about that. Just tell him we're almost there with the petition."

"Mom, quiet." Fin inched closer to the door. "One more appeal," he said into the phone, "that's all we need and then the drug will expire."

"What did he say, Fin?"

"He said we need to calm down and then he hung up on me."

Fin stared out the window at the signs touting Huntsville's main tourist attractions, billboards advertising places he had never seen and never cared to see: the Sam Houston statue, largest freestanding sculpture in the United States next to the Statue of Liberty—Sam Houston State University, one of the largest and oldest criminal-justice programs in the country focused on the special needs of crime victims—the Prison Museum, honored home of "Old Sparky," the electric chair that fried 361 prisoners in its day. He shivered and looked away.

As the tires screamed from Bernadette's too-sharp turn against the curb in front of the Walls Unit, Fin cursed under his breath and then breathed a sigh of relief. Finally, they were here.

***

Bernadette yanked the key from the ignition, opened the door, and lifted her foot out onto the curb. Caring only about what they came to do, she had narrowed her focus down to one person, one life. But Fin grabbed her arm and pulled her back into the car.

"We can't just go in there," he said. "Mr. Pearl said to wait."

She collapsed back onto the seat and found herself staring at the thirty-two-foot-high brick wall encasing the Walls Unit like a lock box. She moaned and covered her face with her hands.

"Mom?"

"We have to get this to Mr. Pearl," she said. "*Now*. Right now."

"There's something we should talk about."

"No time," she said.

"Have you considered the possibility that Rae might find out that she and Veronica are sisters now?"

Fear drilled into Bernadette's stomach and started twisting it into a knot. She shook her head. "It will break her heart," she said.

"It could save her life."

"We can't let it come to that, Fin."

"We need to be prepared, in case it does."

Bernadette had the same suffocatingly helpless feeling she had the night Veronica died. But there had been nothing she could do then. There had been no choice to be made. This time, there was a chance. This time, there was hope. She bowed her head and prayed to the God she'd spurned for so long, hoping he might still be willing to listen to her. *Please let her live,* she pleaded, *and please, spare her the truth so she will want to.*

FORTY

It was almost midnight and there were no other customers in the coffee shop, just the three of them and the barista out back cleaning up and getting ready to close for the night. In spite of her exhaustion, Bernadette was ready to confront Jimmy Pearl—to ask him why he didn't get them in to see Rae, what took him so long to call them back, why he kept them waiting outside The Walls for over an hour, and why, after all that waiting, he had told them to meet him here, of all places—but Fin took charge before she had a chance to say anything.

"So here's the petition," he said, unfolding the legal document and pushing it in front of Rae's lawyer.

Jimmy Pearl, looking tired and drawn around his eyes, didn't even glance at the papers.

"Come on, read it," Fin said, tapping on them with his forefinger, his eyes shining with anticipation, still hopeful.

The lawyer pulled his reading glasses from his shirt pocket, first reading the cover letter and then turning to the petition itself. Bernadette leaned forward, waiting for him to nod at how well written the petition was, maybe comment on the soundness of the clemency arguments. But Jimmy Pearl said nothing, and when he finished reading, he turned the petition face down on the table with a long sigh.

"Well, here's the thing, folks," he said in that slow, drawling voice that right now made Bernadette want to scream, "after sending that letter to the governor, I promised Miss Blackwell I would never take any action again without discussing it with her first."

"Of course," Bernadette said. "But you *did* tell her about this, didn't you?"

"Yes, Ma'am, I did."

"And?" Fin's eyes were suspicious now, as was his tone of voice.

"We did talk on and on, all right, about the petition." Jimmy Pearl stared out the window at the empty parking lot.

"What did she say?" Bernadette held her breath, waited for the other shoe to drop.

"She was stunned, Mrs. Baker. She doesn't feel worthy."

"I hope you told her she is," Fin said.

"I did." A shadow crossed Jimmy Pearl's eyes and moved into the down-turned lines around his mouth, making him suddenly seem much older than he was.

"Did you tell her we were here?" Bernadette asked, in spite of the trepidation she was now feeling.

"Yes, as a matter of fact I did."

"And?" Fin motioned with his hands to hurry it up.

"Okay. I'm going to give it to you straight. Miss Blackwell doesn't want any more delays. I told her we could get one easy because the sentencing court did not set or even approve the expedited execution date, and she still refused."

"Why?" they both asked at the same time.

"She said she gave you her word, Mrs. Baker, that she was done with appeals."

"Let me see her," Bernadette said. "Let me talk to her."

"I thought you might be saying that, so I asked her if she'd be willing to meet with you."

"Is she?"

"I'm afraid not, Mrs. Baker. But she wants you to know she's most grateful to you for trying."

"You weren't able to convince her about filing the petition?" Fin said.

Jimmy Pearl sighed and shook his head. "She believes she's supposed to die now. She believes it's her time."

"You have to go ahead and file this anyway." Fin picked up the petition and waved it in front of the lawyer's face.

"She has to be depressed," Bernadette said.

"She's not unhappy, Mrs. Baker. She's at peace."

"So what do we do now?" Fin asked.

"Nothing to do but respect her decision," Jimmy Pearl said. "We have to let her go."

"No," Fin said, fighting tears. "It's not over. It can't be. Tell him, Mom."

Bernadette looked up at the ceiling. She squeezed her temples with the palms of her hands so hard it made her wince from the pain. What could they do? What could anyone do? She lowered her head and dropped her hands onto the table, then looked up at Jimmy Pearl.

"Are you sure?" she asked, looking into his eyes. "Are you absolutely sure?"

"I've known Miss Blackwell for ten years now, Mrs. Baker, and I have never seen her this certain about anything. I believe she's of sound mind and she believes this is what's right for her."

Bernadette sat back in her chair and sighed. "Okay, then," she said. "Okay, then."

At first she wondered if sheer exhaustion had sucked up all the fight in her—or maybe it was the look of resignation on Jimmy Pearl's face or the tears in his tired eyes that did her in. But even as the lifeblood of hope drained from her body, so, too, did all fear, anxiety, panic. She felt a strange detachment that made her wonder if she was going to die now, too.

"We have to do *something*," Fin sobbed. "We have to save her."

She touched her son's face with her fingertips and gazed into his sad, loving eyes.

"She has already saved herself," she said.

FORTY-ONE

It felt to Bernadette as if they were in a silent movie. The protesters' mouths were moving, their signs flailing the air, but there was no sound, no chanting. She tightened her grip on Marty's arm, glad that he was with her to help forge the way through the strangely silent, undulating sea of bodies. Suddenly Fin was there, too, appearing unannounced from behind. He hugged her and whispered something in her ear, but without any sound she couldn't tell whether it was important or not. And then Marty was guiding her up the steps to the entrance of the Walls Unit. Fin did not come with them. Somehow, she knew he wasn't going to, but she didn't know how she knew. Maybe he'd just told her that he would show his respect in his own way, by standing outside with the protesters.

And then they were in the Turnout Room and Regis was with them. She lowered her body into a plastic chair, knowing Marty was next to her because she felt the warmth of his hand on her knee.

"Would either of you like coffee?" With the volume of the world turned to mute, she had to guess at what Regis said by the way he pointed to the coffee urn over in the corner. She shook her head. She didn't know what Marty did.

Regis sat down next to her and took one of her hands in his. But when she looked at him, the devastation in his eyes made her turn away. *He doesn't want her to die.*

Marty's lips moved, but his voice couldn't cut through the silence. From the wave of his hand, Bernadette assumed he was commenting on the sterility of the room, but she wasn't sure. She glanced at the bare walls, the plastic chairs scattered about, the tall stack of Styrofoam cups and huge coffee urn on the Formica table, the super-sized numbers on the big round clock on the wall. Everything was the same as before, only this time there was no color; everything was in black and white. She'd redecorated the room in her head last time she was here to make it more welcoming, more comforting for the witnesses, but she realized now that that would be a mistake. The room looked lifeless and the coffee smelled bitter, just as it should be.

She felt Marty's hand on her shoulder. His lips moved. He looked worried. She placed her hand on top of his, reminding herself that Marty was there to help her, not the other way around. That was why she'd asked him to come, and that was why he'd agreed. He wouldn't be here otherwise. Or would he?

She wished she could tell him she was okay, but she didn't know if she was or not. All she could think about was Rae. She hoped the chaplain would stay with her so she wouldn't be left alone. She wondered if Maxine Blackwell might change her mind at the last minute and come to be with her daughter at the end, but she knew that was impossible. She didn't even know if Rae's mother was still alive.

Amy Whitehall stood in front of her now, mouthing hello.
Bernadette reached out to shake her hand, a formality that neither
of them was able to complete with the requisite smile. But unlike
last time, the trauma counselor made no attempt to be reassuring,
no offer of help. It was as if her presence was all she had to offer—
or was she waiting for Bernadette to tell her what to do? There was
a deep sadness etched in Amy Whitehall's face as she stood there
with her trembling hand gripping the information packet. *She
doesn't want Rae to die, either.*

"Thank you for being here," Bernadette said, reaching out to
take the folder.

Amy Whitehall nodded, paused, then turned. With heavy
steps, she walked to the other side of the room. Bernadette
examined the faces of the other members of the trauma team as
they made a space for Amy to sit down next to them. *They hate their
jobs.*

She opened the folder and was puzzled to find the Offenders
Rap Sheet indecipherable, as if it had been written in code. When
she squinted, a few words formed on the page:

*Raelynn Blackwell... Execution date (August 8, 2011).
Amount of time on death row (3,755 days – 10 yrs., 3
mo., 12 days).*

She turned the page then, realizing that what she wanted
to know, *had* to know, was what Rae had requested for her last
meal. Wasn't that information supposed to be in these folders?
She was frantic to know that Rae had ordered something good to
eat, something she liked, that she had given herself that. She kept
flipping the pages, but found nothing about Rae's last meal. And

when she got to the last page, which showed a map of the country with symbols indicating which methods of execution were used in each state—noose for hanging, round target for firing squad, chair for electrocution, door for gas chamber, syringe for lethal injection—she threw the folder onto the floor. Marty put his arm around her and pulled her closer to him.

"Do you think anyone told her to drink lots of liquids," she said, "to make it easier to find her vein?" Marty shook his head.

She couldn't expect him to know why she was worried. It was because Rae's arms were so skinny that her veins had to be tiny and, because of her drug use, more delicate, too. And then there was the needle they used, so much bigger than an ordinary IV. *Please don't let it hurt.* What if they missed her vein altogether or passed through it? What if they found a vein but the injection made it rupture or collapse? It could happen.

"Good lord," she said. "I hope the medical technicians remember to adjust the IV pressure for her size."

She shivered, and Marty rubbed her shoulder. If only his warming her could warm Rae as well. Rae wasn't used to air-conditioning; she would get cold in the death chamber.

The door opened then, and in walked Warden Fredrick with his round face still looking friendly, but this time without the smile. His bushy salt-and-pepper eyebrows formed a V under the worry ripples on his forehead as he made his way toward them with slow, deliberate steps. He sat on a chair facing her, the kindness in his blue eyes overshadowed by sorrow. He leaned forward and put his hand on hers; she assumed it was his attempt to assure her that this time there wouldn't be any problems.

"She never had a chance," she found herself saying.

The warden nodded. She read his lips and thought he said, "poor kid," but then he looked apologetic, as if he'd said something wrong or inappropriate, so she tried to smile to set his mind at rest. All at once he stood, shook Marty's hand, and made a hasty retreat for the door. She didn't know why.

"He has to tell them when to do it," she said after he was gone.

Marty nodded.

"He doesn't want to."

She wondered then what would happen if the warden refused to give the signal. Would the executioner release the poison anyway? Everyone said it was too late now for anyone except the courts to change things, but she didn't know if that was true or not. She'd lost her ability to tell the difference between what could be changed and what couldn't be. That was something she used to know.

"Will the witnesses please follow me?"

She jumped. The sound was back, the volume turned up to loud. Her heart pounded against her chest as Marty and Regis helped her up from the chair.

FORTY-TWO

Bernadette's forehead brushed against the window, the rest of her body in her throat as she stood between Marty and Regis in the viewing room. The curtain was still closed, and she was afraid it was because they were having trouble finding Rae's vein. Memories crashed over her like a blow to her stomach as she remembered how Veronica's tiny veins had always been hard to find, too, how she had screamed in pain the few times she had to have blood drawn at the doctor's office.

With no announcement or warning, the curtain opened, and Bernadette gasped, almost collapsed. Marty and Regis gripped her elbows and pulled her up, the trauma team behind her made sure she didn't fall backward, and Amy Whitehall's hands squeezed her trembling shoulders.

Instead of the standard white prison uniform, Rae was wearing a pale pink blouse and light brown slacks with crisp pleats down the front this time. Someone had bought new clothes for her. Someone cared. A lump caught in Bernadette's throat and her eyes stung as she stared at the straps across Rae's body that fastened her onto the gurney. She looked like a small child held captive. Her arms were extended out on boards, her small hands secured by leather straps. Then Bernadette saw it. She drew in her breath and her hand flew up to her mouth.

"The IV. It's in the wrong arm." She stared at the discoloration and swelling on Rae's left arm and saw how exhausted she looked. Bernadette's worst fear had come true. How many times had they tried to find a vein before giving up and using her right arm instead?

Marty put his arm around her shoulder and pulled her close, kissing the top of her head, his way of telling her there was nothing to worry about. But she knew better. She knew things he didn't know, things about other botched executions, things that had prolonged the dying and caused excruciating pain. She knew there was a lot to worry about. Like them inserting the IV into an artery by mistake so the blood carrying the chemicals had to go the long way around before it stopped Rae's heart. Like the catheter clogging. Or the needle passing through the vein. Or the catheter coming out of her vein altogether and spraying the chemicals across the room. It had happened before. So many things could go wrong. The IV in Rae's right arm was supposed to be the backup in case the one in her left arm didn't work. So what was their backup now? Did they even have one?

Don't hurt her, she wanted to shout at the top of her lungs, *please don't hurt her.* A scream started in her stomach and made its way up through her heart and her lungs, into her throat. But she swallowed the scream—not to be compliant, not because she knew that executions required the proper behavior of witnesses as well as the cooperation of those carrying them out. No, the reason she didn't let the scream out was because it was Rae's choice to die and it was her job to accept that choice, because what Rae needed now was her support and she had to be strong for her.

With tears trickling down her cheeks, she squeezed Marty's hand. Rae was shaking now, as if it was all she could do to hold it together. If only she could touch Rae, stroke her head the way she always had when her children were little and sick.

"I'm here. You're not alone." She mouthed the words, but Rae didn't see her because she was looking up at the ceiling, her mouth grimacing, eyes blinking rapidly. She looked scared. *Oh, god, when someone is frightened, their veins contract.*

A microphone began its tortuous downward journey from the ceiling then, stopping within inches of Rae's face. With a look of terror in her eyes, she opened her mouth and licked her lips but didn't say anything. Bernadette's eyes followed a tear making its way down Rae's cheek, and she wondered what Rae would say now if she were asked if she wanted to live, whether she would still say "It don't matter what I want" as she had before.

Bernadette pressed her hand against the window. "Look at me," she whispered. "Look at me."

Rae's head made a jerky movement as if she was pulling it into a turtle shell. But then her chest started heaving up and down, and she turned her head to face the viewing window. Her eyes were wide, frozen with fear.

"Jesus." Bernadette tried to smile as she mouthed the word. She patted at her own throat and then pointed at the silver cross Rae was wearing. "Jesus is here."

Rae's mouth twisted into a half smile, half grimace, and she turned back to the microphone.

"Please." The word was a sob, followed by a coughing spasm that made Rae pull against the restraints and lift her head from the pillow. When the coughing subsided, she bit her bottom lip and tried again.

"Please."

During the silence that followed, Warden Fredrick touched Rae's head with the tips of his fingers. His eyes were filled with tears as he leaned down and whispered something in her ear. When she shook her head and closed her eyes, he pointed up to the ceiling and the microphone ascended. Rae's leg started to twitch, and the chaplain, with a heartrending look on his face, pressed his hand down on her knee.

Bernadette braced herself for what was to come. The warden would give the signal, and the poison would flow out through the tubes from the hole in the wall and enter Rae's body. Unlike Rae, who didn't even know she'd murdered Veronica until the police told her what she'd done, did the invisible executioner behind the one-way window know that he was about to commit murder? *Forgive them, Lord, for they know not what they do.*

When Rae's arms started to shake, Bernadette had to turn away. The unmistakable smell of death in the air was so cold that it made the hair on her arms stand upright. She looked down at a crack in the floor and followed its jagged route to a whisper behind her. She couldn't move her head, and her eyes froze. She tried to lift her arms, but it was as if they had been amputated. While a nightmarish paralysis consumed her muscles and bones, the sensitivity of her skin was heightened so that when Marty touched her hand ever so lightly, spasms took hold of her and grabbed at her jaws, her neck, contracted her stomach. Her legs started to give way.

"Do you want to leave?" she heard Marty ask.

If she could have spoken, she would have told him no, she had to stay for Rae, that there was nothing she could do but accept Rae's decision to die—if, in fact that still was her decision—but even though it was Rae's decision and not hers to make, that nonetheless it was wrong; it was horribly, horribly wrong.

But she could say none of those things because right now all she could hear was Rae speaking to her, her voice saying *I wish you was my ma, Mrs. Baker, I wish you was my ma.* If Bernadette were able to say anything to Rae right now, it would be that she was trying to keep her promise, that she was trying to be here for her. She would tell her that she would look at her, that she wouldn't turn away again—that no matter what, she wouldn't turn away.

Bernadette blinked, lifted her head, and kept her promise, wishing she could do more than just watch. But it was all she could do. At least it was something.

Rae's hands tightened then, and her body went rigid. She looked scared. She was in pain.

"Please stop," Bernadette said out loud.

Marty pulled her close. The room was still. She could hear people breathing around her. Someone coughed, and she shuddered. Her muscles contracted, threatened to freeze again.

Then the warden took off his glasses. The signal.

Rae was looking at the viewing window now, her face fixed on Bernadette. Their eyes locked as Rae's body writhed, almost convulsed, and went limp. Her eyes closed and she took in a breath, deep, drawing in all the air she could. Then her diaphragm deflated like a balloon with air being squished from it, and Bernadette released her own breath at the same time. She had read once that it was easier, more comfortable and more natural not to breathe than to breathe. *Please let that be true.* Rae's body vibrated and then went still, and at that moment Bernadette felt as if her own heart had stopped.

After a few minutes, Warden Fredrick tipped his head toward the door and a man in a white coat entered the death chamber. He checked with his stethoscope for Rae's heartbeat. He checked her wrist for a pulse. He lifted her eyelids and shone a light in her eyes. Then he looked at his watch and said, "Time of death: 6:27 p.m."

"Miss Raelynn Blackwell was pronounced dead at 6:27 p.m." The warden's voice cracked as he repeated the declaration.

Bernadette stood in the silent room, her eyes still fixed on Rae as the curtain closed across the window. She felt as if her head wasn't attached to her shoulders. She balled her hands into fists.

"You got her body," she whispered, "but you never got her soul."

Marty gathered her up in his arms then, and she fell into him, sobbing.

FORTY-THREE

When the doctor told them the good news about the success of Marty's prostate surgery, Bernadette felt true happiness, a pure joy that she had never thought she'd be able to feel again. And now, over dinner, all their individual responses merged into one huge wave of relief that they ecstatically surfed all night.

"To Dad." Fin lifted his coffee cup in a toast.

"To long life," Marty said, his cheeks flushed.

"Hear, hear." Annamaria.

As Marty plopped scoops of Ben & Jerry's ice cream into the dessert dishes Patty compared the amount in her dish with that of the others. Fin teased that he had the most and Marty joked that maybe they should get a scale and weigh them. They all laughed and then, to the sounds of slurping and spoons clinking against glass, everyone set about capturing their desserts before they melted. The ice cream's frostiness stuck to Bernadette's throat, like the envelope that was stuck to the inside of her apron pocket.

Her anticipation about the envelope had swelled like a balloon all through dinner and now it expanded almost to the point of bursting. Enough time had passed. Tonight was the night. She pulled the envelope out of her pocket and raised her eyebrows at Marty. He smiled and nodded. Now was the time. The moment was right.

"This came in the mail," she said. When she opened the envelope, something fell onto the table with a tinkling sound.

Fin's hands flew up, covered his open mouth. "Rae was wearing that," he said.

"She never took it off," Bernadette said.

She handed the silver cross to Fin as the mood in the room changed from celebratory to somber. He cupped the cross in his hands like a prayer.

Bernadette unfolded a piece of yellowed paper and held it up so everyone could see the childlike print on its wide elementary-school lines. "You can tell no one helped her write this," she said as she laid the letter on the table in front of her and started to read it out loud.

Dear Mrs. Baker, This is my last wish. For you to have my most preshus possesion for your kindness to me. If you can forgive me then I can forgive me to. Thank you. Miss Raelynn Blackwell.

A tear slipped down Bernadette's cheek just as it had all the other times she'd read the letter before tonight. "There was a note from the warden with it," she said. "He said Rae wrote it just before they came for her. She asked him to put the cross in the envelope and mail it after she was gone."

She handed the letter to Fin, and he stared at it for a long time before passing it and the cross on to his dad. Marty laid the letter on the table and placed the cross on top of it, then covered them with his hands as if he was giving them a silent blessing.

"So that's it," he said as he handed them to Annamaria. She

passed the letter and the cross on without even a glance.

"Wow." Patty let the cross dangle from her fingertips as she stared at the letter.

"Come with me," Bernadette said after Patty gave the letter and silver cross back to her and she slipped them into her apron pocket. She motioned for everyone to follow as she stood up and headed for the stairs in the front hallway.

When her foot landed on the creaky step, she turned and looked back at her family: Fin and Patty a step behind, holding hands and looking up at her with bewildered faces—Marty after them, looking solemn with his hands in his pockets—Annamaria, with grief-stretched eyes, several steps behind everyone, but at least she was coming. Bernadette shifted her weight and the step creaked again. How many nights had she waited for Veronica's reappearance, how many hours had she re-experienced her death in the lack of the sound of her foot on that step? Four sets of concerned eyes stared up at her as she turned and resumed her climb, wishing she could wrap words around what she was feeling and what she had come to so clearly understand.

At the top of the stairs, she stepped into Veronica's room and walked over to the antique cedar chest in the corner. She ran her fingers over its lid and kissed its smooth polished surface, then slipped her hand down its back until her fingers found the edge of the masking tape that held the key in place. Then, with key in hand, she lowered herself to the floor. Marty sat next to her, their shoulders touching. She reached for his hand, brought it up to her lips, and kissed it. Fin sat on the other side of Bernadette in his usual lotus position, and Patty plopped onto her knees at one end

of the chest, her eyes bright with anticipation. Annamaria stood
and leaned with her back against the doorjamb—half in the room,
half out—and watched the others out of the corner of her eye.

The oversized key slipped with ease into the crest-shaped brass
lock, but before she turned it, Bernadette closed her eyes and let her
fingers linger for a few minutes. Marty lifted the lid and a pungent
cedar smell burst forth from its ten-year captivity. With it came a
yearning in Bernadette so powerful that she toppled forward and
almost fell headfirst into the chest. A giant white A blazed up at
her like a flashlight beaming into her eyes. She traced the letter
on Veronica's maroon and white letter sweater with her fingertips,
then lifted the sweater from the chest, brought it up to her lips, and
kissed it.

"Remember how she screamed when she made cheerleader?"
Fin said with a laugh.

"She went wild," Marty said.

"Aunt Veronica was, like, so beautiful," Patty said. "I always
wanted to be like her." She snatched the sweater from Bernadette's
hands and measured one of its sleeves against her arm.

"Why don't *you* try out, kiddo?" Fin said.

"So, maybe I will." Patty jumped to her feet and pulled the
sweater over her head. It fit as if made for her. "What do you think,
Mom?"

Annamaria stared, wide-eyed, at her daughter from the
doorway, her mouth twisted in a failed smile.

"Come here, Annie." Bernadette tipped her head toward the
chest and patted the floor with her hand.

Annamaria shook her head and looked down.

Bernadette hesitated, considered asking her one more time to join them. But she'd learned long ago that it was best not to push Annamaria, best to let her come around on her own if she was going to. She turned back to the chest and started to pull out Veronica's things one by one. Each item contained a tale, and they took their time telling different versions of the stories, weaving the sequence of events—each precious memory—into an exuberant and gratifying narrative of Veronica's life. At some of the stories, they laughed out loud. At some, they cried.

"Remember this, Annamaria, from our trip to Disneyland?" Fin held Veronica's Mickey Mouse doll up, pointed it toward his sister at the door.

"Remember how sick you got of her singing 'It's a small world after all' over and over and over again?" Marty added.

Annamaria turned her head away.

"And this is where we went every summer." Fin held up a picture of the five of them standing in front of a small log cabin.

"You guys always talk about that lake," Patty said, "but I never saw it."

"Remember how you always pushed me off the dock, Annamaria?" The way Fin said it sounded like a tease, not an indictment.

"What I remember is how Veronica would keep track on her calendar of how much time was left before we would go," Bernadette said.

Marty chuckled. "Her breakfast announcement. It was always only ten more weeks, only six more weeks, eight more days, two more days."

"Can we go there sometime, Mom?" Patty asked.

They all looked at Annamaria, but she didn't look at them.

"We should go back," Bernadette said. "I'm serious. Let's all go."

Marty squeezed her shoulder and said, "Why not? I have a clean bill of health now. And for you, my sweet, I would go anywhere."

"Maybe Uncle Fin could bring Chuck," Patty said with a mischievous smile.

Bernadette raised her eyebrow. She and Marty gave each other a knowing look. Fin broke out in a smile.

"Actually," he said, "I think I will."

"See? You know, Uncle Fin, I like Chuck, too."

"Then it's settled." Bernadette laughed and tickled Fin on the back of his neck, the tickle of a promise of all the good that was yet to come.

At midnight, Patty looked into the chest and declared it empty, gesturing at its contents now scattered about on the floor. Bernadette couldn't believe how alive she felt as she picked up each item in turn, smelled it, kissed it, placed it back in the cedar chest. It was like tucking Veronica in bed for the night. Carefully. Lovingly.

Now only the letter sweater remained. But Patty wouldn't give it up. When they coaxed her, she laughed. Teased. "Goooo maroons!" She jumped into a cheer, her legs splitting the air, the maroon and white pom-poms fluttering from her fingertips.

Bernadette stared at her granddaughter. It was the way her head tilted. The brilliance of her smile. Her exuberant spirit. How could she not have noticed before? Veronica had been with them all this time. She glanced at Marty and Fin. They saw it, too. So did Annamaria. She was sitting on the floor now, still in the doorway, wide-eyed, looking stunned.

"Come sit next to me, Annie," Bernadette said.

Annamaria shook her head, vehemently this time, and turned her back on them. With a pained expression, Fin started to get up. But when Bernadette shook her head and placed her hand on his arm, he nodded and sat back down. She took his hand and squeezed it, affirming what they both knew: that you can't save someone who doesn't want to be saved, and if you insist on trying anyway, you need to ask who it is you are really trying to save—the other person or yourself. The clarity with which she now understood this was a gift from Rae, one that, because she had come to accept it, sustained and nourished her even as her heart bled for Annamaria.

She turned to Patty then and reached into her apron pocket for the silver cross and envelope containing Rae's letter. "Help me with these, sweetie," she said.

Patty, looking pleased to be asked, dropped the pom-poms back into the chest and pulled the sweater over her head. Then Bernadette folded the sweater carefully, neatly. She lifted it to her face and smelled it. Kissed it. Laid it on everything else in the chest. Then she placed the envelope on top of the letter sweater.

"Let's do this together." She brought Rae's cross up to her lips and kissed it before handing it to her granddaughter.

Patty felt each link of the chain as if they were rosary beads. "Aunt Veronica," she said as she placed the silver cross on the envelope in the chest, "this is your sister."

"I wish the two of you could have lived," Bernadette said as she gazed into the chest. "You both would have done so much good."

Fin leaned forward, reached into the chest so his fingertips could caress the cross. "You would have liked each other," he whispered.

His words touched the deepest part of Bernadette, the place where she knew wisdom resided. When it came right down to it, the struggle wasn't about ideas or stances; it wasn't even about doing the right thing. It was about the connection of one human being with another. Fin's compassion had taught her that. She placed her hand on her son's cheek and smiled. She no longer worried about him. As always, he was going to do what he was going to do. That was just fine with her.

Marty glanced around to make sure no one objected and then closed the lid to the chest. Bernadette turned the key and left it in the lock.

With a collective sigh, they all stood up and stretched their legs. Except for Annamaria, who was now curled into herself on the floor with her hands on the back of her head. Splotches of crimson covered her neck. Bernadette ran to the doorway, fell onto her knees, and held her daughter's body, now wracked with violent sobs, against her breasts. She stroked her corkscrew curls and kissed the top of her head, tasting the years of grief that poured out in one long keening lament. It was a good sign. A very good sign.

"I miss her so much, Mom." Annamaria's shaky voice was childlike, almost inaudible.

"I know, sweetie, I know."

Patty dropped to her knees with her arms outstretched, grabbed her mom, and held on for dear life.

"I'm so scared for you, Patty," Annamaria sobbed.

Bernadette stood up, leaving mother and daughter to weep in each other's arms. She felt Marty's arm around her shoulder. He was shaking. Then she felt Fin's hand as he slipped it through her arm on the other side. He was shaking, too. Crying, the three of them huddled close together, providing with their bodies a tent, a shelter in which Annamaria's grief could be laid bare, her naked pain exposed. She was going to be okay now. They were all going to be okay now.

ACKNOWLEDGEMENTS

Several exceptional people, who strive to make forgiveness and healing possible in the aftermath of violent crime, were the inspiration for *Just Mercy*. They include: David Doerfler—former Director, Victim Offender Mediation/Dialogue program for the Texas Department of Criminal Justice, Victim Services Division—and the victim and offender participants in that program; Ronnie Earle, former Travis County Texas District Attorney and passionate proponent of restorative justice; Sister Helen Prejean, author of *Dead Man Walking* and leading advocate for the abolishment of the death penalty; Marilyn Peterson Armour, PhD, Professor and Director, Institute for Restorative Justice and Restorative Dialogue, The University of Texas at Austin, and relentless seeker of meaning in the aftermath of homicide.

The seeds of *Just Mercy*, although I wasn't aware of it at the time, were planted years ago when I decided to investigate the lifelong personal and environmental risk factors experienced by murderers who were executed by Texas in 1997. I focused on Texas because it has the highest rate of executions in the United States since the death penalty was reinstated in the late 1970s, and on the

37 men because they represented half of the people put to death in the country in 1997. I am most grateful to the many people—too many to name without inadvertently leaving someone out—that made that research possible.

What I learned from the 37 Men study proved invaluable to me in the development and writing of *Just Mercy*. The character of Raelynn Blackwell, who murdered Veronica Baker, is the female prototype of one of the profiles that emerged of the men in the study and turned out to be one of the key findings: that virtually all of the men whose childhood backgrounds included sexual abuse, physical abuse and physical or emotional neglect had committed the most-heinous crimes. In *Just Mercy*, Bernadette Baker's reaction to a public information packet she is given at Raelynn Blackwell's execution reflects my own reaction when I first saw how the death penalty was normalized in the packet's contents (e.g., a history of the death penalty and detailed execution procedures; pages of statistics such as current death row and prior execution lists; a map of the United States with symbols—noose, needle, chair, target, gas chamber door—to show the methods of execution used in each state with the death penalty).

My decision to write fiction in general and *Just Mercy* in particular grew out of a growing conviction that people become empowered to work for personal and social change, not through objective data and studies, but through personal connections that lead them to care enough to take action. Instead of continuing to conduct research about complex and controversial social issues, I wanted to show how ordinary people find the courage to embrace the rough places of life and make deeply personal and moral choices that transform themselves and the world in important ways. I am deeply indebted to the teachers and writers who taught me how to give voice to my passion for social justice in a way that privileges human emotion and personal experience over detached objectivity.

Best selling author and writing coach Hal Zina Bennett guided me through the first years of transition from academic writer to novelist by providing just the kind of encouragement, support and advice I needed. Max Regan (internationally published poet, writer, and founder of Hollowdeck Press) has been my writing coach, developmental editor, cheerleader and dear friend for many years. Without his extraordinary skill, honesty, insight and genuine caring *Just Mercy* would not have been possible. The inspiration and skills I get each year at Max's annual Boulder Writers' Retreats are living proof of his assertion that writing is a team sport. Mary Kabrich and Roger Roffman, writing group members who have endured listening to innumerable drafts of my work over the years, provide me with priceless critiques without fail twice a month. Huge thanks to my writing team for badgering and pushing me, for giving me feedback I don't always want to hear, for laughing at and with me, and always, always, for their support, encouragement, and friendship.

My sincere appreciation to everyone who made *Just Mercy* better by reading and commenting on early drafts: Deede Colbath, Pauline Erera, Larry Fitzgerald, Wendy Gross, Evelyn McChesney, Dorothy Sturdevant, Richard Walker, and Diane Young. Extra thanks go to Larry Fitzgerald who, as former Texas Department of Criminal Justice Public Information Officer in Huntsville, shared details about the Walls Unit that would otherwise have been inaccessible to me.

I am most grateful to Kevin Atticks and the Apprentice House team for publishing *Just Mercy* and getting it into readers' hands. Thank you to Christy Karras for her tireless and meticulous copyediting. Thanks to Andrea Dunlop for her expertise as a book publicist and kudos for making me a social media convert.

Words can never fully express the appreciation and gratitude I have for my wife Susan, the love of my life, who shares my passion for social justice and makes it possible every day for me to try to make the world a better place.

JUST MERCY

Dorothy Van Soest

A Book Club and Readers' Guide

Questions and Topics for Discussion

1. What is the significance of the novel's title, *Just Mercy?* Discuss its possible different meanings and why you think the author selected this title.

2. In chapter one, the murderer presses the sharp point of the knife into the tip of each of her fingers. What do you think is the significance of this symbolism?

3. How do the personalities and perspectives of members of the Baker family impact how they face Veronica's death and Raelynn Blackwell's punishment? What holds them together in spite of their differences?

4. With which character(s) did you feel the most sympathy and connection? How did your opinions or feelings about them change as the story unfolded?

5. Bernadette seems driven, to the point of compulsivity at times. What do you think motivates her?

6. How would you characterize the relationship between Fin and Annamaria? How does it compare to their relationship with their murdered sister, Veronica?

7. How does the shifting point-of-view allow the reader numerous opportunities to understand members of the Baker family?

8. What are your feelings about Raelynn Blackwell? Do they change and, if so, how?

9. Each of the characters in *Just Mercy* made a choice or took a position that had moral implications. Would you have made the same decision? Why? Why not?

10. Did your notion of what was best or right shift in the course of your reading?

11. How does the setting of Texas figure into the book? Is the setting a character? Does it come to life? Did you feel you were experiencing the time and place in which the book was set?

12. Right after witnessing Raelynn's execution, Bernadette whispered: "You got her body, but you never got her soul." What do you think she meant by that?

13. Is the plot engaging—does the story interest you? Were you surprised by the plot's complications?

14. What main ideas—themes—does the author explore? What do you think is the main theme?

15. Is the ending satisfying? If so, why? If not, why not... and how would you change it?

For More Information about the Topics in *Just Mercy*:

The Death Penalty

Death Penalty Information Center: www.deathpenaltyinfo.org/

Murder Victims Families for Human Rights: www.mvfhr.org/

Prejean, Sister Helen. *Dead Man Walking.* New York: Vintage Books, 1993.

Texas Coalition to Abolish the Death Penalty: http://tcadp.org/

Restorative Dialogue and Restorative Justice

Being with the Energy of Love and Forgiveness, A Film: www.youtube.com/watch?v=8OUnOpbmb7g

Center for Restorative Justice & Peacemaking, University of Minnesota: www.cehd.umn.edu/ssw/rjp/

The Institute for Restorative Justice and Restorative Dialogue, The University of Texas at Austin: www.utexas.edu/research/cswr/rji/

Parents of Murdered Children: www.pomc.com

Umbreit, Mark. *Dancing With the Energy of Conflict and Trauma: Letting Go, Finding Peace in Families, Communities & Nations.* CreateSpace Independent Publishing Platform, 2013.

Umbreit, Mark & Armour, Marylin. *Restorative Dialogue: An Essential for Research and Practice.* New York: Springer Publishing, 2010.

ABOUT THE AUTHOR

Dorothy Van Soest is a writer, social worker, political and community activist, as well as a retired professor and university dean who holds an undergraduate degree in English literature and a Masters and Ph.D. in Social Work. She is currently Professor Emeritus at the University of Washington with a research-based publication record of nine books and over fifty journal articles, essays, and book chapters that tackle complex and controversial issues related to violence, oppression, and injustice. *Just Mercy* was informed by her widely acclaimed investigation of the lives of thirty-seven men who were executed by Texas in 1997 and inspired by the Texas Department of Criminal Justice's Victim Offender Mediation/Dialogue program. Dorothy Van Soest lives in Seattle, Washington where she is currently working on her next novel, a mystery that grew out of her experiences with the child welfare system. Her website is www.dorothyvansoest.com/

Apprentice House is the country's only campus-based, student-staffed book publishing company. Directed by professors and industry professionals, it is a nonprofit activity of the Communication Department at Loyola University Maryland.

Using state-of-the-art technology and an experiential learning model of education, Apprentice House publishes books in untraditional ways. This dual responsibility as publishers and educators creates an unprecedented collaborative environment among faculty and students, while teaching tomorrow's editors, designers, and marketers.

Outside of class, progress on book projects is carried forth by the AH Book Publishing Club, a co-curricular campus organization supported by Loyola University Maryland's Office of Student Activities.

Eclectic and provocative, Apprentice House titles intend to entertain as well as spark dialogue on a variety of topics. Financial contributions to sustain the press's work are welcomed. Contributions are tax deductible to the fullest extent allowed by the IRS.

To learn more about Apprentice House books or to obtain submission guidelines, please visit www.apprenticehouse.com.

Apprentice House
Communication Department
Loyola University Maryland
4501 N. Charles Street
Baltimore, MD 21210
Ph: 410-617-5265 • Fax: 410-617-2198
info@apprenticehouse.com • www.apprenticehouse.com

CPSIA information can be obtained at www.ICGtesting.com
Printed in the USA
BVOW05s0745060815

411937BV00009B/203/P

9 781627 200226